Chosen

A House of Night Novel

P. C. and KRISTIN CAST

Book Three of the
HOUSE OF NIGHT
Series

www.atombooks.co.uk

ATOM

First published in the United States in 2008 by St. Martin's Press
First published in Great Britain in 2009 by Atom
This edition published in 2010 by Atom

A CIP catalogue record for this book
is available from the British Library.

£185.203

ISBN 978-1-90741-013-0

£9.00

Typeset in Granjon by Palimpsest Book Production Limited,
Grangemouth, Stirlingshire
Printed in the UK by CPI Mackays, Chatham ME5 8TD

Papers used by Atom are natural, renewable and
recyclable products sourced from well-managed forests and certified
in accordance with the rules of the Forest Stewardship Council.

Mixed Sources
Product group from well-managed
forests and other controlled sources
www.fsc.org Cert no. SGS-COC-004081
© 1996 Forest Stewardship Council
FSC

Atom
An imprint of
Little, Brown Book Group
100 Victoria Embankment
London EC4Y 0DY

An Hachette UK Company
www.hachette.co.uk

www.atombooks.co.uk

Chosen

I thought adult vampyres weren't supposed to have relationships with fledglings.' We were so close that I didn't have to speak much above a whisper for him to hear me.

'We're not supposed to. It's highly improper. But sometimes there's an attraction that happens between two people that transcends the vampyre-fledgling boundary, as well as age and propriety. Do you believe in that kind of attraction, Zoey?'

He was talking about us! We were staring into each other's eyes, and I felt lost in him. His tattoos were a bold pattern of intricate slashing lines that gave the impression of lightning bolts, and they went perfectly with his dark hair and eyes. He was so insanely handsome and so much older that he made me feel at the same time incredibly attracted to him *and* scared to death that I was playing with something so far beyond what I'd ever experienced that it could easily spiral out of control. But the attraction was there – and if he was right, it definitely transcended the vampyre-fledgling boundary. So much so that Erik had even noticed how Loren looked at me.

Erik . . . Guilt washed through me. He would just die if he could see what was going on between Loren and me. A mean little thought snaked through my mind, *Erik isn't here to see me*, and I drew in a deep, shaky breath and heard myself say, 'Yes. I believe in that kind of attraction. Do you?'

BY P. C. AND KRISTIN CAST

The House of Night Series
Marked
Betrayed
Chosen
Untamed
Hunted
Tempted

This one is for all of you who have e-mailed us wanting more and more and more of Zoey and the gang. We heart you!

Acknowledgments

Thank you to our fabulous agent, Meredith Bernstein, who had the idea for the vampyre finishing school.

A huge thanks to our St Martin's team: Jennifer Weis, Stefanie Lindskog, Katy Hershberger, Carly Wilkins, and the excellent marketing and cover design geniuses.

From P. C.:
Thank you to all my students who are always begging me to put them in these books and kill them off. Y'all are great comedic fodder.

CHAPTER ONE

'YEP, I HAVE A SERIOUSLY SUCKY BIRTHDAY,' I TOLD MY CAT, Nala. (Okay, truthfully she's not so much my cat as I'm her person. You know how it is with cats: They don't really have owners, they have staff. A fact I mostly try to ignore.)

Anyway, I kept talking to the cat as if she hung on my every word, which is soooo not the case. 'It's been seventeen years of sucky December twenty-fourth birthdays. I'm totally used to it by now. No big deal.' I knew I was saying the words just to convince myself. Nala 'mee-uf-owed' at me in her grumpy-old-lady cat voice and then settled down to lick her privates, clearly showing that she understood I was full of b.s.

'Here's the deal,' I continued as I finished smudging a little liner on my eyes. (And I mean a *little* – the line-your-eyes-till-you-look-like-a-scary-raccoon is definitely not the look for me. Actually, it's not the look for anyone.) 'I'm gonna get a bunch of well-meaning presents that aren't really birthday presents – they're stuff that's Christmas themed because people always try to mush my birthday with Christmas, and that seriously doesn't work.' I met Nala's big green eyes in the mirror. 'But we're going to smile and pretend we're fine with the dorky birthmas gifts because people do not get that they can't mush a birthday into Christmas. At least not successfully.'

Nala sneezed.

'Exactly how I feel about it, but we'll be nice 'cause it's even worse when I say something. Then I get crappy gifts *and* everyone's upset and things turn all awkward.' Nala didn't look convinced, so I focused my attention on my reflection. For a second I thought I might have gone too heavy on the eyeliner, but I looked closer and realized that what was making my eyes look so huge and dark wasn't anything as ordinary as eyeliner. Even though it had been two months since I'd been Marked to become a vampyre, the sapphire-colored crescent-moon tattoo between my eyes and the elaborate filigree of interlocking lacework tattoos that framed my face still had the ability to surprise me. I traced one of the curving jewel-blue spiral lines with the tip of my finger. Then almost without conscious thought I pulled the already wide neck of my black sweater down so that it exposed my left shoulder. With a flick

2

of my head I tossed back my long dark hair so that the unusual pattern of tattoos that began at the base of my neck and spread over my shoulder and down either side of my spine to the small of my back was visible. As always, the sight of my tattoos gave me an electric thrill that was part wonder and part fear.

'You're not like anyone else,' I whispered to my reflection. Then I cleared my throat and continued in an overly perky voice. 'And it's okay not to be like anyone else.' I rolled my eyes at myself. 'Whatever.' I looked up over my head, half surprised that it wasn't visible. I mean, I could definitely feel the ginormic dark cloud that had been following me around for the past month. 'Hell, I'm surprised it's not raining in here. And wouldn't that be just great for my hair?' I sarcastically told my reflection. Then I sighed and picked up the envelope I'd laid on my desk. *THE HEFFER FAMILY* was embossed in gold above the sparkling return address. 'Speaking of depressing . . . ,' I muttered.

Nala sneezed again.

'You're right. Might as well get it over with.' I reluctantly opened the envelope and pulled out the card. 'Ah, hell. It's worse than I thought.' There was a huge wooden cross on the front of the card. Staked to the middle of the cross (with a bloody nail) was an old time scroll-like paper. Written (in blood, of course) were the words: *He IS the reason for the season*. Inside the card was printed (in red letters): MERRY CHRISTMAS. Below that, in my mom's handwriting, it said: *I hope you're remembering your family during this blessed time of the year. Happy Birthday, Love, Mom and Dad*.

3

'That's so typical,' I told Nala. My stomach hurt. 'And he is not my dad.' I ripped the card in two and threw it into the wastepaper basket, then stood staring at the torn pieces. 'If my parents aren't ignoring me, they're insulting me. I like being ignored better.'

The knock on my door made me jump.

'Zoey, everyone wants to know where you are.' Damien's voice carried easily through the door.

'Hang on – I'm almost ready,' I yelled, shook myself mentally, and gave my reflection one more look, deciding, with a definitely defensive edge, to leave my shoulder bare. 'My Marks aren't like anyone else's. Might as well give the masses something to gawk at while they talk,' I muttered.

Then I sighed. I'm usually not so grumpy. But my sucky birthday, my sucky parents . . .

No. I couldn't keep lying to myself.

'Wish Stevie Rae was here,' I whispered.

And that was it, what had me withdrawing from my friends (including *boy*friends – both of them) during the past month and impersonating a large, soggy, disgusting, rain cloud. I missed my best friend and ex-roommate, who everyone had watched die a month ago, but who I knew had actually been turned into an undead creature of the night. No matter how melodramatic and bad B movie that sounded. The truth was that right now, when Stevie Rae should have been downstairs puttering around with my lame birthday details, she was actually lurking about somewhere in the old tunnels under Tulsa, conspiring with other disgusting undead creatures who were truly evil, as well as definitely bad-smelling.

'Uh, Z? You okay in there?' Damien's voice called again, interrupting my mental blahs. I scooped up a complaining Nala, turned my back on the terrible birthmas card from my 'rentals, and hurried out the door, almost running over a worried-looking Damien.

'Sorry . . . sorry . . . ,' I mumbled. He fell in step beside me, giving me quick little sideways glances.

'I've never known anyone before who was as *not* excited as you about their birthday,' Damien said.

I dropped the squirming Nala and shrugged, trying for a nonchalant smile. 'I'm just practicing for when I'm old as dirt – like thirty – and I need to lie about my age.'

Damien stopped and turned to face me. 'Okayyyy.' He dragged the word out. 'We all know that thirty-year-old vamps still look roughly twenty and definitely hot. Actually one-hundred-and-thirty-year-old vamps still look roughly twenty and definitely hot. So the whole lying about your age issue is a nonissue. What's really going on with you?'

While I hesitated, trying to figure out what I should or could say to Damien, he raised one neatly plucked brow and, in his best schoolteacher voice, said, 'You know how sensitive my people are to emotions, so you may as well just give up and tell me the truth.'

I sighed again. 'You gays are freakishly intuitive.'

'That's us: homos – the few, the proud, the hypersensitive.'

'Isn't homo a derogatory term?'

'Not if it's used by a homo. By the by, you're stalling and it's so not working for you.' He actually put his hand on his hip and tapped his foot.

I smiled at him, but knew that the expression didn't reach my eyes. With an intensity that surprised me, I suddenly, desperately wanted to tell Damien the truth.

'I miss Stevie Rae,' I blurted before I could stop my mouth.

He didn't hesitate. 'I know.' His eyes looked suspiciously damp.

And that was it. Like a dam had broken open inside me the words came spilling out. 'She should be here! She'd be running around like a crazy woman putting up birthday decorations and probably baking a cake all by herself.'

'A really awful cake,' Damien said with a little sniffle.

'Yeah, but it'd be one of her *mama's favorite recipes*.' I gave my best exaggerated Okie twang as I mimicked Stevie Rae's countrified voice, which made me smile through my own tears, and I thought how weird it was that now that I was letting Damien see how upset I really felt – and why I felt that way – my smile actually reached my eyes.

'And the Twins and I would have been pissed because she would have insisted we all wear those pointed birthday hats with the elastic string that pinches your chin.' He shuddered in not-so-pretended horror. 'God, they're so unattractive.'

I laughed and felt a little of the tightness in my chest begin to loosen. 'There's just something about Stevie Rae that makes me feel good.' I didn't realize that I'd used the present tense until Damien's teary smile faltered.

'Yeah, she *was* great,' he said, with an extra emphasis on the *was* while he looked at me like he was worried about my sanity.

If only he knew the whole truth. If only I could tell him.

But I couldn't. If I did it would get either Stevie Rae or me, or both of us, killed. For good this time.

So instead I grabbed my obviously worried friend's arm and started pulling him toward the stairs that would lead us down to the public rooms of the girls' dorm and my waiting friends (and their dorky presents).

'Let's go. I'm feeling the need to open presents,' I lied enthusiastically.

'Ohmygod! I can*not* wait for you to open mine!' Damien gushed. 'I shopped for it forevah!'

I smiled and nodded appropriately as Damien went on and on about his Quest for the Perfect Present. Usually he isn't so overtly gay. Not that the fabulous Damien Maslin isn't actually gay. He totally is. But he's also a tall, brown-haired, big-eyed cutie who looks like he'd be excellent boyfriend material (which he is – if you're a boy). He's not a fluttery-acting gay kid, but get the boy talking about shopping and he definitely shows some girlish tendencies. Not that I don't like that about him. I think he looks cute when he gushes about the importance of buying really good shoes, and right then his babbling was soothing. It was helping me to get ready to face the bad presents that (sadly) waited for me.

Too bad it couldn't help me face what was really bothering me.

Still talking about his Shopping Quest, Damien led me though the main room of the dorm. I waved at the various clumps of girls clustered around the pods of flat-screen TVs as we headed to the little side room that served as a computer lab and library. Damien opened the door and my friends broke into a totally off-key chorus of 'Happy Birthday to You.' I heard Nala hiss and from the edge of my vision watched her back from the doorway and trot away down the hall. *Coward*, I thought, even though I wished I could escape with her.

Song over (thankfully), my gang swarmed me.

'Happy-happy!' said the Twins together. Okay – they're not genetically twins. Erin Bates is a very white girl from Tulsa and Shaunee Cole is a lovely caramel-colored girl of Jamaican-American descent who grew up in Connecticut, but the two are so freakishly alike that skin tone and region make absolutely no difference. They're soul twins, which is way closer than mere biology.

'Happy birthday, Z,' said a deep, sexy voice I knew very, very well. I stepped out of the twin sandwich and walked into the arms of my boyfriend, Erik. Well, technically, Erik is one of my two boyfriends, but the other is Heath, a human teenager I dated before I was Marked and I'm not supposed to be dating him now, but I kinda sorta accidentally sucked his blood and now we're Imprinted and so he's my boyfriend by default. Yes, it's confusing. Yes, it makes Erik mad. Yes, I expect him to dump me any day because of it.

'Thanks,' I murmured looking up at him and getting trapped all over again in his incredible eyes. Erik is tall and

8

hot, with Superman dark hair and incredibly blue eyes. I relaxed in his arms, a treat I hadn't allowed myself much of during the past month, and temporarily basked in his yummy smell and the sense of security I felt when I was close to him. He met my gaze and, just like in the movies, for a second everyone else went away and it was just us. When I didn't move out of his arms his smile was slow and a little surprised, which made my heart hurt. I'd been putting the kid through way too much – and he didn't even really understand why. Impulsively, I tiptoed and kissed him, much to the general merriment of my friends.

'Hey, Erik, why don't you spread some of that birthday sugar around?' Shaunee wagged her eyebrows at my grinning boyfriend.

'Yeah, sweet thang,' Erin said, and in typical twin fashion mirrored Shaunee's eye waggle. 'How about a little b-day kiss over here.'

I rolled my eyes at the Twins. 'Uh, it's not *his* birthday. You only get to kiss the birthday boy or girl.'

'Damn,' Shaunee said. 'I lurve ya, Z, but I don't want to kiss ya.'

'Just please with the same-sex kissing,' Erin said, then she grinned at Damien (who was gazing adoringly at Erik). 'I'll leave that to Damien.'

'Huh?' Damien said, clearly paying more attention to Erik's cuteness than the Twins.

'Again, we say—' Shaunee started.

'Wrong team!' and Erin finished.

Erik laughed good-naturedly, gave Damien a very guy-like punch on the arm, and said, 'Hey, if I ever decide to change teams, you'll be the first to know.' (Yet another reason why I adore him. He's mega-cool and popular, but he accepts people how they are and never gets an I'm-all-that attitude.)

'Uh, I hope I'll be the first to know if you change teams,' I said.

Erik laughed and hugged me, whispering, 'Not something you ever need to worry about,' in my ear.

While I was seriously considering sneaking another Erik kiss, a mini-whirlwind in the form of Damien's boyfriend, Jack Twist, burst into the room.

'Yea! She hasn't opened her presents yet. Happy birthday, Zoey!' Jack threw his arms around us (yes, Damien and me) and gave us a big hug.

'I told you that you needed to hurry up,' Damien said, as we untangled.

'I know, but I had to make sure it was wrapped *just right*,' Jack said. With a flourish that only a gay boy can pull off, he reached into the man purse looped over his arm and lifted out a box wrapped in red foil with a green sparkly bow on it that was so big it practically swallowed the package. 'I made the bow myself.'

'Jack's really good at crafts,' Erik said. 'He's just not good at cleaning up the crafts.'

'Sorry,' Jack said sweetly. 'I promise I'll clean up right after the party.'

Erik and Jack are roommates, further proving Erik's

coolness. He's a fifth former (in normal language that's a junior) and he's also easily the most popular guy at school. Jack is a third former (a freshman), a new kid, cute but kinda dorky, and definitely gay. Erik could have made a big deal about being stuck with a queer and could have gotten out of rooming with him, and made Jack's life hell at the House of Night. Instead he totally took him under his wing and treats him like a little brother, a treatment he extends to Damien, who has been officially going out with Jack for two point five weeks as of today. (We all know because Damien is ridiculously romantic and he celebrates the half-week anniversaries as well as the weekly ones. Yes, it makes the rest of us gag. In a nice way.)

'Hello! Speaking of presents!' Shaunee said.

'Yeah, bring that overbowed box over here to the present table and let Zoey get to opening,' Erin said.

I heard Jack whisper to Damien, 'Overbowed?' and caught Damien's *help* look, as he assured Jack, 'No, it's perfect!'

'I'll carry it over to the table and open it first.' I snatched the package from him, hurried to the table, and started to carefully extract the ginormous green sparkly bow from the red foil saying, 'I think I'm going to save this bow because it's so cool.' Damien gave me a thank-you wink. I heard Erik and Shaunee snickering and managed to kick one of them, which shut both of them up. Putting the bow aside I unwrapped and opened the little box and pulled out ...

Oh, jeesh.

'A snow globe,' I said, trying to sound happy. 'With a

snowman inside it.' Okay, a snowman snow globe is *not* a birthday present. It's a Christmas decoration. A cheesy Christmas decoration at that.

'Yeah! Yeah! And listen to what it plays!' Jack said, practically hopping up and down in excitement as he took the globe from me and wound a knob in its base so that 'Frosty the Snowman' started tinkling out around us in painfully cheap and off-key notes.

'Thank you, Jack. It's really pretty,' I lied.

'Glad you like it,' Jack said. 'It's kinda a theme for your birthday.' Then he shot his eyes over to Erik and Damien. The three of them grinned at each other like bad little boys.

I planted a smile on my face. 'Oh, well, good. Then I'd better open the next present.'

'Mine's next!' Damien handed me a long, soft box.

Smile wedged in place, I started to open the box, though I couldn't help wishing I could turn into a cat and hiss and run from the room.

CHAPTER TWO

'OOOH, IT'S BEAUTIFUL!' I STROKED MY HAND OVER THE folded material of the scarf, thoroughly shocked that I'd actually gotten a cool gift.

'It's cashmere,' Damien said smugly.

I lifted it from the box, thrilled that it was a chic, shimmery cream color instead of the red or green birthmas presents I usually get. Then I froze, realizing I'd been thrilled too soon.

'See the snowmen embroidered on the ends?' Damien said. 'Aren't they adorable?'

'Yep, adorable,' I said. Sure — *for Christmas* they're adorable. For a birthday present, uh, not so much.

'Okay, we're next,' Shaunee said, passing me a big box haphazardly wrapped in green Christmas-tree foil.

'And we didn't follow the snowman theme,' Erin said, frowning at Damien.

'Yeah, no one told us,' Shaunee frowned at Damien, too.

'That's okay!' I said a little too quickly and enthusiastically, and then tore into their package. Inside was a pair of black leather stiletto boots that would have been utterly cool and chic and fabulous . . . had it not been for the Christmas trees, complete with red and gold ornaments, that were stitched in full color on the side of each boot. This. Can. Only. Be. Worn. At. Christmas. Which makes it definitely a lame birthmas present.

'Oh, thanks.' I tried to gush. 'They're really cute.'

'Took us forever to find them,' Erin said.

'Yeah, plain boots would not do for Ms Born-on-the-Twenty-Fourth,' Shaunee said.

'No indeed. Plain old black leather stiletto boots would never do,' I said, feeling like crying.

'Hey, there's another present left.'

Erik's voice pulled me out of the black hole of my birthmas-present depression. 'Oh, something else?' I hoped it was only to my ears that my tone said, 'Oh, yet another tragic non-present present?'

'Yeah, one more something else.' Almost shyly, he handed me a very small rectangular shaped box. 'I really hope you like it.'

I glanced down at the box before I took it and almost

14

squealed in happy surprise. Erik was holding a silver and gold wrapped present with a Moody's Fine Jewelry sticker plastered classily in the middle of it. (I swear I heard the 'Hallelujah Chorus' crescendo somewhere in the background.)

'It's from Moody's!' I sounded breathless, but I couldn't help myself.

'I hope you like it,' Erik repeated, lifting his hand and offering the little silver and gold box like a shining treasure.

I ripped through the lovely wrapping to expose a black velvet box. Velvet. I swear. Real velvet. I bit my lip to keep from giggling, held my breath, and opened it.

The first thing I saw was the gleaming platinum chain. Speechless with happiness my eyes followed the chain down to the beautiful pearls that were nestled into the plush velvet. Velvet! Platinum! Pearls! I sucked in air so that I could begin my gushing *ohmygodthankyouErikyou'rethebestboyfriendever* when I realized that the pearls were oddly shaped. Were they defective? Had the fabulously exclusive and amazingly expensive Moody's Fine Jewelry Store ripped off my boyfriend? And then I realized what I was seeing.

The pearls were shaped into a snowman.

'Do you like it?' Erik asked. 'When I saw it, it just screamed Zoey's birthday at me, and I had to get it for you.'

'Yeah. I like it. It's, uh, unique.' I managed.

'It's Erik who came up with the snowman theme!' Jack cried happily.

'Well, it wasn't really a theme,' Erik said, his cheeks getting a little pink. 'I just thought it was different, not like those typical hearts and such that everyone gets.'

'Yep, hearts and such would be so ordinarily birthday-fied. Who would want that?' I said.

'Let me put it on you,' Erik said.

There was nothing else to do but pull my hair out of the way and let Erik step back to clasp the delicate chain around my throat. I could feel the snowman hanging heavy and disgustingly festive just above my cleavage.

'It's cute,' Shaunee said.

'And very expensive,' Erin said. Both Twins gave mirrored nods of approval.

'It matches my scarf perfectly,' Damien said.

'And my snow globe!' Jack added.

'It's definitely a Christmas birthday theme,' Erik said, giving the Twins a sheepish look, which they responded to with forgiving grins.

'Yes, yes, it certainly is a Christmas birthday theme,' I said, fingering the pearl snowman. Then I beamed to everyone a very bright, very painted-on smile. 'Thanks, you guys. I really appreciate all the time and effort it took y'all to find such-special gifts. I mean it.' And I did mean it. I may loathe the gifts, but the thoughts behind them were a totally different thing.

My absolutely clueless friends came together and we all did a kinda awkward group hug that left us laughing. Just then the door swung open and the light from the hall glistened on very blond, very big hair.

'Here.'

Thankfully, my turning-into-vampyre reflexes were pretty good, and I caught the box she tossed at me.

'Mail call came for you while you were back here with your nerd herd,' she sneered.

'Go away, Aphrodite, ya hag,' Shaunee said.

'Before we throw some water on you and you melt,' Erin added.

'Whatever,' Aphrodite said. She started to turn away, but paused and gave me a wide, innocent smile before saying, 'Nice snowman necklace.' Our eyes met and I swear she winked at me before tossing her hair and flitting away, her laughter floating in the air after her like mist.

'She's such a total bitch,' Damien said.

'You'd think she would have learned her lesson when you took the Dark Daughters from her, and Neferet proclaimed that the Goddess has withdrawn her gifts from Aphrodite,' Erik said. 'But that girl will never change.'

I looked sharply at him. *So says Erik Night, her ex-boyfriend.* I didn't need to say the words aloud. I knew by the way Erik looked hastily away from me that they were easy enough to read in my eyes.

'Don't let her mess up your birthday, Z,' Shaunee said.

'Ignore the hateful hag. Everyone else does,' Erin said.

Erin was right. Since Aphrodite's selfishness had caused her to be publicly kicked out of leadership of the Dark Daughters, the school's most prestigious student group, and the position of Lead Dark Daughter as well as priestess in

17

training had been given to me, she had lost her standing as most popular and powerful fledgling. Our High Priestess, Neferet, who was also my mentor, had made it clear that our goddess, Nyx, has withdrawn her favor from Aphrodite. Basically, Aphrodite was shunned where she was once put on a big ol' popularity pedestal and worshipped.

Unfortunately, I knew there was more to the story than what everyone else believed. Aphrodite had used her visions, which had clearly *not* been taken away from her, to save my grandma as well as Heath, my human boyfriend. Sure, she'd been bitchy and selfish during the saving, but still. Heath and Grandma were alive, and a good part of the credit for that goes to Aphrodite.

Plus, recently I'd found out that Neferet, our High Priestess – my mentor, the vamp most looked up to at the school – was also not what she appeared to be. Actually, I was coming to believe that Neferet was probably as evil as she was powerful.

Darkness does not always equate to evil, just as light does not always bring good. The words that Nyx had said to me the day I was Marked flitted through my mind, summarizing the problem with Neferet. She wasn't what she appeared to be.

And I couldn't tell anyone – or at least not anyone who was alive (which left me with my undead best friend who I hadn't managed to talk to during the entire past month). Thankfully, I also hadn't talked to Neferet for the past month. She'd left for a winter retreat in Europe and wasn't scheduled to be back until the New Year. I figured I'd come up with a plan about how to deal with her when she returned.

So far my plan consisted of just that: coming up with a plan. Which was no plan at all. Crap.

'Hey, what's in the package?' Jack said, pulling me out of my mental nightmare back to my birthmas party nightmare.

We all looked at the brown paper package I was still holding.

'I dunno,' I said.

'I'll bet it's another birthday present!' Jack cried. 'Open it!'

'Oh, boy . . ,' I said. But when my friends gave me confused looks I got real busy unwrapping the box. Inside the generic brown wrapper was another box, this one wrapped in beautiful lavender paper.

'It *is* another birthday present!' Jack squealed.

'Wonder who it's from?' Damien asked.

I was just wondering the same thing, and thinking that the paper reminded me of my grandma, who lived on an awesome lavender farm. But why would she send my present through the mail when I was meeting her later tonight?

I uncovered a smooth, white box, which I opened. Inside was another, much smaller white box fitted snuggly inside a bunch of lavender tissue paper. Curiosity completely killing me, I lifted the little box from its lavender tissue nest. Several pieces of the paper clung all static-electricified to the bottom of the newly freed box, and I brushed them off before opening it. As they floated to the table I peeked inside the box and sucked in a shocked breath. Lying on a bed of white cotton was the most beautiful sliver bracelet I'd ever seen. I picked it up, oohing and ahing at the twinkling charms. There were starfish and seashells and seahorses, and each of them was separated by adorable little silver hearts.

'It's absolutely perfect!' I said, fastening it to my wrist. 'I wonder who could have sent it to me?' Laughing, I turned my wrist this way and that, letting the gaslights that were so easy on our sensitive fledgling eyes catch the polished silver and make it glisten like faceted jewels. 'It must be my grandma, but that's weird because we're meeting in just . . . ,' and I realized everyone was totally, absolutely, uncomfortably silent.

I looked from my wrist to my friends. Their expressions ranged from shock (Damien) to annoyance (the Twins) to anger (Erik).

'What?'

'Here,' Erik said, handing me a card that must have slipped out of the box with the clinging tissue paper.

'Oh,' I said, instantly recognizing the scrawling handwriting. *Oh, hell*! It was from Heath. Better known as boyfriend no. 2. As I read the short note I felt my face getting hot and knew I was turning a totally unattractive shade of bright red.

> *Zo – HAPPY BIRTHDAY!! I know how much you hate those lame birthmas presents that try to mush your b-day with Christmas, so I sent you something I know you'll like. Hey! It doesn't have anything to do with Christmas! Duh! I'm hating the stupid Cayman Islands and this boring vacation with my parents and I'm counting the days till I can be with you again. See you on the 26th! I heart you! Heath*

'Oh,' I repeated like a total moron. 'It's, uh, from Heath.' I wished I could make myself disappear.

'Please. Just please. Why didn't you tell anyone that you don't like birthday presents that have anything to do with Christmas?' Shaunee asked in her usual no-nonsense way.

'Yeah, all you had to do was say something,' Erin said.

'Uh,' I said succinctly.

'We thought the snowman theme was a cute idea, but it's not if you hate Christmas stuff,' Damien said.

'I don't hate Christmas stuff,' I managed to say.

'I like snow globes,' Jack said softly, looking like he was about to cry. 'The snowy part makes me happy.'

'Looks like Heath knows more about what you like than we do.' Erik's voice was flat and emotionless, but his eyes were dark with hurt, which made my stomach clench.

'No, Erik, it's not like that,' I said quickly, taking a step toward him.

He moved back like I had some kind of awful disease he might catch, and suddenly it really pissed me off. It wasn't my fault that Heath had known me since I was in third grade and had figured out the mushed birthmas present issue years ago. Okay, yes, he knew stuff about me that the rest of them didn't. There was nothing weird about that! The kid had been in my life for seven years. Erik and Damien, the Twins and Jack had been in my life for two months – or less. How was that my fault?

Purposefully, I made a show of looking at my watch. 'I'm supposed to meet my grandma at Starbucks in fifteen minutes.

I better not be late.' I walked over to the door, but paused before I left the room. I turned around and looked at my group of friends. 'I didn't mean to hurt anyone's feelings. I'm sorry if Heath's note made you guys feel bad – but that's not my fault. And I did tell someone that I don't like it when people try to mush my birthday together with Christmas – I told Stevie Rae.'

CHAPTER THREE

THE STARBUCKS AT UTICA SQUARE, THE COOL OUTDOORS shopping center that was right down the street from the House of Night, was a lot busier than I'd thought it would be. I mean, sure, it was an unusually warm winter night, but it was also December 24, and almost nine o'clock. You'd think people would be home getting ready for visions of sugarplums and whatnot, and not out looking for a caffeine buzz.

No, I told myself sternly, *I am not going to be in a bad mood for Grandma. I hardly ever get to see her, and I'm not going to spoil the little time we have together.* Plus, Grandma was totally hip to the fact that birthmas presents were lame. She always got me something as unique and wonderful as she is.

'Zoey! I'm over here!'

At the far edge of the Starbucks sidewalk area I could see Grandma's arms waving at me. This time I didn't have to plant a fake smile on my face. The rush of happiness that seeing her always brought me was authentic and had me dodging through the crowd as I hurried to her.

'Oh, Zoeybird! I've missed you so, *u-we-tsi-a-ge-ya!*' The Cherokee word for daughter wrapped around me, along with my grandma's warm, familiar arms that held the sweet, soothing scent of lavender and home. I clung to her, absorbing love and security and acceptance.

'I've missed you, too, Grandma.'

She squeezed me one more time and then held me back at arm's length. 'Let me look at you. Yes, I can tell that you're seventeen. You look so much more mature, and I think a little taller than you did when you were merely sixteen.'

I grinned. 'Oh, Grandma, you know I don't look any different.'

'Of course you do. Years always add beauty and strength to a certain type of woman – and you're that type.'

'So are you, Grandma. You look great!' I wasn't just saying that. Grandma was a zillion years old – at least somewhere in her fifties – but she looked ageless to me. Okay, not ageless like vamp women who looked twenty-something at fifty-something (or one-hundred-and-fifty-something). Grandma was an adorable human ageless with her thick silver hair and her kind brown eyes.

'I do wish you didn't have to cover your lovely tattoos to meet me here.' Grandma's fingers rested briefly on my cheek where I'd hastily patted the thick concealing makeup fledglings were required to wear when they left the House of Night campus. Yes, humans knew vampyres existed – adult vamps didn't conceal themselves. But the rules for fledglings were different. I guess it made sense – teenagers didn't always handle conflict well – and the human world did tend to conflict with vampyres.

'That's just the way it is. Rules are rules, Grandma,' I shrugged it off.

'You didn't cover the beautiful Marks on your neck and shoulder, did you?'

'No, that's why I'm wearing this jacket.' I glanced around to make sure no one was watching us, then I brushed back my hair and flipped down the shoulder of the jacket so that the sapphire lacework on the back of my neck and shoulder was visible.

'Oh, Zoeybird, it's just so magical,' Grandma said softly. 'I'm so proud that the goddess has Chosen you as special and Marked you so uniquely.'

She hugged me again, and I clung to her, incredibly glad that I had her in my life. She accepted me for *me*. It didn't matter to her that I was turning into a vampyre. It didn't matter to her that I was already experiencing blood-lust and that I had the power to manifest all five of the elements: air, fire, water, earth, and spirit. To Grandma I was her true *u-we-tsi-a-ge-ya*, the daughter of her heart, and everything else that came along with me was just secondary stuff. It was weird and wonderful that she and I could be so close and so much alike when her real daughter, my mom, was so completely different.

'There you are. The traffic was just awful. I hate leaving Broken Arrow and fighting my way to Tulsa during the holiday rush.'

As if my thoughts had somehow tragically conjured her, my mother's voice threw cold water on my happiness. Grandma and I let go of each other to see my mom standing beside our table, holding a rectangular bakery box and a wrapped present.

'Mom?'

'Linda?'

Grandma and I spoke together. It was no surprise that Grandma looked as shocked as me by my mother's sudden appearance. Grandma would never have invited my mother without letting me know. Both of us saw totally eye to eye about my mother. One, she made us sad. Two, we wished she would change. Three, we knew she probably wouldn't.

'Don't look so surprised. Like I wouldn't show up at my own daughter's birthday celebration?'

'But, Linda, when I talked with you last week you said you were going to send Zoey's birthday present to her through the mail,' Grandma said, looking as annoyed as I felt.

'That was before you said you were meeting her here.'

Mom told Grandma, then she frowned at me. 'It's not like Zoey invited me to come herself, but then I'm used to having an inconsiderate daughter.'

'Mom, you haven't talked to me in a month. How was I supposed to invite you anywhere?' I tried to keep my tone neutral. I really didn't want Grandma's visit to deteriorate into a big drama scene, but my mom hadn't said ten sentences and she was already totally pissing me off. Except for the stupid Christmas-birthday card she'd sent me, the only communication I'd had with my mom had been when she and her awful husband, the step-loser, had come to parent visitation at the House of Night a month ago. It had been a complete nightmare. The step-loser, who was an Elder for the People of Faith Church, had been his usual narrow-minded, judgmental, bigoted self and had ended up basically being thrown out and told never to come back. As usual, my mom had scampered along after him like a good little submissive wife.

'Didn't you get my card?' Mom's brittle tone started to crumble under my steady look.

'Yes, Mom. I did.'

'See, I've been thinking about you.'

'Okay, Mom.'

'You know, you could call your mother once in a while,' she said a little tearfully.

I sighed. 'Sorry, Mom. School's just been crazy with semester finals and all.'

'I hope you're getting good grades at that school.'

'I am, Mom.' She made me feel sad and lonely and angry at the same time.

'Well, good.' Mom wiped her eyes and started bustling around with the packages she'd brought. In an obviously forced cheerful voice she added, 'Come on, let's all sit down. Zoey, you can go into Starbucks and get us something to drink in a minute. It's a good thing your grandma invited me. As usual, no one else thought to bring a cake.'

We sat down and Mom wrestled with the tape on the bakery box. While she was busy, Grandma and I shared a look of complete understanding. I knew she hadn't invited Mom, and she knew I absolutely hated birthday cake. Especially the cheap, overly sweet cake my mom always ordered from the bakery.

With the kind of horrible fascination usually reserved for gawking at car wrecks I watched Mom open the bakery box and reveal a small square one-layer white cake. The generic *Happy Birthday* was written in red, which matched the red poinsettias blobbed at each corner. Green icing trimmed the whole thing.

'Doesn't it look good? Nice and Christmassy,' Mom said as she tried to pick off the half-price sticker from the lid of the box. Then she froze and looked at me with overly wide eyes. 'But you don't celebrate Christmas anymore, do you?'

I found the fake smile I'd been using earlier and replanted it on my face. 'We celebrate Yule, or Winter Solstice, which was two days ago.'

'I'll bet the campus is beautiful right now.' Grandma smiled at me and patted my hand.

'Why would the campus be beautiful?' Mom's brittle tone was back. 'If they don't celebrate Christmas, why should they decorate Christmas trees?'

Grandma beat me to the explanation. 'Linda, Yule was celebrated a long time before Christmas. Ancient peoples have been decorating *Christmas trees*,' she said the words with a slightly sarcastic intonation, 'for thousands of years. It was Christians who adopted that tradition from Pagans, not the other way around. Actually, the church chose December twenty-fifth as the date of Jesus' birth to coincide with Yule celebrations. If you'll remember, the whole time you were growing up we rolled pinecones in peanut butter, strung apples and popcorn and cranberries together, and decorated an outside tree that I always called our Yule tree, along with our inside Christmas tree.' Grandma smiled a kinda sad, kinda confused smile at her daughter before turning back to me. 'So did you decorate the trees on campus?'

I nodded. 'Yeah, they look amazing, and the birds and squirrels are going totally nuts, too.'

'Well, why don't you open your presents, then we can have cake and coffee?' My mom said, acting like Grandma and I had never spoken.

Grandma brightened. 'Yes, I've been looking forward to giving you these for a month now.' She bent and withdrew two presents from under her side of the table. One was big and tented with brightly colored (and definitely not Christmas) wrapping paper. The other was book-sized and covered in cream-colored tissue paper like you'd get from a chic boutique.

'Open this one first.' Grandma pushed the tented present to me and I eagerly unwrapped it to find the magic of my childhood underneath.

'Oh, Grandma! Thank you so much!' I pressed my face into the brightly blooming lavender plant she'd potted in a purple clay pot and inhaled. The aroma of the wonderful herb brought visions of lazy summer days and picnics with Grandma. 'It's perfect,' I said.

'I had to rush grow it in the hothouse so that it would be blooming for you. Oh, and you'll need this.' Grandma handed me a paper bag. 'There's a grow light inside there and a mounting for it so that you can be sure it gets enough light without having to open your bedroom curtains and hurt your eyes.'

I grinned at her. 'You think of everything.' I glanced at my mom, and saw that she had the blank look on her face that I knew meant she wished she was someplace else. I wanted to ask her why she had bothered to come at all, but pain closed my throat, which surprised me. I had thought that I had grown up beyond her ability to hurt me. Seems the actual truth of being seventeen wasn't as old as I'd imagined.

'Here, Zoeybird, I got you one other thing,' Grandma said, handing me the tissue-paper-wrapped present. I could tell that she'd noticed Mom's stony silence and, as usual, she was trying to make up for her daughter's crappy parenting.

I swallowed down the clog in my throat and unwrapped the present to reveal a leather-bound book that was obviously

old as dirt. Then I noticed the title and I gasped. '*Dracula!*
You got me an old copy of *Dracula!*'

'Look at the copyright page, honey,' Grandma said, eyes
shining with delight.

I turned to the publisher's page and could not believe what
I saw. 'Ohmygod! It's a first edition!'

Grandma was laughing happily. 'Turn a couple of pages.'

I did, and found Stoker's signature scrawled across the
bottom of the title page and dated January, 1899.

'It's a *signed* first edition! It must have cost a zillion dollars!'
I threw my arms around Grandma and hugged her.

'Actually, I found it in a very junky used book store that
was going out of business. It was a steal. After all, it's only a
first edition of Stoker's American release.'

'It's cool beyond belief, Grandma! Thank you so much.'

'Well, I know how much you love that spooky old story,
and in light of recent events I thought it would be ironically
funny for you to have a signed edition,' Grandma said.

'Did you know Bram Stoker was Imprinted by a vampyre, and
that's why he wrote the book?' I gushed as I oh-so-carefully
turned the thick pages, checking out the old illustrations, which
were, indeed, spooky.

'I had no idea Stoker had a relationship with a vampyre,'
Grandma said.

'I wouldn't call being bitten by a vampyre and then put
under her spell a *relationship*,' my mother said.

Grandma and I looked at her. I sighed. 'Mom, it's way
possible for a human and a vampyre to have a relationship.

That's what Imprinting is about.' Well, it was also about bloodlust and some serious desire, along with a psychic link that could be pretty disconcerting, all of which I knew from my experience with Heath. But I wasn't going to mention that to Mom.

My mother shivered like something nasty had just run its finger up her spine. 'It sounds disgusting to me.'

'Mother. Do you not get that there are two very specific choices for my future? One would be that I become the thing that you're saying is disgusting. The other would be that sometime in the next four years I die.' I hadn't wanted to get into it with her, but her attitude was seriously pissing me off. 'So would you rather see me dead or see me an adult vampyre?'

'Neither, of course,' she said.

'Linda,' Grandma put her hand on my leg under the table and squeezed. 'What Zoey is saying is that you need to accept her and her new future, and that your attitude is hurting her feelings.'

'*My* attitude!' I thought Mom was going to launch into one of her tirades about 'why are you always picking on me,' but instead she surprised me by taking a deep breath and then looking me straight in the eyes. 'I don't mean to hurt your feelings, Zoey.'

For a moment she looked like her old self, like the mom she'd been before she'd married John Heffer and turned into the Perfect Stepford Church Wife, and I felt my heart squeeze. 'You do hurt my feelings, though, Mom.' I heard myself say.

'I'm sorry,' she said. Then she held her hand out to me. 'How about we try this birthday thing again?'

I put my hand in hers, feeling cautiously hopeful. Maybe there was part of my old mom left inside her. I mean, she'd come alone, without the step-loser, which was pretty darn close to a miracle. I squeezed her hand and smiled. 'Sounds good to me.'

'Well, then, you should open your present and then we can eat cake,' Mom said, sliding over the box that sat next to the as yet untouched cake.

'Okay!' I tried to keep the enthusiasm in my voice, even though the present was wrapped in paper covered with a grim nativity scene. My smile held until I recognized the white leather cover and gold-tipped pages. With my heart sinking down into my stomach, I turned the book over to read: *The Holy Word, People of Faith Edition* printed in expensive gold leaf cursive across the cover. Another glittering of excess gold caught my eye. Across the bottom of the cover it read, *The Heffer Family*. There was a red velvet bookmark with a gold tassel stuck inside the front pages of the book and, trying to buy time so I could think of something to say other than 'this is a truly awful present,' I let the pages fall open there. Then I blinked, hoping what I was reading was just a trick of my eyes. No. It was really there. The book had opened to the family-tree page. In the weird back-slanted left-handed writing that I easily recognized as belonging to the step-loser, my mom's name LINDA HEFFER had been penned in. A line had been drawn attaching it to JOHN HEFFER, with the date of their marriage off to the side. Underneath their names, written in as if we had been born to them, were the names of my brother, my sister, and me.

Okay, my bio dad, Paul Montgomery, had left us when I was just a kid and had promptly disappeared from the face of the earth. Once in a while a pathetically small child-support check would arrive from him with no return address, but other than those rare instances, he hadn't been part of our lives in upward of ten years. Yes, he was a crappy dad. But he was my dad, and John Heffer, who seriously hated my guts, was not.

I looked up from the bogus family tree and into my mom's eyes. My voice sounded surprisingly steady, calm even, but inside I was a big mess of emotions. 'What were you thinking when you decided on this for my birthday present?'

Mom seemed annoyed at my question. 'We were thinking that you'd like to know that you're still part of this family.'

'But I'm not. I haven't been for a long time before I was Marked. You know that and I know that and John knows that.'

'Your father most certainly does not—'

I held up my hand to cut her off. 'No! John Heffer is not my father. He's your husband, and that's all he is. Your choice – not mine. That's all he's ever been.' The wound that had been bleeding inside me from the time my mother had walked up broke open and hemorrhaged anger throughout my body. 'Here's the deal, Mom. When you bought my present you were supposed to be picking something you thought I might actually like, not something your husband wanted crammed down my throat.'

'You don't know what you're talking about, young lady,' my mother said. Then she glared at Grandma. 'She gets this attitude from you.'

My grandma raised one silver brow at her daughter and said, 'Thank you, Linda, that might be the nicest thing you've ever said to me.'

'Where is he?' I asked my mom.

'Who?'

'John. Where is he? You didn't come here for me. You came here because he wanted you to make me feel bad, and that's not something he'd miss. So where is he?'

'I don't know what you mean.' Her eyes flicked around guiltily, and I knew I'd guessed right.

I stood up and called down the sidewalk, 'John! Come out, come out, wherever you are!'

Sure enough, a man detached himself from one of the stand-up tables that were situated at the opposite end of the sidewalk near the Starbucks entrance. I studied him as he walked up to us, trying to understand what my mother had ever seen in him. He was a totally unspectacular guy. Average height – dark, graying hair – weak chin – narrow shoulders – skinny legs. It wasn't till you looked in his eyes that you saw anything unusual, and then what was revealed was an unusual absence of warmth. I'd always thought it was weird that such a cold, soulless guy would constantly spout religion.

He reached our table and started to open his mouth, but before he could speak I tossed my 'gift' at him.

'Keep it. It's not my family and it's not my beliefs,' I said, looking him squarely in the eyes.

'So you're choosing evil and darkness,' he said.

'No. I'm choosing a loving goddess who has Marked me as her own and gifted me with special powers. I choose a different way than you. That's all there is to it.'

'As I said, you choose evil.' He rested his hand on my mom's shoulder, like she needed his support to be able to sit there. Mom covered his hand with hers and made sniffling sounds.

I ignored him and focused on her.

'Mom, please don't do this again. If you can accept me, and if you really want to see me, then call and we'll meet. But pretending you want to see me because John tells you what to do hurts my feelings and isn't good for either of us.'

'It is good for a wife to submit unto her husband,' John said.

I thought about mentioning how chauvinistic and patronizing and just plain wrong that sounded, but instead I decided not to waste my breath and said, 'John, go to hell.'

'I wanted you to turn away from the evil,' Mom said, crying softly.

My grandma spoke up. Her voice was sad but stern. 'Linda, it is unfortunate that you found and then bought completely into a belief system that insists as one of its basic tenants that different means evil.'

'What your daughter has found is God, no thanks to you,' John snapped.

'No. My daughter has found you, and it is sad but true that she never liked to think for herself. Now you're doing her thinking for her. But here's a little independent thought that Zoey and I would like to leave with you,' Grandma continued speaking as she handed me my lavender plant and first edition of *Dracula*, and then grabbed my elbow and pulled me to my feet. 'This is America, and that means you don't have the right to think for the rest of us. Linda, I agree with Zoey. If you can find some sense in that head of yours and want to see us because you love us *as we are*, then give me a call. If not, I don't want to hear from you again.' Grandma paused and shook her head in disgust at John. 'And you, I don't ever want to hear from again, no matter what.'

As we walked away, John's voice whipped out at us, sharp and cutting with anger and hatred. 'Oh, you'll hear from me again. Both of you will. There are many good, decent, God-fearing people who are tired of tolerating your evil, who believe enough is enough. We won't live side by side with worshippers of darkness for much longer. Mark my words . . . wait and see . . . it is time you repented . . .'

Thankfully, we were soon beyond hearing his rant. I felt like I was going to cry until I realized what my sweet old grandma was muttering to herself.

'That man is such a damn turd monkey.'

'Grandma!' I said.

'Oh, Zoeybird, did I call your mother's husband a damn turd monkey out loud?'

'Yes, Grandma, you did.'

She looked at me, her dark eyes sparkling. 'Good.'

CHAPTER FOUR

GRANDMA TRIED TO SAVE THE REST OF MY BIRTHDAY celebration. We walked across Utica Square to the Stonehorse Restaurant, where we decided to have some decent birthday cake. Which meant Grandma had two glasses of red wine and I had a brown pop and a huge, gooey slice of devil's food cake. (Yes, we enjoyed the irony.)

Grandma didn't try to make it all better by fabricating some crap about my mom not meaning it . . . she'd come around . . . just give her time . . . blah . . . blah . . . blah. Grandma's way more practical and tons cooler than that.

'Your mom's a weak woman who can only find her identity

through a man,' she said as she sipped her red wine. 'Unfortunately, she chose a really bad man.'

'She'll never change, will she?'

Grandma touched my cheek gently. 'She might, but I honestly doubt it, Zoeybird.'

'I like it that you don't lie to me, Grandma,' I said.

'Lies don't fix things. They don't even make things easier, at least not in the long run. Best to tell the truth and then clean up an honest mess.'

I sighed.

'Honey, do you have a mess you need to clean up?' Grandma asked.

'Yeah, but unfortunately it's not an honest one.' I gave Grandma a sheepish smile and told her about my disastrous birthday party.

'You know, you're going to have to straighten out this boyfriend issue. Heath and Erik are only going to put up with each other for about this long.' She held up her fingers, measuring out roughly an inch's worth of 'this long.'

'I will, but Heath was in the hospital for almost a week after that whole serial killer thing that I saved him from, and then his parents jetted him off to the Cayman Islands for their Christmas vacation. I haven't even seen him in a month. So I really haven't had the chance to do much about the Heath and Erik issue.' I focused on scraping the bottom of my plate instead of looking at Grandma. The 'whole serial killer thing' was utter b.s. I'd saved Heath, but it hadn't been from something as simple as a crazy human. I'd saved him from a group of creatures that my best friend, the undead Stevie Rae, had been (and probably still was) leader of. But I couldn't tell Grandma that. I couldn't tell anyone that, because behind it all was the High Priestess of the House of Night, my mentor, Neferet, and she was way too psychic for my own good. She can't seem to read my mind, at least not very well, but I tell someone – she reads his or her mind – we're all in a lot of trouble.

Talk about stress.

'Maybe you should go home and make it right,' Grandma said. Then, when she saw my startled look she added, 'I mean, make the birthmas present issue right, not the Heath and Erik issue.'

'Oh, good. Yeah, I should do that.' I paused, thinking about what she had just said. 'You know, it really has turned into my home.'

'I know.' She smiled. 'And I'm glad for you. You're finding your place, Zoeybird, and I'm proud of you.'

Grandma had walked me back to where I'd parked my vintage VW Bug, and hugged me good-bye. I'd thanked her for the great presents again, and neither of us had mentioned my mother. There are just some things it doesn't do any good to talk about. I'd told Grandma I was going back to the House of Night to make things right with my friends, and I'd meant to. But instead I found myself driving downtown. Again.

For the past month every night I could make a lame excuse or sneak out by myself, I'd been haunting the streets of downtown Tulsa. Haunting . . . I snorted to myself. That was an excellent word to use for me searching for my best friend, Stevie Rae, who had died a month ago, and then become undead.

Yes, it was as weird as it sounded.

Fledglings died. We all knew that. I'd witnessed the death of two of the three who had died since I'd been at the House of Night. Okay, so everyone knew we could die. What everyone didn't know was that the last three fledglings who had died had resurrected, or come alive again, or . . . hell! I suppose the easiest way to describe it is that they had become the stereotype for vampyres: the walking undead who were bloodsucking monsters with no humanity left within them at all. And they smelled bad, too.

I knew because I'd been unlucky enough to see what I had at first thought were the ghosts of the first two dead fledglings. Then human teenagers started being killed, and it had looked like someone was trying to set up a vampyre as the killer. That sucked, especially since I'd known the first two boys who had been killed, and the police's attention turned on me for a little while. What sucked even worse was when Heath had been the third human taken.

Well, I couldn't let him be killed. Plus, we'd kinda sorta accidentally Imprinted. With Aphrodite's help I'd figured out how to follow the Imprint to Heath. The police thought that I'd rescued a pretty messed-up Heath from a human serial killer.

What had I really discovered?

My undead best friend and her disgusting minions.

I'd gotten Heath out of there (the 'there' had been the old downtown Prohibition tunnels under the abandoned Tulsa depot) and confronted Stevie Rae. Or what was left of her.

See, one problem was that I didn't believe all of her humanity had been destroyed, like it appeared to have been with the other undead and very nasty ex-fledglings who had been trying to chomp on Heath.

The second problem was Neferet. Stevie Rae had told me that Neferet was behind their undeadness. I knew it was true because Neferet had put a really awful spell on Heath and me right before the police had showed up. It was supposed to make us forget everything that had happened in the tunnels. I think it worked on Heath. It had only worked on me temporarily. I'd used the power of the five elements to break through mine.

So, long story short. Since then I'd been worried about what the hell I was going to do about: one, Stevie Rae; two, Neferet; three, Heath. It might seem that it helped that none of my three worries had been around during the past month, but it didn't.

'All right,' I said aloud, 'it's my birthday, and an exceedingly crappy birthday it has been, even for me. So, Nyx, I'm going to ask for only one birthday favor from you. I want to find Stevie Rae.' I added a hasty 'Please.' (As Damien would remind me, when speaking to one's goddess it was best to be polite.)

I hadn't really expected any kind of answer, so when the words *roll down your window* kept drifting around and around my mind, I thought they were the lyrics to a song on the radio. But my radio wasn't on, and the words had no music with them – plus, they were inside my head and not inside my radio.

Feeling more than a little nervous I rolled down my window.

It had been unusually warm all week. Today the high had been almost sixty, which was weird for December, but it was Oklahoma, and weird was just another word for Oklahoma weather. Still, it was close to midnight and the night had definitely cooled off. Not that that bothered me. Adult vamps don't feel the cold with the same intensity as humans. No, it isn't because they are cold, dead, pieces of walking reanimated flesh (eesh, that might be what Stevie Rae is, though). It's because their metabolism is way different than humans. As a fledgling, especially one who is more advanced than most kids who have only been Marked for a couple of months, my resistance to the cold was already way better than a human kid's. So the cool air rushing into my Bug didn't bother me, which was why it was strange that I suddenly started to sneeze and felt kinda creepy.

Ugh, what was that smell? It was like a musty basement and egg salad that hadn't been refrigerated soon enough and dirt all mixed together to make a disgusting whiff of something that was nastily familiar.

'Ah, hell!' I realized what I was smelling and jerked my Bug across all three one-way lanes to park a little bit north of the downtown bus station. I barely took time to roll up my window and lock the door (I'd just die if my first edition of

Dracula was ripped off) before I got out of the car and hurried to the sidewalk where I stood very still and sniffed the air. I caught the scent right away. Ugh. It was too horrible to ignore. Still sniffing like a retarded dog, I began following my nose down the sidewalk away from the comforting lights of the bus station.

I found her in an alley. At first I thought she was leaning over a big trash bag full of garbage and my heart squeezed. I had to get her out of this kind of life – I had to figure out a way to keep her safe until this awful thing that had happened to her could be fixed. *Or she needs to die once and for all.* No! I closed my mind to that kind of thinking. I'd watched Stevie Rae die once. I wasn't going to do it again.

But before I could get to her and wrap her in my arms (while I held my breath) and tell her I'd make all of this okay, the bag of garbage moaned and moved and I realized that Stevie Rae wasn't digging through the trash, she was biting a street person on the neck!

'Oh, gross! Jeesh, would you just stop!'

With inhuman quickness, Stevie Rae whirled around. The street person fell to the ground, but Stevie Rae kept hold of one of her dirty wrists. Teeth bared and eyes glowing a very creepy red she hissed at me. I was too disgusted to be scared or even freaked out. Plus, I'd just had a really terrible birthday and people, even undead best friend people, were on my last nerve.

'Stevie Rae, it's me. You can turn off the hissing crap. Plus, it's a ridiculous vampyre cliché.'

She didn't say anything for a second, and I had the horrible thought that she might have somehow deteriorated in the month since I'd last seen her, to a point where she was actually like the rest of them – bestial and unreachable. My stomach gave a painful flip, but I met her red eyes and rolled my own. 'And, please, you smell really bad. Are there no showers in Creepy Undead Land?'

Stevie Rae frowned, which was actually an improvement, because then her lips covered her teeth. 'Go away, Zoey,' she said. Her voice was cold and flat, making what used to be a sweet Okie accent sound like rough trailer trash, but she'd said my name, which was all the encouragement I needed.

'I'm not going anywhere until we talk. So let go of that street person – eesh, Stevie Rae, she probably has lice and who knows what else – and let's talk.'

'If you want to talk you'll have to wait till I'm done eating.' Stevie Rae cocked her head to the side in a movement that looked insectile. 'Don't I remember that you Imprinted your little human boy toy? Looks like you have a taste for blood your own self. Want to join me in a bite?' She smiled and licked her fangs.

'Okay, nasty, just nasty! And for your information Heath is not my boy toy. He's my boy*friend*, or one of them anyway. I sucked his blood kinda sorta by accident. I was going to tell you about it, but you died. So, no. I do not want to bite that person. I don't even know where she's been.' I gave the poor, wide-eyed, matted-hair woman a weak smile. 'Uh, no offense, ma'am.'

'Good. More for me.' Stevie Rae began to bend back over the woman's throat.

'Stop it!'

She looked over her shoulder at me. 'Like I said, go away, Zoey. You don't belong here.'

'Neither do you,' I said.

'That's just one of the many things you're wrong about.'

When she turned back to the woman, who was now crying and repeating 'please, oh please' over and over, I took a couple of steps forward and raised my hands over my head. 'I said let her go.'

Stevie Rae's answer was to hiss and open her mouth to chomp the woman's neck. I closed my eyes and quickly centered myself. 'Air, come to me!' I commanded. Instantly my hair began to lift in the breeze that surrounded me. I circled one hand in front of me, imagining a mini-tornado. I opened my eyes as I flicked my wrist and tossed the power of air toward the crying homeless woman. Exactly as I'd imagined it, the whirling air surrounded her, and hardly rustling one hair on Stevie Rae's very nappy head, it picked up her victim and carried her down the alley, letting go of her only when she reached the safety of a streetlight. 'Thank you, air,' I murmured, and felt the breeze brush my face caressingly before it dissipated.

'You're getting good at that.'

I turned back to Stevie Rae. She was watching me with an obviously leery expression, as if she thought I was going to conjure another tornado and suck her up into oblivion.

I shrugged. 'I've been practicing. It's really just concentration and control. You'd know that if you'd been practicing, too.'

A flash of pain crossed Stevie Rae's gaunt face so quickly that I wondered if I'd really seen or just imagined it. 'The elements have nothing to do with me now.'

'That's crap, Stevie Rae. You have an affinity for earth. You had it before you died, or whatever,' I faltered over how awkward it was to be talking to undead dead Stevie Rae about being dead. 'That kind of thing just doesn't go away. Plus, remember the tunnels? You still had the affinity then.'

Stevie Rae shook her head and her short blond curls, the ones that weren't all nappy and dirty, bounced, reminding me of how she used to look. 'It's gone. Whatever I once had died with the part of me that was human. You need to accept it and move on. I have.'

'I'll never accept it. You're my best friend. I'm not going to move on.'

Suddenly Stevie Rae hissed a nasty, feral sound, and her eyes blazed blood red. 'Do I look like your best friend?'

I ignored the way my heart was beating around inside my chest. She was right. What she had become was absolutely not like the Stevie Rae I'd known. But I wouldn't believe that she was all the way gone. I'd seen glimpses of my best friend in the tunnels and that meant I couldn't give up on her. I felt like crying, but instead I pulled myself together and forced my voice to sound normal.

'Well, hell no, you don't look like Stevie Rae. How long

has it been since you've washed your hair? And what are you wearing?' I pointed at the sweat pants and oversized shirt that were covered by a long, nastily stained black trench coat like the ones those freaky goth kids like to wear even when it's a hundred degrees outside. 'I wouldn't look like me if I was dressed like that either.' I sighed and took a couple steps closer to her. 'Why don't you just come with me? I'll sneak you back into the dorm. It'll be easy – practically no one's there. Neferet's not there,' I added, and then hurried on (I doubted if either of us wanted to talk about Neferet just then – hell, if ever). 'Most of the teachers are on winter break and the kids are taking short trips to see their families. Absolutely nothing is going on. We won't even be bothered by Damien and the Twins and Erik 'cause they're pissed at me. So you can take a long, soapy shower, and I'll get you some real clothes, then we can talk.' I was looking into her eyes, so I saw the longing that filled them. It lasted only an instant, but I knew it had been there. Then she looked quickly away.

'I can't come with you. I have to feed.'

'That's no problem. I'll get you something to eat from the dorm kitchen. Hey, I'll bet I can find a bowl of Lucky Charms,' I smiled. 'Remember, they're magically delicious – and have absolutely no nutritional value at all.'

'Like Count Chocula does?'

My smiled widened into a relieved grin as Stevie Rae took up the thread of our old argument about which of our personal favorite breakfast cereals was the best. 'Count Chocula has coco-flavored goodness. Coco is a plant. It's healthy.'

Stevie Rae's eyes met mine. Hers weren't glowing red anymore, and she also wasn't trying to hide the tears that were filling them and flowing down her cheeks. I automatically moved to hug her, but she stepped back.

'No! I don't want you to touch me, Zoey. I'm not who I was. I'm dirty and disgusting.'

'Then come back to the school with me and wash up!' I pleaded. 'We'll figure this out – I promise.'

Stevie Rae shook her head sadly and wiped at her eyes. 'There's no figuring this out. When I said that I'm dirty and disgusting I didn't mean on the outside. What you see on the outside of me isn't half as nasty as what I'm really like on the inside. Zoey, I have to feed. That's not eating cereal or sandwiches and drinking brown pop. I have to have blood. Human blood. If I don't—' She paused and I saw a terrible shudder move through her body. 'If I don't, the pain is a gnawing, burning hunger that I can't stand. And you need to understand that I *want* to feed. I *want* to tear open human throats and drink that warm blood so filled with terror and anger and pain that it makes me dizzy.' She paused again, this time breathing heavily.

'You can't really want to kill people, Stevie Rae.'

'You're wrong. I do.'

'You say that, but I know there are still parts of my best friend inside you, and Stevie Rae wouldn't be comfortable spanking a puppy, let alone killing someone.' I hurried on when she opened her mouth to disagree with me. 'What if I can get you human blood so that you don't have to kill anyone?'

In that horrid emotionless tone she said, 'I like the kill.'

'Do you also like to be filthy and smelly and disgusting-looking?' I snapped.

'I don't care about how I look anymore.'

'Really? What if I said I could get you a pair of Roper jeans, cowboy boots, and a nice long-sleeved, tuck-in shirt that is very crisply ironed?' I saw the flicker in her eyes and knew I'd managed to touch the old Stevie Rae. My mind rushed around, trying to come up with the right thing to say while I still had some piece of her listening. 'So here's the deal. Meet me tomorrow at midnight – no, wait. Tomorrow's Saturday. No way things will be settled down enough by midnight for me to sneak out. So make it 3:00 A.M. at the gazebo on the Philbrook grounds.' I paused for a second to grin at her. 'You remember the place, right?' Of course I knew she definitely remembered where I meant. She'd been there with me before, only that night she'd been trying to save me, and not the other way around.

'Yes. I remember.' She clipped the word in that same cold, flat voice.

'Okay, so meet me there. I'll have your outfit with me and I'll also have blood. You can eat, or drink, or whatever, and change your clothes. Then we can start to figure this out.' I added to myself that I'd also have soap and shampoo and do some conjuring of water so the girl could wash up. Eesh, she smelled as terrible as she looked. 'Okay?'

'There's really no point.'

'Can you please let me decide that for myself? Plus, I haven't told you the horrors of my birthday yet. Grandma and I had a nightmare scene with my mom and step-loser. Grandma called the step-loser a turd monkey.'

A laugh burst out of Stevie Rae that sounded so much like her old self that my vision got all blurry with the tears I had to frantically blink away.

'Please come,' I said, my voice rough with emotions. 'I've missed you so much.'

'I'll come,' Stevie Rae said. 'But you'll be sorry.'

CHAPTER FIVE

ON THAT NOT-SO-POSITIVE NOTE, STEVIE RAE WHIRLED around and then dashed down the alley, disappearing into its dark stinkyness. Much more slowly, I got in my Bug. I was sad and restless and had way too much thinking to do to head straight back to the school, so instead I drove to the twenty-four-hour IHOP that was in south Tulsa on Seventy-first Street, ordered a big chocolate milk shake and a stack of chocolate-chip pancakes, and did my thinking while I did some serious stress eating.

I guess it had gone okay with Stevie Rae. I mean, she had agreed to meet me tomorrow. And she hadn't tried to bite me, which was a plus. Of course, the whole trying-to-eat-the-street-person was highly disturbing, as was the totally gross way she looked and smelled. But underneath all of that hateful crazy undead girl exterior I swear I could still sense *my* Stevie Rae, my best friend. I was going to hold tight to that and see if I could coax her back into the light. Figuratively speaking anyway. I think the actual light bothers her even more than it bothers me or adult vamps. Which figured. The gross undead dead kids were definitely vamp stereotypes. I wondered if she'd burst into flame if sunlight touched her. Crap. That would definitely be bad, especially since we're meeting at 3:00 A.M., which was only a couple hours before dawn. Crap again.

As if worrying about sunlight and whatnot wasn't enough, I had to start thinking about what I was going to do when all the profs (Neferet in particular) came back to school in the too-near future, and the fact that I had to keep the knowledge that Stevie Rae was undead versus dead dead from everyone. No. I'd worry about that after I got Stevie Rae cleaned up and someplace safe. I'd just take it one little tiny baby step at a time and hope that Nyx, who had clearly led me to Stevie Rae, was going to give me some help figuring things out.

By the time I got back to school it was almost dawn. The parking lot of the school was mostly deserted, and I didn't meet anyone as I walked slowly around the side of the castle-like cluster of buildings that made up the House of Night. The girls' dorm was at the opposite end of the campus, but

I still wasn't in any hurry. Plus, I had something I needed to do before I went to the dorm and more than likely ran into at least a couple of my disgruntled friends. (Ugh, I really *really* hate my birthday.)

The building that sat across from the main House of Night structure was made of the same odd mixture of old bricks and jutting rocks as the rest of the school, but this one was smaller and rounder, and in front of it was a marble statue of our goddess, Nyx, with her arms upraised as if her hands were cupping a full moon. I stood gazing at the goddess. The old-fashioned gaslights that illuminated the campus weren't just easy on our changing eyesight. They created a soft, warm light that flickered like a caress, breathing life into Nyx's statue.

Feeling more than a little in awe of the goddess, I put down my lavender plant and *Dracula* (gently), and then I searched around in the winter grass at the base of Nyx's statue until I found the tall green prayer candle that had fallen over on its side. I set it upright and then closed my eyes and focused myself, concentrating on the warmth and beauty of the gaslight flame and on how one candle could cast enough light to change the whole atmosphere of a dark room.

'I call flame – light for me, please,' I whispered.

I heard the wick sputter and felt the flash of heat against my face. When I opened my eyes, I saw that the green candle, which represents the element earth, was burning cheerily. I smiled in satisfaction. I hadn't been exaggerating to Stevie Rae. I had been practicing calling the elements during the past month, and I was getting really good at it. (Not that my awesome, goddess-given power would help me soothe my friends' hurt feelings, but still.)

I placed the lighted candle carefully at Nyx's feet. Instead of bowing my head, I tilted it back, so that my face was open and looking up at the majesty of the night sky. And then I prayed to my goddess, but I'll admit that the way I pray sounds a lot like just talking. This isn't because I mean any disrespect to Nyx. It's just the way I am. From the first day I was Marked and the goddess appeared to me, I've felt close to her – like she really cares about what happens in my life, versus being a nameless God on High who looks down on me with a frown and a notebook he's all too ready to fill out passes to hell on.

'Nyx, thanks for helping me tonight. I'm confused and completely weirded out by the Stevie Rae situation, but I know if you'll help me – help us – we can get through this. Take care of her, please, and help me to know what to do. I know you've Marked me and given me special powers for a reason, and I'm beginning to think that the reason might have something to do with Stevie Rae. I won't lie to you; it scares me. But you knew what a sissy I was when you picked me,' I smiled up at the sky. During my first conversation with Nyx I had told her that I couldn't be Marked as special by her because I couldn't even parallel park. It hadn't seemed to matter to her then, and I was hoping it still didn't matter to her. 'Anyway, I just wanted to light this for Stevie Rae to symbolize the fact that I won't forget her, and I won't walk away from what you need me to do, no matter how clueless I am about the details.'

I planned to sit there for a while and hoped that maybe I'd get another whisper in my mind that would give me some idea about how I should handle meeting Stevie Rae tomorrow. So I was still sitting in front of Nyx's statue and staring up at the sky when Erik's voice scared the bejeezus right out of me.

'Stevie Rae's death has really shaken you up, hasn't it?'

I jumped and let out an unattractive squeak. 'Jeesh, Erik! You scared me so bad I almost peed myself. Do not sneak up on me like that.'

'Fine. Sorry. I shouldn't have bothered you. Later.' He started to walk away.

'Wait, I don't want you to go. You just surprised me. Next time rustle a leaf or cough or something. Okay?'

He stopped walking and turned back to me. His face was guarded, but he gave me a tight nod and said, 'Okay.'

I stood up and smiled what I hoped was an encouraging smile. Undead friend and Imprinted human boyfriend aside, I really did like Erik and definitely didn't want to break up with him. 'Actually I'm glad you're here. I need to apologize for what happened before.'

Erik made a brusque gesture with his hand. 'Don't worry about it, and you don't have to wear that snowman necklace, or you can take it back and exchange it. Or whatever. I kept the receipt.'

My hand went up to touch the pearl snowman. Now that I could lose it (and Erik) I suddenly realized it was kinda cute. (Erik was more than kinda cute.) 'No! I don't want to take it back.' I paused and collected myself so I didn't sound so psycho and desperate. 'Okay, here's the thing. There's a distinct possibility that I might be a little overly sensitive about the whole birthday-Christmas issue. I really should have told you guys how I felt about it, but I've had sucky birthdays for so long that I guess I just didn't even think about it. Or at least not until today. And then it really was too late. I wasn't going to say anything and you guys wouldn't even have known if you hadn't seen that note from Heath.' I remembered I still had Heath's gorgeous bracelet on my wrist so I dropped my hand down and pressed it against my side, wishing the adorably cute little hearts would stop jingling so merrily. Then I added lamely, 'Plus, you're right. Stevie Rae has really shaken me up.' Then I clamped my mouth shut because I realized I had (again) talked about the supposedly dead Stevie Rae as if she was alive, or in her case I guess I should say not dead. And, of course, I was babbling like the desperate psycho I was trying not to appear to be.

Erik's blue eyes seemed to look inside me. 'Would things be easier for you if I just backed off and left you alone for a while?'

'No!' He was really making my stomach hurt. 'It definitely wouldn't be easier if you backed off.'

'You've just been so *not here* since Stevie Rae died. I can understand if you need some space.'

'Erik, the truth is it's not just Stevie Rae. There's other stuff going on with me that's really hard to talk about.'

He moved closer and took my hand, lacing his fingers through mine. 'Can't you tell me? I'm pretty good at fixing problems. Maybe I could help.'

I looked up into his eyes and wanted so damn bad to tell him everything about Stevie Rae and Neferet and even Heath that I could feel myself sway toward him. Erik closed the little space left between us and I slid into his arms with a sigh. He always smelled so good and felt incredibly strong and solid.

I rested my cheek against his chest. 'Are you kidding, of course you're good at fixing problems. You're good at everything. Actually, you're freakishly close to perfect.'

I felt his chest rumble as he laughed. 'You say that like it's a bad thing.'

'It's not a bad thing – it's an intimidating thing,' I mumbled.

'Intimidating!' He pulled back so that he could look at me. 'You've got to be kidding!' He laughed again.

I frowned up at him. 'Why are you laughing at me?'

He hugged me and said, 'Z, do you have any clue what it's like to date a girl who is the most powerful fledgling in the history of vampyres?'

'No, I don't date girls.' Not that there's anything wrong with lesbians.

He took my chin in his hand and tilted my face up. 'You can be scary, Z. You *control the elements*, all of them. Talk about having a girlfriend it'd be best not to piss off.'

'Oh, please! Don't be silly. I've never zapped you.' I didn't mention that I have actually zapped people. Most specifically undead people. Well, and his ex-girlfriend, Aphrodite (who is about as hateful and annoying as the undead dead). But it was probably a good idea not to bring all that up.

'I'm just saying that you don't need to be intimidated by anyone. You're amazing, Zoey. Don't you know that?'

'I guess not. Things have been kinda foggy lately.'

Erik pulled back again and looked at me. 'Then let me help clear things up for you.'

I felt myself swimming in his blue eyes. Maybe I could tell him. Erik was a fifth former, and in the middle of his third year at the House of Night. He was almost nineteen and an amazingly talented actor. (He can sing, too.) If any fledgling could keep a secret it would be him. But as I opened my mouth to blurt the truth about undead Stevie Rae a terrible feeling clenched my stomach and made the words freeze in my throat. It was *that* feeling again. The gut-deep feeling I get that tells me to keep my mouth shut or run like hell or sometimes just take a breath and think. Right now it was telling me in an impossible to ignore way that I needed to keep my mouth shut, which Erik's next words just reinforced.

'Hey, I know you'd rather talk to Neferet, but she won't be back for maybe another week or so. I could stand in for her until then.'

Neferet was the one person or vampyre I absolutely could not talk to. Hell, Neferet and her psychic-ness was the reason I couldn't talk to my friends or Erik about Stevie Rae.

'Thanks, Erik.' Automatically, I started to pull out of his arms. 'But I have to work through this myself.'

He let go of me so suddenly I almost fell backward. 'It's him, isn't it?'

'Him?'

'That human guy. Heath. Your old boyfriend. He's coming back in two days and that's why you're acting weird.'

'I'm not acting weird. At least not that weird.'

'Then why won't you let me touch you?'

'What are you talking about? I let you touch me. I just hugged you.'

'For about two seconds. Then you pulled away, like you've been doing for a while now. Look, if I've done something wrong you need to let me know and—'

'You haven't done anything wrong!'

Erik didn't say anything for several breaths, and when he did speak he sounded way older than almost nineteen and more than a little sad. 'I can't compete with an Imprint. I know that. And I'm not trying to. I just thought you and I had something special. We'll last a lot longer than some biological thing you have with a human. You and I are alike, and you and Heath aren't. At least not anymore.'

'Erik, you're not competing with Heath.'

'I researched Imprinting. It's about sex.'

I could feel my face getting hot. Of course he was right. Imprinting was sexual because the act of drinking a human's blood turned on the same receptor in the vamp's brain and the human's brain that was turned on during orgasm. *Not that*

I wanted to discuss that with Erik. So instead I decided to stick with the surface facts and not get into the deeper stuff. 'It's about blood, not sex.'

He gave me a look that said he had (unfortunately) been telling the truth. He'd done his research.

Naturally, I got defensive. 'I'm still a virgin, Erik, and I'm not ready to change that.'

'I didn't say you—'

'Sounds like you're getting me mixed up with your last girlfriend,' I interrupted. 'The one I saw on her knees in front of you trying to give you *another* blow job.' Okay, it was really not fair of me to bring up the nasty incident I'd accidentally witnessed between Aphrodite and him. I hadn't even known Erik then, but at the moment picking a fight with him seemed a lot easier than talking about the bloodlust I definitely felt for Heath.

'I am not getting you mixed up with Aphrodite,' he said between clenched teeth.

'Well, maybe this isn't about me acting weird. Maybe this is about you wanting more than I can give you right now.'

'That's not true, Zoey. You know damn well I'm not pressuring you about sex. I don't want someone like Aphrodite. I want you. But I want to be able to touch you without you pulling away from me like I'm some kind of leper.'

Had I been doing that? Crap. I probably had. I drew a deep breath. Fighting like this with Erik was stupid, and I was going to end up losing him if I didn't figure out some way to let him get close to me without letting him know things he couldn't accidentally let Neferet know. I looked down at the ground, trying to sort through what I could and couldn't say to him. 'I don't think you're a leper. I think you're the hottest guy at this school.'

I heard Erik's deep sigh. 'Well, you've already said you don't date girls, so that should mean you would like it when I touch you.'

I looked up at him. 'It does. I do.' Then I decided I was going to tell him the truth. Or at least as much of the truth as I could. 'It's just hard to let you get close to me when I'm dealing with, well, *stuff*.' Oh, great. I called it *stuff*. I'm a moron. Why does this kid still like me?

'Z, does this *stuff* have to do with figuring out how to deal with your powers?'

'Yeah.' Okay, that was pretty much a lie but not totally. All the *stuff* (i.e., Stevie Rae, Neferet, Heath) had happened to me because of my powers and I was having to deal with it, though clearly I wasn't doing a very good job of that. I felt like I should cross my fingers behind my back, but was afraid Erik would notice.

He took a step toward me. 'So the *stuff* is not that you hate it when I touch you?'

'Hating it when you touch me is not the *stuff*. Definitely nope. Definitely.' I took a step toward him.

He smiled and suddenly his arms were back around me, only this time he bent to kiss me. He tasted as good as he smells, so the kiss was nice and somewhere in the middle of it I realized how long it had been since Erik and I had had a good hot make-out session. I mean, I'm no ho like Aphrodite, but I'm not a nun either. And I wasn't lying when I told Erik I liked him to touch me. I slid my arms up around his broad shoulders, leaning into him even more. We fit together nice. He's really tall, but I like that. He makes me feel little and girly and protected, and I like that, too. I let my fingers play with the back of his neck where his dark hair brushes down thick and a little curly. My fingernails teased the soft skin there, and I felt him shiver and heard the little moan in the back of his throat.

'You feel so good,' he whispered against my lips.

'So do you,' I whispered back. Pressing myself against him I deepened the kiss. And then on impulse (ho-ish impulse at that) I took his hand from the small of my back and moved it up so that it was cupping the side of my breast. He moaned again and his kiss got harder and hotter. He slid his hand down and under my sweater, and then back up so that he had my breast in his hand, bare except for my lacy black bra.

Okay, I'll just admit it. I liked him touching my boob. It felt good. It especially felt good that I was proving to Erik that I hadn't rejected him. I moved so that he could get a better feel and somehow that little, innocent (well, semi-innocent) movement caused our mouths to slip and my front tooth nicked his bottom lip.

The taste of his blood hit me hard and I gasped against his mouth. It was rich and warm and indescribably salty sweet. I know it sounds gross, but I couldn't help my instant response to it. I cupped Erik's face in my hands and pulled his lip down to my mouth. I licked it lightly, which made the blood flow faster.

'Yes, go ahead. Drink,' Erik said, his voice rough and his breathing coming quicker and quicker.

That was all the encouragement I needed. I sucked his lip into my mouth, tasting the wonderful magic of his blood. It wasn't like Heath's blood. It didn't give me a pleasure so intense that it was almost painful, almost out of control. Erik's blood wasn't the burst of white hot passion Heath's was. Erik's blood was like a small campfire, something warm and steady and strong. It filled my body with a flame that heated a liquid pleasure all the way down to my toes, and it made me want more – more of Erik and more of his blood.

'Uh-hum!'

The sound of a throat being conspicuously (and loudly) cleared had Erik and me jumping away from each other like we'd been electrocuted. I watched Erik's eyes widen as he looked up and behind me, and then saw his smile, which made him totally look like a little boy caught with his hand in a cookie jar (apparently my cookie jar).

'Sorry, Professor Blake. We thought we were alone.'

CHAPTER SIX

OH. MY. GOD. I WANTED TO DIE. I WANTED TO DIE AND turn to dust and have the breeze blow me *anywhere* just as long as it was away. Instead I turned around. Sure enough, Loren Blake, Vampyre Poet Laureate and the Best-Looking Male in the Known Universe, was standing there with a smile on his classically handsome face.

'Oh, uh, hi,' I stuttered, and because that didn't sound stupid enough I blurted, 'You're in Europe.'

'I was. Just got back this evening.'

'So how was Europe?' Calm and collected, Erik draped an arm nonchalantly around my shoulders.

Loren's smile got wider and he looked from Erik to me. 'Not as friendly as it is here.'

Erik, who seemed to be having fun, laughed softly. 'Well, it's not where you go, it's who you know.'

Loren lifted one perfect brow. 'Obviously.'

'It's Zoey's birthday. We were just doing the birthday kiss thing,' Erik said. 'You know Z and I are going out.'

I looked from Erik to Loren. Testosterone was practically visible in the air between them. Jeesh, they were acting totally guy-like. Especially Erik. I swear I wouldn't have been surprised if he knocked me over the head and started dragging me around by my hair. Which was not an attractive mental image.

'Yes, I heard that you two were dating,' Loren said. His smile looked weird – kinda sarcastic so that it was almost a sneer. Then he pointed at my lip. 'You have a little blood there, Zoey. Might want to clean that up.' My face flamed. 'Oh, and happy birthday.' He turned down the sidewalk and headed to the section of the school that housed the professors' private rooms.

'I don't know how that could have been more embarrassing,' I said after licking the blood from my lip and straightening my sweater.

Erik shrugged and grinned.

I smacked him across the chest before reaching down for my plant and my book. 'I don't know why you think this is funny,' I said as I started to march away toward the dorm. Naturally, he followed me.

'We were just kissing, Z.'

'You were kissing. I was sucking your blood.' I looked sideways at him. 'Oh, and there's that little your-hand-up-my-shirt detail. Better not forget that.'

He took the lavender plant from me and grabbed my hand. 'I won't forget that, Z.'

I didn't have a hand free to smack him again with, so I settled for a glare. 'It's embarrassing. I cannot believe Loren saw us.'

'It was just Blake, and he's not even a full professor.'

'It's *embarrassing*,' I repeated, wishing my face would cool off. I also wished I could suck some more of Erik's blood, but I was not going to mention that.

'I'm not embarrassed. I'm glad he saw us,' Erik said smugly.

'You're glad? Since when has public making-out become a turn-on for you?' Great. Erik was a kinky freak boy and I was just now finding out.

'Public making-out isn't a turn-on, but I'm still glad Blake saw us.' All the fun had gone out of Erik's voice, and his smile had turned grim. 'I don't like the way he looks at you.'

My stomach lurched. 'What do you mean? How does he look at me?'

'Like you're not a student and he's not a teacher.' He paused. 'So you haven't noticed?'

'Erik, I think you're crazy.' I carefully didn't answer the question. 'Loren doesn't look at me like anything.' My heart was thumping like it would beat its way out of my chest. Hell yes, I'd noticed how Loren looked at me! *Way* noticed it.

I'd even talked to Stevie Rae about it. But with all that had happened lately, plus Loren being gone for almost a month, I'd just about convinced myself that I'd imagined most of what happened between us.

'You call him Loren,' Erik said.

'Yeah, like you said, he's not a real professor.'

'I don't call him Loren.'

'Erik, he helped me do research for the new rules for the Dark Daughters.' That was more of an exaggeration than an outright lie. I'd been researching. Loren had been there. We'd talked about it. Then he touched my face. Definitely not thinking about that, I hurried on, 'Plus, he's asked me about my tattoos.' And he had. Under the full moon I'd bared most of my back so that he could see them . . . and touch them . . . and let them inspire his poetry. I jerked my mind away from that line of thinking, too, and finished with, 'So I kinda know him.'

Erik grunted.

My mind felt like a bunch of gerbils were zooming around in big wheels inside it, but I made my voice sound light and kidding. 'Erik, are you jealous of Loren?'

'No.' Erik looked at me, looked away, and then met my eyes again. 'Yes. Okay, maybe.'

'Don't be. There's no reason for you to be jealous. There's nothing going on between me and him. Promise.' I bumped my shoulder into his. And at that moment I meant it. It was stressful enough trying to figure out what I was going to do with Imprinted Heath. The last thing I needed was a secret affair with someone who was even more off limits than a human ex-boyfriend. (Sadly, it seemed like the last thing I need is usually the first thing I get.)

'He just doesn't feel right to me,' Erik said.

We'd stopped in front of the girls' dorm and, still holding his hand, I turned to him and fluttered my lashes innocently. 'So you felt up Loren, too?'

He scowled. 'Not even vaguely a possibility.' He pulled me to him and put his arm around me. 'Sorry about getting all nuts about Blake. I know there's nothing going on with you two. I guess I was being jealous and stupid.'

'You're not stupid, and I don't mind you being jealous. Or at least a little bit.'

'You know I'm crazy about you, Z,' he said as he bent and nuzzled my ear. 'I wish it wasn't so late.'

I shivered. 'Me, too.' But I could see the sky starting to get light over his shoulder. Plus, I was exhausted. Between my birthday, my mom and step-loser, and my undead best friend, I really needed some alone time to think and a good solid night's (or in our case, day's) sleep. But that didn't stop me from snuggling into Erik.

He kissed me on the top of my head and held me close. 'Hey, have you figured out who's going to represent earth during the Full Moon Ritual?'

'No, not yet,' I said. Crap. The Full Moon Ritual was in two nights and I'd been avoiding thinking about it. Replacing Stevie Rae would be gruesome enough if she was dead dead. Knowing that she's undead dead and hanging around the stinky alleys and nasty tunnels downtown made replacing her just plain depressing. Not to mention wrong.

'You know I'll do it. All you have to do is ask.'

I tilted my head up to look at him. He was on the Prefect Council, along with the Twins, Damien, and, of course, me. I was Senior Prefect even though I'm technically a freshman and not a senior. Stevie Rae had been part of the council, too. And, no, I hadn't decided who should replace her. Actually, I had to Tap or choose two students for the council and I hadn't thought about that, either. God, I was stressed out. I drew a deep breath. 'Would you please represent earth in the circle for our Full Moon Ritual?'

'No problem, Z. But don't you think it might be a good idea if we had a practice circle casting before then? With all the rest of you having an affinity for an element, or in your case all five elements, we better make sure everything goes smoothly when a nongifted guy stands in.'

'You're not exactly nongifted.'

'Well, I wasn't talking about my vast make-out skills.'

I rolled my eyes. 'Neither was I.'

He pulled me closer so that my body was molded against him. 'Guess I need to show you more of my talent.'

I giggled and he kissed me. I could still taste a hint of blood on his lip, which made the kiss even sweeter.

'Guess you two made up,' Erin said.

'Looks more like a make-out than a makeup, Twin,' Shaunee said.

This time Erik and I didn't spring apart. We just sighed.

70

'There's no such thing as privacy at this school,' Erik muttered.

'Hello! You're sucking face out here in plain sight,' Erin said.

'I think it's kinda sweet,' Jack said.

'That's because you're kinda sweet,' Damien said, twining his arm through Jack's as they walked down the wide front stairs of the dorm.

'Twin, I may vomit. How about you?' Shaunee said.

'Definitely. As in projectile,' Erin said.

'So this lovey-dovey stuff makes you two sick, huh?' Erik asked with an evil gleam in his eyes. I wondered what he was up to.

'Utterly nauseous,' Erin said.

'Ditto,' Shaunee agreed.'

'Then you wouldn't be interested in what Cole and T.J. wanted me to pass along to you?'

'Cole Clifton?' Shaunee said.

'T. J. Hawkins?' Erin said.

'Yep and yep,' Erik said.

I watched the twinly cynical Shaunee and Erin instantly change their negative attitudes.

'Cole is so *fiiiine*,' Shaunee practically purred. 'That blond hair of his and those naughty blue eyes make me want to spank him.'

'T. J.' – Erin fanned herself dramatically – 'that boy can *sing*. And he's tall . . . Ooh, he's *so* damn fine.'

'Does all this drama mean you two are actually interested

in some lovey-dovey stuff?' Damien asked with a smug raise of his eyebrows.

'Yes, Queen Damien,' Shaunee said, while Erin narrowed her eyes at him and nodded.

'So did you have something you wanted to pass along to the Twins from Cole and T. J.?' I prompted Erik before Damien could fire back at the Twins, which made me for the zillionth time miss Stevie Rae. She was a better peacekeeper than me.

'Just that we all thought it would be cool if Shaunee and Erin and you' – he squeezed my shoulders – 'went to the IMAX tomorrow night with us.'

'Us as in you, Cole, and T. J.?' Shaunee asked.

'Yep. Oh, and Damien and Jack are invited, too.'

'What are we gonna see?' Jack asked.

Erik paused for dramatic effect, then said, '*300* is rerunning as a special holiday IMAX event.'

It was Jack's turn to fan himself.

Damien grinned. 'We're in.'

'Us, too,' Shaunee said, while Erin nodded so vigorously in agreement that her long blond hair bounced around, making her look like a crazed cheerleader.

'You know, *300* may be the perfect movie. It has something in it for everyone,' I said. 'Man titties for those of us who like that. And girl boobies for those of us who like that. Plus a very large dose of heroic guy action, and who doesn't like that?'

'And a midnight IMAX show for those of us who don't like the daylight,' Erik said.

'Sheer perfection,' Damien said.

'Ditto,' said the Twins together.

I just stood there and grinned. I was crazy about them. Each and every one of the five of them. I still missed Stevie Rae constantly, but for the first time in a month I was feeling like myself – content, happy even.

'So it's a date?' Erik said.

Everyone chimed in with their yeses.

'Better get back to our dorm. Wouldn't want to be caught on sacred girl ground after dorm curfew,' he teased.

'Yeah, we better go,' Damien said.

'Hey Zoey, happy birthday,' Jack said.

Jeesh, he's a sweet kid. I grinned at him, 'Thanks, honey.' Then I looked at the rest of my friends. 'I'm sorry I was such a butt earlier. I really do like my presents.'

'Which means you'll be *wearing* your presents?' Shaunee said with her sharp chocolate-colored eyes narrowed at me.

'Yeah, you'll be wearing those totally hot boots we spent $295.52 on?' Erin added.

I gulped. Shaunee and Erin's families had money. I, on the other hand, was definitely *not* used to owning $300 boots. Actually, now that I realized how expensive they were, I was liking them more and more. 'Yep. I will be wearing those *fiiiine* boots.' I mimicked Shaunee.

'The cashmere scarf wasn't exactly cheap, either,' Damien said haughtily. 'Did I mention it's cashmere? One hundred percent.'

'More times than we can count,' Erin mumbled.

'I love me some cashmere,' I assured him.

Jack was frowning and looking at his feet. 'My snow globe wasn't that expensive.'

'But it's cute, and it follows the snowman theme, perfectly matching my gorgeous snowman necklace, which I'm never going to take off.' I smiled up at Erik.

'Even in the summer?' He asked.

'Even in the summer,' I said.

Erik whispered, 'Thanks, Z.' And kissed me softly.

'Feeling my gorge rise again,' Shaunee said.

'Puking a little bit in my mouth,' Erin said.

Erik hugged me one more time before jogging after the already-retreating Jack and Damien. Over his shoulder he called, 'So do I tell Cole and T. J. that you two aren't really into the whole kissing thing.'

'Do and we'll kill you,' Shaunee said sweetly.

'You'll be dead like a rock,' Erin said, just as sweetly.

I echoed Erik's fading laughter as I grabbed my lavender pot, hugged *Dracula* to my bosom, and went into the dorm with my friends. And I began to actually think that maybe I could figure out a solution to the Stevie Rae issue and we could all be together again.

Sadly, that thought proved to be as naïve as it was impossible.

CHAPTER SEVEN

SATURDAY EVENING (WHICH IS REALLY OUR SATURDAY morning) is usually a lazy time. Girls hang around the dorm in pj's and nappy, uncombed hair, sleepily eating bowls of cereal or cold popcorn and staring at reruns on the different wide-screen TVs in the dorm's main room. So it's not surprising that Shaunee and Erin gave me confused, groggy frowns when I grabbed a granola bar and a can of brown pop (*not* diet, eesh) and appeared between their glazed stares and the TV.

'What?' Erin said.

'Z, why are you so awake?' Shaunee said.

'Yeah, it's not healthy to be perky so early,' Erin said.

'Exactly, Twin. Each person has only so much perkiness. If they use it up early in the day, then it's gone and you're left with grumpiness,' Shaunee said.

'I'm not perky. I'm busy.' Thankfully, that stopped their lecture. 'I'm going to go to the library to research some ritual stuff.' That wasn't a lie. They just assumed I was talking about the coming Full Moon Ritual when I was actually talking about a ritual to make poor undead dead Stevie Rae un-undead. 'While I'm doing that, I want you guys to find Damien and Erik and tell them that we're going to meet under the tree by the wall at—' I glanced at my watch. 'It's five thirty right now. I should be done with my research by seven-ish. So how about we meet at seven fifteen?'

''Kay,' the Twins said.

'But how come we're meeting?' Erin said.

'Oh, sorry. Erik is going to be representing earth tomorrow.' I swallowed around the sudden clog in my throat. The Twins looked equally sad. Clearly, none of us had really gotten over Stevie Rae, even those of us who believed she was dead. 'Erik thought that it might be a good idea to practice casting a circle before the actual ritual. You know, what with all the rest of us having elemental affinities and him not. I thought it was a good idea, too.'

'Yeah . . . sounds good . . . ,' the Twins mumbled.

'Stevie Rae wouldn't want us to mess up a ritual because we're missing her,' I said. 'She'd be all *Y'all better act right and not make big ol' butts outta yourselves.*' My twang made the Twins smile.

'We'll be there, Z,' Shaunee said.

'Good, then we'll go watch *300* after that,' I said.

That really made them grin.

'Oh, and would you two be sure that all the elemental candles are there?'

'Will do, Z,' Erin said.

'Thanks, guys.'

'Hey, Z,' Shaunee called across the room when I was almost out the door.

I paused and looked back at them.

'Nice boots,' Erin said.

I grinned and held out one foot. I was wearing jeans, but they were the kind that rolled up to just under my knees, which meant that everyone had a clear view of the sparkling Christmas trees that adorned the side of each boot. I was also sporting Damien's snowman scarf, which really was soft as a cashmere dream. A couple of girls sitting on the love seat closest to the door made noises like they thought the boots were cute, too, and I saw the Twins share a smug, told-ya-so look.

'Thanks, the Twins gave them to me for my birthday.' I said, loud enough for Shaunee and Erin to hear. They blew me kisses as I went out the door.

I munched my granola bar and headed to the media center in the main school building. Surprisingly, I was feeling okay about the Full Moon Ritual. Sure, it would be weird not having

Stevie Rae represent earth, but I'd be surrounded by my friends. It was still *us*, even if we were short one of us.

The school was even more deserted today than it had been during the past month, which made sense. It was Christmas, and even though fledglings have to stay in physical contact with adult vamps, we are allowed to stay off campus for up to a full day. (There's some kind of pheromone vamps secrete that semi-controls the physical Change taking place within us and allows us to complete the metamorphosis into adult vamps, or at least allows some of us to do that. The rest of us die.) So lots of kids were spending Christmas with their human families.

As I'd expected, the library was deserted. I didn't need to worry about it being locked up and alarmed like a typical school. Vamps, with their psychic and physical powers, didn't need locks to make us act right. Actually, I wasn't for sure what they did when a fledgling did something typically teenage and moronic. Rumor had it that the vamps would banish the miscreant (hee-hee, 'miscreant,' that was one of Damien's vocab words) for varying periods of time. Which meant the kid could get really sick – as in drowning in his own disintegrating bodily tissues and dying.

All in all, it was best not to piss off the vampyres. Naturally, I'd made an enemy of the most powerful High Priestess at our school. Sometimes being me was good – like when Erik was kissing me or when I was hanging with my friends – but mostly being me was a big ball of stress and angst.

I searched the musty old books in the metaphysical section

of the library (as you can probably imagine, at this particular library it was a big section). It was slow going because I'd decided not to use the computer catalogue search engine. The last thing I needed was to leave an electronic trail that screamed: Zoey Redbird is trying to find information about fledglings that die and have been reanimated as bloodsucking fiends by a High Priestess who is an evil control freak with some kind of as-yet-unknown Master Plan! No. Even I knew that would not be a good idea.

I'd been there for more than an hour and was getting frustrated by my snail-like pace. I really wished I could ask for Damien's help. Not only was the kid smart and a fast reader, he was also seriously good at research. I was clutching *Rituals to Heal Body and Spirit* and trying to get a top-shelf copy of a leather-bound old-as-dirt book titled *Combating Evil with Spells and Rituals*, when a strong arm reached up and plucked it easily from over my head. I turned around and almost banged dorkishly right into Loren Blake.

'*Combating Evil*, huh? Interesting choice of reading material.'

His nearness did not help my nerves. 'You know me' (which he really didn't). 'I like to be prepared.'

His brow wrinkled in confusion. 'Are you expecting an attack of evil?'

'No!' I said way too quickly. So I laughed, trying for a gay, carefree tone (gay, hee-hee), but was sure I came across as totally fake. 'Well, a couple months ago no one expected Aphrodite to lose control of a bunch of blood-sucking vampyre

79

spirits and she did. So I figured, you know, better safe than sorry.' God, I'm a moron.

'Guess that makes sense. So there's nothing specific you're preparing for?'

I wondered at the sharp interest in his eyes. 'Nope,' I said nonchalantly. 'Just trying to do a good job as leader of the Dark Daughters.'

He glanced at the rituals book I was holding. 'You know that those rituals are only for adult vampyres, don't you? When fledglings get sick there is, unfortunately, only one reason behind it. Their bodies are rejecting the Change and they will die.' Then he added in a gentler voice, 'You're not feeling ill, are you?'

'Oh, gosh, no!' I said hastily. 'I'm fine. It's just, well—' I hesitated, grasping for an excuse. With a sudden inspiration I blurted, 'It's embarrassing to admit, but I thought I'd do some extra studying for when I become a High Priestess.'

Loren smiled. 'Why would that be embarrassing to admit? I wouldn't have imagined you as one of those silly women who think being well read and well educated is an embarrassment.'

I felt my cheeks start to get warm – he'd called me a 'woman,' which was way better than him calling me a fledgling or a kid. He always made me feel so grown, so *womanly*. 'Oh, no, that's not it. It's embarrassing because it sounds kinda conceited to assume that I'm going to actually be a High Priestess someday.'

'I think that assumption is just good common sense and

justifiable self-confidence.' His smile warmed till I swear I could feel the heat of it against my skin. 'I always have been drawn to confident women.'

God, he made my toes squidge.

'You don't have any idea how special you are, do you, Zoey? You're unique. Not like the rest of the fledglings. You're a goddess among those who think themselves demigods.' When his hand caressed the side of my face, lingering on the tattoos that framed my eyes, I thought I'd melt into the bookshelves. '*I have sworn thee fair, and thought thee bright. Who art as black as hell, as dark as night.*'

'What's that from?' His touch had made my body all tingly and my head woozy, but I did manage to recognize the deep cadence his amazing voice took on when he was reciting poetry.

'Shakespeare,' he murmured as his thumb brushed softly over the line of tattoos that decorated my cheekbone. 'It's from one of the sonnets he wrote to the Dark Lady, who was his true love. We know, of course, that he was a vampyre. But we believe the true love of his life was a young girl who had been Marked and who died as a fledgling without completing the Change.'

'I thought adult vampyres weren't supposed to have relationships with fledglings.' We were so close that I didn't have to speak much above a whisper for him to hear me.

'We're not supposed to. It's highly improper. But sometimes there's an attraction that happens between two people that transcends the vampyre-fledgling boundary, as well as age and propriety. Do you believe in that kind of attraction, Zoey?'

He was talking about us! We were staring into each other's eyes, and I felt lost in him. His tattoos were a bold pattern of intricate slashing lines that gave the impression of lightning bolts, and they went perfectly with his dark hair and eyes. He was so insanely handsome and so much older that he made me feel at the same time incredibly attracted to him *and* scared to death that I was playing with something so far beyond what I'd ever experienced that it could easily spiral out of control. But the attraction was there – and if he was right, it definitely transcended the vampyre-fledgling boundary. So much so that Erik had even noticed how Loren looked at me.

Erik . . . Guilt washed through me. He would just die if he could see what was going on between Loren and me. A mean little thought snaked through my mind, *Erik isn't here to see me*, and I drew in a deep, shaky breath and heard myself say, 'Yes. I believe in that kind of attraction. Do you?'

'I do now.' His smile was sad. It made him look suddenly very young and handsome and so vulnerable that my guilty thoughts of Erik evaporated. I wanted to take Loren in my arms and tell him it would be all right. I was just getting up the nerve to move even closer to him when his next words surprised me so much that I forgot about his little-lost-boy smile. 'I came back yesterday because I knew it was your birthday.'

I blinked in shock. 'You did?'

He nodded, still caressing my cheek with his finger. 'I had

been looking for you when I ran into you and Erik.' His eyes darkened and his voice went deep and harsh. 'I didn't like seeing his hands all over you.'

I hesitated, not sure how to respond to that. I was embarrassed as hell that he'd seen Erik and me making out. Still, even though what we'd been doing had been embarrassing to be caught at, we hadn't really done anything wrong. Erik was, after all, my boyfriend, and what he and I did together wasn't really any of Loren's business. But staring into his eyes I realized that I might want it to be Loren's business.

As if he could read my mind he took his hand from my face and looked away from me. 'I know. I don't have any right to be angry at you for being with Erik. It's not even my business.'

Slowly, I touched his chin, turning his face back to me so that he could meet my eyes. 'Do you want it to be your business?'

'More than I can tell you,' he said. Then he dropped the book – he'd still been holding it – and framed my face in his hands, so that his thumbs rested close to my lips and his fingers splayed back into my hair. 'I believe it's my turn for a birthday kiss.'

He claimed my mouth and at the same time it felt like he claimed my body and soul. Okay, Erik was a good kisser. And I've been kissing Heath since I was in third grade and he was in fourth, so Heath's kisses were familiar and good. Loren was a man. When he kissed me there was none of the awkward hesitation I was used to. His lips and tongue said he knew exactly what he wanted and he also knew how to get it. And a weird, magical thing happened to me. I wasn't just some kid anymore when I kissed him back. I was a woman, mature and powerful, and I knew what I wanted and how to get it, too.

When the kiss ended both of us were breathing hard. Loren still held my face in his hands, but he'd moved away just far enough so that we could look into each other's eyes again.

'I shouldn't have done that,' he said.

'I know,' I said, but that didn't stop me from staring boldly at him. I was still clutching the stupid healing rituals and spells book with one hand, but my other hand was resting on his chest. Slowly I spread my fingers so that they slid within the open neck of his button-up shirt to touch his naked skin. He shivered and I felt that shiver somewhere deep inside me.

'This is going to be complicated,' he said.

'I know,' I repeated.

'But I don't want to stop.'

'Neither do I,' I said.

'No one can know about us. At least not yet.'

'Okay.' I nodded, not sure what there was to know about, but understanding that the thought of his asking me to sneak around with him made a weird knot form in the pit of my stomach.

He kissed me again. This time his lips were sweet and warm and very, very gentle, and I felt the weird knot dissolving. 'I almost forgot,' he whispered against my lips. 'I have something for you.' He gave me one more fast kiss and then fished into the pocket of his black slacks for something. Smiling, he pulled out a small gold jeweler's box. Holding it out to me he said, 'Happy birthday, Zoey.'

My heart was flopping ridiculously around in my chest as I opened the box – and gasped. 'Ohmygod! They're amazing!' Diamond stud earrings glittered at me like a beautiful, captured dream. They weren't huge and gaudy, but small and dainty and so clear and sparkly that they almost hurt my eyes. For an instant I saw Erik's sweet smile as he'd given me the snowman necklace, and then heard my grandma's voice in my conscience telling me that there's no way I should accept such an expensive gift from a man, but Loren's voice drowned out the image of Erik along with Grandma's warning.

'I saw them and they reminded me of you – perfect and exquisite and fiery.'

'Oh, Loren! I've never had anything so beautiful.' I leaned into him, tilting my face up, and he bent and put his arms around me and kissed me until I thought the top of my head would explode.

'Go ahead, put them on,' Loren whispered to me while I was still trying to get my breath back after our kiss.

I hadn't put any earrings on when I got up, so it only took me a second to stick them through my ears.

'There's an old beveled mirror over in the reading corner. Come look at them.' We stuck the books back on the shelf and Loren took my hand, guiding me over to the cozy corner of the media center that had a big, overstuffed sofa and two matching comfy chairs. On the wall between them was a large, obviously antique, gold-framed beveled mirror. Loren stood behind me with his hands on my shoulders so that both of us were reflected in the mirror. I pushed my thick hair behind my ears and turned my head from side to side so that the flickering gaslights caught the diamonds' facets so they glistened brilliantly.

'They're beautiful,' I said.

Loren squeezed my shoulders and pulled me back against him. 'Yes, you are,' he said. Then, still holding my gaze in the mirror, he bent to nuzzle one of my diamond decorated earlobes and whispered, 'I think you've done enough studying for one day. Come back to my room with me.'

I watched my eyes become all heavy-lidded as he kissed my neck, following the path my tattoos took down to my shoulder. Then I realized what it was he was really asking and a jolt of fright bolted through my body. He wanted me to go back to his room and have sex! I didn't want to do that! Okay, well, maybe I did. In theory anyway. But to *actually* lose my virginity to this incredibly hot, experienced, *man* – right now? Today? I gulped for air and stepped kinda awkwardly out of his arms. 'I – I can't.' While my mind was flailing around for something else I could say that wouldn't sound moronic and juvenile, the grandfather clock that stood solemnly behind the sofa began bonging out seven bells and I felt a rush of relief. 'I can't because I made plans to meet Shaunee and Erin and the rest of the Prefect Council at seven fifteen so we can practice for the ritual tomorrow night.'

Loren smiled. 'You are a diligent little Leader of the Dark

Daughters, aren't you? Then it will have to be another time.' He moved to me, and I thought he'd kiss me again. Instead he touched my face, briefly caressing my tattoos. His touch made me all shivery and breathless. 'If you change your mind I'll be in the poet's loft. You know where that is?'

I nodded, still finding it hard to speak. Everyone knew the in-residence Poet Laureate had the whole third floor of the professors' quarters building all to himself. More than once I'd listened to the Twins fantasize about wrapping up like giant presents and having themselves delivered to the lurve loft (as they call it).

'Good. You should know I'll be thinking about you, even if you don't decide to come put me out of my misery.'

He had already turned and was walking away when I found my voice. 'But I really can't come, so when am I going to see you again?'

He looked over his shoulder at me, smiling his sexy, knowing smile. 'Don't worry, my little High Priestess, I will come to you.'

When he was gone I sat heavily on the couch. My legs felt like rubber and my heart was beating so hard it hurt. Shakily, I touched one of the diamond earrings. It felt cold, unlike the snowman made of pearls that rested accusatorily around my neck and the silver bracelet that was clasping my wrist. They felt hot. I put my face in my hands and said miserably, 'I think I'm turning into a ho.'

CHAPTER EIGHT

Everyone was already there when I rushed up. Even Nala was there. I swear she looked at me with eyes that said she knew exactly what I'd been up to in the library. Then she shot a grumpy 'mee-uf-ow!' in my general direction, sneezed, and padded away. God, I'm so glad she can't talk.

Suddenly Erik's arms were around me. He kissed me quickly and then hugged me while he whispered in my ear, 'I've been looking forward to seeing you all day.'

'Well, I was in the library.' I realized my tone was way too abrupt and hateful (in other words, guilty) when he pulled away from me and gave me a sweet but confused smile.

'Yeah, that's what the Twins told us.'

I looked into his eyes, feeling utterly like poo. How could I even take a chance at losing him? I should never have let Loren kiss me. It was wrong. I knew it was wrong and—

'Hey, Z, nice scarf,' Damien said, tugging on the end of one of the snowmen and interrupting my guilty mental tirade.

'Thanks, my boyfriend gave it to me,' I tried a lame tease, but knew that I sounded all weird and overly perkly.

'By that little comment she means her friend who is a boy,' Shaunee said, giving me an eye roll.

'Yeah, don't stress Jack,' Erin said. 'Damien's not changing teams.'

'Shouldn't you be telling me not to stress?' Erik asked playfully.

'No, sweet thang,' Erin said.

'If Z dumps you for Queen Damien we'll be here to help you deal with your grief,' Shaunee said. Then the Twins did a little impromptu bump and grind for Erik's benefit. Despite the guilt I was feeling, the two of them made me laugh, and I covered Erik's eyes.

Damien pointedly frowned at the Twins and then cleared his throat. 'You two are completely incorrigible.'

'Twin, I forget, what does incorrigible mean?' Shaunee said.

'I do believe it means that we're hotter and sexier than a whole herd of corriges,' Erin said, still bumping and grinding.

'You two are dolts, which means you have very little sense.' Damien said, but even he couldn't keep from laughing, especially when a giggling Jack joined in the bump and grind. 'Anyway,' he continued. 'I almost went to the library, but then Jack and I got all involved watching a *Will and Grace* rerun marathon and I totally lost track of time. Next time you want to do research, just let me know, though, and I'll be happy to help you out.'

'He's such a little bookworm,' Jack said, pushing his shoulder playfully.

Damien blushed. The Twins made gagging noises. Erik laughed. I wanted to puke my guts up.

'Oh, no problem. I was just looking up some, well, stuff,' I said.

'More *stuff* again?' Erik grinned down at me.

I hated that he looked so understanding and supportive. If he knew the *stuff* I'd been researching was making out with Loren Blake . . . Oh, God. No. He could never, ever find out.

And, yes, I realize how trifling and ho-ish it was that not long before this I'd been sucking Loren's face and feeling all hot and tingly about him, but now I was practically suffocating in a wave of guilt.

Clearly I need therapy.

'So did you bring the candles?' I asked the Twins, resolving once and for all to think about the Loren mess later.

'Of course,' Erin said.

'Please. It was easy-peasy,' Shaunee said. 'We even have them put in their correct places.' She pointed behind us to a nice flat area under the canopy of the huge oak. I could see the four candles representing the elements in their proper places, with the fifth candle, representing spirit, sitting in the middle of the circle.

'I brought the matches,' Jack said enthusiastically.

'Okay. Well. Let's do this,' I said. The five of us started moving to our candles. Damien surprised me by hanging back a little from the others and whispering, 'If you want Jack to leave, just let me know and I'll tell him to go.'

'No,' I said automatically, and then my mind caught up with my mouth and I added, 'No, Damien. It's okay for him to be here. He's part of us. He belongs.'

Damien gave me a grateful smile and motioned for Jack to bring me the matches. He scampered to me in the middle of the circle.

'I was going to get a lighter, but then I thought about it and it just didn't feel right.' He explained to me very seriously. 'I think it's better to use real wood. You know, *real* matches. A lighter is just too cold and modern for an ancient ritual. So I brought these.' He proudly presented a long cylindrical thing. When I just looked at it like a well, dolt, he pulled off the top and handed the bottom part to me. 'See, long and totally chic fireplace matches. I got them from the den in our dorm. You know, by the fireplace.'

I took the matches from him. They were long and slender and a pretty violet color with red tips. 'They're perfect,' I said, glad I could make someone happy. 'Be sure you bring them tomorrow to the real ritual. I'll use them instead of the usual lighter.'

'Great!' he gushed and then, shooting a pleased grin at

Damien, hurried out of the circle to sit comfortably under the tree, leaning back against the oak.

'Okay, are you guys ready?'

My three friends and one boyfriend (thankfully there was only *one* of my boyfriends present) chorused their yeses.

'Let's just go over the basics and not make this all complicated and involved. You guys will be out in the circle in your appropriate places with the rest of the Dark Daughters and Sons. Then Jack is going to key the music and I'll come in, just like I did last month.'

'Is Professor Blake going to recite a poem again?' Damien asked.

'Oh, baby, I do hope so,' Shaunee said.

'That vamp is so *fiiine* he almost makes poetry interesting,' Erin said.

'No!' I snapped. Then when they all gave me weird looks (I assume they were *all* giving me weird looks – the Twins and Damien did, I avoided looking at Erik.) I continued in a less crazy voice, 'I mean, I don't think he's going to recite anything. I haven't talked to him about it, but whatever,' I said with utter and complete nonchalance, then I hurried on. 'So, I'll come in and move around the circle to the music, with or without poetry, until I get to my place in the center. I'll cast the circle, ask for Nyx's blessing for us specifically at the start of a new year, take the wine around, than close the circle and we'll all go eat.' I glanced at Damien, 'You took care of the food, right?'

'Yep, the chef is back from her winter vacation, and she and I decided on the menu yesterday. We're having chilli about a zillion different ways. And,' he added in a voice that said he thought he was being totally naughty, 'we're also having imported beer.'

'Sounds good,' I smiled my appreciation at him. Yes, it sounds weird and vaguely illegal that minors were going to be drinking beer at what is basically a school-sanctioned event. The truth is that due to the physiological Change that was taking place inside all of our bodies, alcohol just didn't affect us anymore – or at least not enough to cause us to act like typical teenagers (in other words we won't get all wasted and use it as an excuse to have sex with each other).

'Hey, Z, weren't you going to announce at the ritual who you're Tapping for the Prefect Council this coming year?' Erik asked.

'You're right. I'd forgotten that I need to do that.' I sighed. 'So, yeah, before I close the circle I'll announce the two kids I'm Tapping.'

'Who are they?' Damien asked.

'I, uh, haven't narrowed it down to two yet. I'll make my final decision on that tonight,' I lied. Actually, I hadn't come up with any names yet. I hadn't even wanted to think about it since one of those two kids would be taking Stevie Rae's place on the Council. Then I remembered that I was really supposed to let my current Council help me decide which new kids we were choosing. 'Uh, guys. I guess tomorrow before the ritual we can meet and go over the names.'

'Hey, Z, don't stress,' Erik said. 'Just choose two kids. We'll be fine with them.'

I felt a huge wash of relief. 'Are you sure?'

My friends called a chorus of 'okay' and 'sounds good to me' comments. Each of them clearly having the utmost confidence in me. Ugh.

'Okay, good. So, are we all cool with the order of the ritual?' I asked.

They nodded.

'All right. Let's practice the circle casting.' As always, it didn't matter what stress and nonsense was going on in my life. When it came to circle casting and calling forth the five elements with which I have a special bond, or affinity, the sense of excitement and pleasure my gift gives me (thankfully) overshadows everything else. As I approached Damien I felt my stress lift along with my spirit. I took out one long, slender match and struck it against the sandpapery bottom of the cylinder. It lit as I said, 'I call air to our circle. We breathe it in with our first breaths, so it is only right that it be the first element called. Come to us, air!' I touched the match to the yellow candle Damien held and it lit, and stayed lit, even in the wildly gusting wind that whirled around Damien and me like we were in the center of a tamed but playful mini-tornado.

Damien and I grinned at each other. 'I don't think I'll ever get over how amazing it is,' he said softly.

'Me, either,' I said, and blew out the wildly flickering match. Then I moved clockwise, or deosil, around the circle to Shaunee and her red candle. I could hear Shaunee humming something under her breath that I recognized, as I pulled out the next match, as the old Jim Morrison song, 'Light My Fire.' I smiled at her. 'Fire warms us with its passionate flame. I call fire to our circle!' As usual, I barely had to touch the lit match to Shaunee's candle. It instantly combusted, licking light and warmth against our skins.

'I couldn't be hotter if I was on fire,' Shaunee said.

'Well, Nyx sure gave you the right element,' I told her. Then I walked over to Erin, who was practically vibrating with excitement. My match was still flaming, so I simply smiled at Erin and said, 'Water is a perfect balance to flame, just as Erin is a perfect Twin for Shaunee. I call water to our circle!' I touched the match to the blue candle and was instantly engulfed in the scents and sounds of the sea. I swear I could feel warm, tropical water washing against my legs, cooling what fire had just overheated.

'I do love me some water,' Erin said happily.

Then I drew a deep, fortifying breath, made sure my face was set in a calm smile, and I walked over to where Erik was standing at the head of the circle and holding the green candle that represents the fourth element of the circle, earth.

'Are you ready?' I asked him.

Erik looked a little pale, but he nodded and his voice was strong and sure when he said, 'Yes. I'm ready.'

I lifted the still burning match and 'Ouch! Crap!' Feeling like an utter moron and not High Priestess in training and the only fledgling ever to have been gifted with an affinity for all five elements, I dropped the match that I'd let burn too long and scorch my fingers. I looked sheepishly at

Erik and then around the almost completed circle. 'Sorry, guys.'

They shrugged off my dorkishness good-naturedly. I was just turning back to Erik and digging in the cylinder for the next match when what I had seen – or rather, what I *hadn't* seen – registered in my mind.

There was no thread of light binding Damien, Shaunee, and Erin. Their candles were lit. Their elements had manifested. But the connection we'd felt since the five of us had cast our first circle together, which was so powerful it had been visible as a beautiful, binding thread of light, was definitely missing. Not sure what to do, I sent up a silent plea to Nyx, *Please, Goddess, show me what I need to do to reform our circle without Stevie Rae!* Then I lit the match and smiled encouragement at Erik.

'Earth supports us and nurtures us. As the fourth element I call earth to our circle!'

I took the long match and touched it to the wick of the green candle. Erik's reaction was instant. He cried out in pain as the green candle flew from his hand away from the circle and into the thickening shadows behind the tree. Erik was rubbing his hand and muttering something about it feeling like he'd been stung, at the same time a string of cussing was coming from the darkness as someone who was, apparently, very pissed off, was heading our way.

'Dammit! Ouch! Shit! What the—'

Aphrodite emerged from the shadows holding the unlit green candle and rubbing a red mark on her forehead that was already beginning to swell.

'Oh, wonderful. I should have fucking figured. I'm told to come out here in the' – she paused, looked around at the tree and the grass, then wrinkled up her perfect nose – '*wilderness* all surrounded by *nature*, and what do I find besides insects and dirt? The nerd herd throwing shit at me,' she said.

'I only wish we'd thought of it,' Erin said sweetly.

'Aphrodite, you are a hateful hag from hell,' Shaunee said just as sweetly.

'Dorks, don't talk to me.'

Ignoring their bickering I said, 'Who told you to come out here?'

Aphrodite met my eyes. 'Nyx,' she said.

'Please!'

'Whatever!'

'Not likely!'

Damien and the Twins all shouted together. I noticed that Erik was keeping suspiciously silent. I held up my hand. 'Enough!' I snapped and they shut up.

'Why did Nyx tell you to come out here?' I asked Aphrodite.

Still meeting my gaze squarely, she approached me. Barely giving Erik a glace she said, 'Move out of the way, lame ex-boyfriend.' Surprising me, Erik actually stepped out of her way so that she took earth's place in front of me. 'Call earth and light it, and you'll see,' Aphrodite said.

Before anyone could protest I followed my gut, already knowing from the premonition it was giving me what would happen. 'Earth supports us and nurtures us. As the fourth element I call earth to our circle!' I repeated and then touched my newly lit match to the green candle. It flamed instantly, surrounding Aphrodite and me in the scents and sounds of a lush meadow at full bloom in the middle of summer.

Aphrodite spoke softly. 'Nyx decided I needed more shit in my already crap-filled life. So now I have an affinity for earth. Ironic enough for you?'

CHAPTER NINE

'OH, NO DAMN WAY!' SHAUNEE SHOUTED.

'Ditto, Twin! Only no *fucking* damn way!' Erin said.

'I can't believe this is right,' Damien said.

'Believe it,' I said, my back still to the rest of the circle as I continued to stare at Aphrodite. Before my friends could freak out any more I added, 'Look at the circle.' I hadn't needed to look at it. I already knew what I'd see, and their gasps told me I was right. Still, I turned slowly, awed anew by the beauty of the powerful thread of goddess-given light that bound the four of them together. 'She's telling the truth. Nyx sent her out here. Aphrodite has an affinity for earth.'

Shocked into silence, my friends just stared as I moved to the center of the circle and picked up my purple candle. 'Spirit is what makes us unique, what gives us courage and strength, and it is what lives on after our bodies are no more. Come to me, spirit!' I was engulfed in all four elements as spirit rushed into me, filling me with peace and joy. I walked around the circle, meeting my friends' confused, upset gazes, trying to help them understand something I didn't really get myself, but what I could feel was, indeed, Nyx's will.

'I don't pretend to understand Nyx. The Goddess's ways are mysterious and sometimes she asks really hard things of us. This is one of those hard things. Like it or not, Nyx has made it clear that Aphrodite should take Stevie Rae's place in our circle.' I looked at Aphrodite. 'I don't think she's exactly thrilled about it.'

'Understatement,' Aphrodite mumbled.

I continued. 'But we have a choice. Nyx doesn't force our will. We need to be in agreement about letting Aphrodite in, or—' I hesitated, not knowing how to finish. We'd tried to cast the circle with someone else, and Erik hadn't been allowed to represent earth. Maybe it was *just* Erik the Goddess didn't want standing in the circle, but I found that hard to believe. Not only was Erik a good guy and already a member of our Council, but my gut was telling me that the problem wasn't that Nyx didn't want Erik. The problem was that Nyx specifically wanted Aphrodite. I sighed and blundered on. 'Or I guess we can start trying a bunch of different kids and seeing if any of them are allowed to manifest earth.' I looked outside the circle and met Erik's shadowed eyes. 'But I don't think Erik's the issue.' He smiled at me, but it was just a movement his mouth made; the smile didn't reach his eyes or touch his face.

'I think we have to do what Nyx wants us to do. Even if we don't like it,' Damien said.

'Shaunee?' I turned to her. 'What's your vote?'

Shaunee and Erin shared a look and I swear, weird as it sounds, I could almost see words pass in the air between them.

'We'll let the hag join the circle,' Shaunee said.

'But only because Nyx wants it,' Erin said.

'Yeah, but we want to go on the record as saying we totally do *not* understand what Nyx is up to,' Shaunee added, while Erin nodded in agreement.

'Do they get to keep calling me a hag?' Aphrodite said.

'Are you breathing?' Shaunee asked.

'Then if you're breathing you're still a hag,' Erin said.

'Which is what we call you,' Shaunee finished.

'No,' I said firmly. The Twins turned their glares on me. 'You guys don't have to like her. You don't even have to like that Nyx wants her here. But if we accept Aphrodite, then we *accept* her. That means the name-calling has to stop.' The Twins sucked air, obviously getting ready to argue with me, so I hurriedly added, 'Look inside yourselves, especially right now when you have manifested your element. What is your conscience telling you?' Then I held my breath and waited.

The Twins paused.

'Yeah, okay,' Erin said unhappily.

'We see your point. We just don't like it,' Shaunee said.

'And what about her? So we stop calling her a hag and such, but she still gets to act like one?' Erin said.

'Now Erin has a point,' Damien said.

I looked over at Aphrodite. By her expression she was bored, but I could see that she kept taking big gulps of air, like she couldn't get enough of smelling the meadow earth had manifested around her. Every once in a while I noticed that she trailed her fingers down around her as if she was letting them brush through tall, fragrant grasses. Clearly, she wasn't as unmoved by what had just happened as she pretended to be.

'Aphrodite's going to do the same thing the two of you just did. She's going to search her conscience and then do the right thing.'

Aphrodite looked mockingly around like she was searching for something that might be hidden in the night. Then she shrugged. 'Oops. Seems I don't have a conscience.'

'Stop it!' I snapped, and the energy I'd evoked with the circle whipped between Aphrodite and me, snaking dangerously around her body. The power augmented my voice, making Aphrodite's blue eyes widen in surprise and fear. 'Not here. Not in this circle. You will not lie and pretend. Decide now. You have a choice, too. I know you've ignored Nyx before. You can choose to ignore her again. But if you choose to stay and do the Goddess's will, you're not going to do it with lies and hate.'

I thought she'd break the circle and walk away. I almost wished she would. It'd be easier not to have anyone represent earth. I could just light the green candle myself and put in on the ground. Whatever. But Aphrodite surprised me, and it would only be the first of many surprises Nyx had in store for me.

'Fine. I'll stay.'

'Fine,' I said. I glanced around at my friends. 'Fine?'

'Yeah, fine,' they grumbled.

'Good. So we have our circle,' I said.

Before anything else bizarre could happen I moved counterclockwise around the circle, bidding each element good-bye. The silver thread of power disappeared, leaving behind the scents of the ocean and wildflowers on a warm breeze. No one said anything, and the awkward silence grew until I was starting to feel sorry for Aphrodite. Of course, she opened her mouth and, as usual, destroyed any pity anyone might feel for her.

'Don't worry. I'm leaving so you can get back to your Dungeons and Dragons meeting or whatever,' Aphrodite sneered.

'Hey, we don't play Dungeons and Dragons!' Jack said.

'Come on, we have time to go down to the IHOP for something to eat before the movie starts,' Damien said, and the whole group of them completely ignored Aphrodite as they walked away, chattering among themselves about how fine the Spartans are and how this time when they watch *300* they're going to keep track of how many vamp actors are in it.

They were several feet away before Erik noticed I wasn't with them.

'Zoey?' he called. The gang stopped and looked back at me, obviously surprised to see Aphrodite and me still standing in the dissolved circle. 'Aren't you coming?' His voice was carefully neutral, but I could see his jaw tightening with a mixture of what might be annoyance or worry.

'You guys go ahead. I'll meet you at the movies. I need to talk to Aphrodite.'

I expected Aphrodite to make a smart-ass comment, but she didn't. I snuck a sideways glance at her and saw she was staring off into the darkness and not paying any attention to my friends or me.

'But, Z, you're gonna miss the chocolate-chip pancakes,' Jack said.

I smiled at him. 'It's okay. I had some last night – it being my birthday and all.'

'They need to talk, so let's go,' Erik said.

I didn't like how he sounded – almost like he didn't care – but before I could say anything else he was walking away. Crap. I was definitely going to have some making-up to do with him.

'Erik likes things his way. He also likes a girlfriend who puts him first. Guess you're just finding that out,' Aphrodite said.

'I'm not going to talk about Erik with you. I just want to hear about what Nyx has shown you of her will.'

'Shouldn't you already know about Nyx's will, blah, blah, whatever? Aren't you her Chosen one?'

'Aphrodite, I have a really bad headache right now. I'd like to be with my friends eating chocolate chip pancakes. Then I want to go see *300* with my boyfriend. So I'm already tired of the whole I'm-such-a-bitch-all-the-time act you put on. Here's the deal – just answer the question and we can both go do whatever we want to do.' I was rubbing my forehead. The last thing I expected was the bomb she suddenly dropped on me.

'You really mean just answer the question so that you can go meet the creature Stevie Rae's turned into, don't you?'

I felt all the color drain from my face. 'What in the hell are you talking about Aphrodite?'

'Let's walk,' she said and started to walk alongside the huge stone wall that borders the school.

'Aphrodite, no.' I grabbed her arm. 'Tell me what you know.'

'Look, it's hard for me to hold still so soon after I've had a vision, and the one I had that made me come out here was not like my normal visions.' Aphrodite pulled free from me and brushed a hand across her brow like she had a headache, too. I noticed for the first time that her hands were shaking – actually that her whole body was trembling and she looked abnormally pale.

'All right. We'll walk.'

She didn't say anything for a little while, and I had to fight with myself not to grab her and shake her and *make* her tell me how she knew about Stevie Rae. When she finally started talking, she didn't look at me and seemed to be speaking to the night more than to me.

'My visions have been changing. It started with the one I had when those human kids were being killed. I used to be able to see things like I was just an observer. I watched what was happening but wasn't touched by it. Everything and everyone were clear, easy to understand. With those boys it was different. I wasn't detached anymore. I was one of them. I could feel myself being killed with them.' She paused and shuddered. 'I also couldn't see things clearly anymore. Stuff becomes a big jumble of fear and panic and crazy emotions. I get some flashes of things I can identify or understand, like when I told you that you had to get Heath out of those tunnels or he'd die. But mostly I'm freaked and confused, and afterward I feel awful.' Aphrodite glanced at me as if she was just then remembering I was really there. 'Like it was with the vision I saw of your grandma drowning. I actually was your grandma, and it was just lucky that I caught glimpses of the bridge and knew where she'd go into the water.'

I nodded, 'I remember you couldn't tell me very much. I thought it was more because you didn't want to tell me than that you couldn't tell me.'

Her smile was sarcastic. 'Yes, I know. Not that I care what you thought.'

'Just get on with the Stevie Rae part.' God, she was annoying.

'I haven't had a vision for a month. Good thing, too, since my parents insist I visit during winter break. Often.'

Her grimace said that visiting her parents wasn't exactly a good thing, which I already knew. At the last parent visitation night I'd sorta accidentally watched a majorly nightmarish scene between Aphrodite and her parents. Her dad's the mayor of Tulsa. Her mom might be Satan. Basically, they made my 'rentals look like the Brady parents (yes, I'm a dork and watch Nickelodeon reruns).

'I had to have a birthday scene with my parents yesterday.'

'Your stepdad's one of the People of Faith psychos, isn't he?'

'Totally. My grandma called him a turd monkey.'

That made her laugh. I mean really laugh. I watched her, amazed at how it transformed her face from cold and pretty to warm and beautiful.

'Yep. I hate my 'rentals,' I said.

'Who doesn't,' she said.

'Stevie Rae doesn't. Or at least she didn't before . . .' My voice trailed off and I had to fight the urge not to burst into embarrassing tears.

'So that part of the vision's already happened. Stevie Rae has been turned into a monster.'

'She's *not* a monster! She's just different than she used to be.'

Aphrodite lifted one perfect blond brow. 'I'd say that could be an improvement if I hadn't seen what she's changed into.'

'Just tell me what you saw.'

'I saw vampyres being killed. Horribly.' Aphrodite had to pause to swallow, like she was trying hard not to throw up.

'By Stevie Rae?' I squeaked.

'No. That was a different vision.'

'Okay, I'm confused.'

'Try having the damn visions, or at least these new visions

107

I've been having. Confusion is what they're all about. And pain. And fear. They completely suck.'

'So Stevie Rae wasn't in the one where the vampyres died?'

She shook her head. 'No, but the two felt like they went together.' Aphrodite sighed. 'I saw Stevie Rae. She was horrible. Real dirty and thin and her eyes glowed a weird red. And you wouldn't believe what she was wearing. I mean, not that she was ever Miss Fashion Sense, but still.'

'Yeah, yeah, I get it. So you saw her undead.'

'That's what she is, isn't it. She's turned into some kind of horrible vampyre cliché, the monster humans have been calling us for centuries.'

'Not *all* humans. You know, you really need to get over your completely crappy attitude about humans. You used to be one,' I said.

'Whatever. I used to be in love with Sean William Scott, too. Talk about old news.' She flipped her hair back. 'Anyway, I saw Stevie Rae when she died. Again. This time for real. And I knew if the vision was allowed to come true that it would somehow mean all of the vamp deaths I saw would really happen. So we have to figure out a way to save Stevie Rae because Nyx is seriously not happy about a bunch of vamps being killed.'

'How did Stevie Rae die?'

'Neferet killed her. She pulled Stevie Rae out into the direct sunlight and she burned up.'

CHAPTER TEN

'CRAP. THEN SHE REALLY CAN'T GO OUT IN THE SUNLIGHT,' I said.

'You didn't already know that?' Aphrodite said.

'Stevie Rae hasn't been exactly easy to talk to since she, well, died.'

'But you have seen her and talked to her?'

I stopped walking and stood in front of Aphrodite so that she had to face me. 'Look, you can't tell anyone about Stevie Rae.'

'No kidding? I thought I'd put it in the school paper.'

'I'm serious, Aphrodite.'

'Don't treat me like I'm a moron. If anyone besides us knows about Stevie Rae, Neferet will know. She's bound to since she can practically read everyone's mind. Well, except us that is.'

'She can't read your mind, either?'

Aphrodite's smile was self-satisfied and more than a little hateful. 'She never has been able to. How do you think I got away with so much crap for so long?'

'Lovely.' I remembered distinctly what a terrible bitch Aphrodite had been as leader of the Dark Daughters. Actually, since the moment I'd met Aphrodite she'd been selfish and mean and downright hateful. Yes, her visions had helped me save my grandma and Heath, but she'd made it clear that she hadn't really cared about saving either of them, and had helped only because she got something out of it. I narrowed my eyes at her. 'Okay, you're going to have to explain why you're bothering to tell me all this stuff. What's in it for you?'

Aphrodite widened her eyes in mock innocence and put on a ridiculous Southern Belle accent, 'Why, what ever do you mean? I'm helping you because you and your friends have always been so sweet to me.'

'Cut the crap, Aphrodite.'

Her expression flattened and her voice returned to normal. 'Let's just say I have a lot to make up for.'

'To Stevie Rae?'

'To Nyx.' She looked away from me. 'You probably won't get this, being all-powerful with new gifts from Nyx and basically Miss Perfect, but once you've had your gifts for a while, you might find out that it's not always easy to do the right thing. Other things – people – get in the way. You'll make mistakes.' Aphrodite scoffed. 'Well, maybe *you* won't. But I did. I might not particularly give a shit about you or Stevie Rae or maybe anyone here at school, but I do care about Nyx.' Her voice faltered. 'I know what it's like to believe the goddess has turned from me and I don't ever want to feel like that again.'

I reached out and touched her arm. 'But Nyx didn't turn from you. Those were just lies Neferet told so that no one would believe your visions. You know Neferet's behind what Stevie Rae's turned into, don't you?'

'I've known since the vision, when I saw Heath dying.' She forced a little laugh. 'Good thing she *can't* read our minds. I don't know what she'd do to a fledgling who knows how awful she is.'

'She knows I know.'

'You've got to be kidding!'

'Well, she knows I'm on to her.' I hesitated, and then figured, what the hell. Weirdly enough, it was turning out that Aphrodite (a.k.a., the hag from hell) was the one person on this earth I could really talk to. 'Neferet tried to erase my memory of the night I saved Heath from those undead dead kids. It worked for a while, but I knew right away something was wrong. I used the power of the elements to heal my memory, and, well, I kinda let Neferet know that I remembered what had happened.'

'You *kinda* let her know?'

I fidgeted. 'Well, she threatened me. Said no one would believe me if I said anything about her. And, uh, it made me mad. So I told her that it didn't matter if no vamp or fledgling believed me, because Nyx does.'

Aphrodite smiled. 'I'll bet that pissed her off.'

'Yeah, I suppose it did.' Actually it made me a little sick to think about just how pissed Neferet probably was. 'But she left right after that for winter break. I haven't seen her since.'

'She'll be back soon.'

'I know.'

'Are you scared?' Aphrodite asked.

'Totally,' I said.

'I don't blame you there. Okay, here's what I know for sure from my visions. We have to get Stevie Rae some place safe and away from the rest of those *things*. And we have to do it now. Before Neferet comes back. There's some connection between the two of them. I don't understand it, but I know it's there, and I know it's wrong.' Aphrodite made a face like she'd just tasted something nasty. 'Actually the whole undead dead monster thing is all wrong. Talk about disgusting creatures.'

'Stevie Rae's different than the rest of them.'

Aphrodite gave me a look that said she definitely didn't believe me.

'Think about it. Why would Nyx have given a fledgling such a powerful gift as an affinity for earth and then let her die. And then un-die.' I paused, struggling with how to make her understand. 'I think her connection to earth is the reason Stevie Rae has kept some of her humanity, and I really believe that if I – I mean *we*, if *we* can help her she'll find the rest of her humanity. Or maybe we'll find a way to heal her. To turn her back into a fledgling or maybe even a grown-up vamp. And maybe if Stevie Rae is fixed, that means there's a chance for the rest of them, too.'

'So do you have a clue how we're going to fix her?'

'Nope. Not one clue.' Then I grinned. 'But now I have a powerful fledgling with visions and an earth affinity helping me.'

'Great. That makes me feel so much better.'

I didn't want to admit it to Aphrodite, but the truth was that being able to talk to her about Stevie Rae and having her help figuring out what we were supposed to do did make me feel better. Much better.

'Anyway,' Aphrodite was saying, 'how are we going to find Stevie Rae?' She curled her lip. 'Do *not* tell me you expect me to crawl around nasty tunnels with you.'

'Actually, Stevie Rae said she'd meet me at the Philbrook gazebo tonight at about three o'clock.'

'Is she going to show?'

I chewed my lip. 'I bribed her with country clothes, so I think so.'

Aphrodite shook her head. 'So she dies, un-dies, and still has a shitty fashion sense.'

'Apparently.'

'Now that's *really* sad.'

'Yeah.' I sighed. I loved Stevie Rae, but even I had to admit she liked to dress like a hick.

'So, where are you taking her after you give her the clothes?'

I didn't think I should mention that I'd like to take her straight to a bathtub. 'I don't know. I haven't thought much past getting her clothes and, uh, blood.'

'Blood!'

'She has to have it. Human blood. Or she goes crazy.'

'Isn't she already pretty much crazy?'

'No! She's just dealing with issues.'

'Issues?'

'Lots of issues,' I said firmly.

'Okay. Whatever. You've gotta decide where you're going to take her. She can't stay with the rest of those things. That won't help her,' Aphrodite said.

'I was going to try to talk her into coming back here. I figured I could hide her pretty easily while most of the vamps are gone.'

'You can't bring her back here.' Aphrodite had gone pale. 'This is where I saw her die. Again.'

'Crap! Then I don't know what the hell I'm going to do,' I admitted.

'I suppose you could take her to my old place,' Aphrodite said.

'Yeah, right. Your parents are so understanding and all. That sounds like a great idea, Aphrodite.'

She rolled her eyes. 'My parents are gone. They left early this morning for three weeks skiing in Breckenridge. Plus, she won't be staying inside the house. My parents live in one of those old oil mansions right down the street from the

Philbrook. They have a garage apartment that used to be a servants' quarters back in the day. It's not used anymore except when my grandma comes to visit, and my mom just stuck her in one of those high-class, high-security, high-dollar nursing homes, so you don't need to worry about that. Still, everything in the apartment should work – you know, electricity and water and such.'

'You think she'd be okay there?'

Aphrodite shrugged. 'She'd be safer there than here.'

'All right. That's where she goes then.'

'Is she gonna be okay with that?'

'Yeah,' I lied. 'I'll tell her the fridge is filled with blood.' I sighed. 'Even though I don't know how the hell I'm going to get her a glass of blood, let alone a fridge full of it.'

'It's in the kitchen.'

'At your house?' Now I was totally confused.

'No, jeesh, stay with me. They have blood here. In a big stainless steel cooler in the kitchen. For the vamps. Fresh shipments come in all the time from human donors. All the upperclassmen know about it. We get to use it sometimes in rituals.'

'That'll work, especially since there's hardly anyone around right now. I should be able to get into the kitchen and grab some blood without being caught.' I frowned. 'Please tell me it's not just sitting in a Tupperware pitcher or something equally disturbing.' Okay, even though I really, *really* liked to drink blood, I was still completely grossed out at the idea of actually drinking blood. I know, I need therapy. Again.

'It's in pouches, like at the hospital. Nothing to stress about.'

By this time we'd made an automatic turn to the right and were meandering back toward the dorm.

'You have to go with me,' I said abruptly.

'To the kitchen?'

'No, I mean to Stevie Rae. You'll have to show us your house and how to get in the apartment and everything.'

'She's not going to want to see me,' Aphrodite said.

'I know, but she'll have to get over it. She knows your vision saved my grandma. When I tell her you've had a vision about her, she's just gonna have to believe it.' I was glad I sounded so sure. I definitely didn't feel sure. 'But it might be best if you hide and wait until I've talked to her for a while before she sees you.'

'Look, I'm trying to do the right thing here, but I'm not going to hide from a kid I used to use as a refrigerator.'

'Don't call her that!' I snapped. 'Did you ever think that a big part of your problem and why so many bad things have happened to you isn't Neferet and all the bullpoop she's up to, but it's the fact that you have such a bitchy, crappy, attitude?'

Aphrodite's brows went up and she cocked her head to the side, which made her look like a blond bird. 'Yeah, I've thought about that, but I'm not like you. I'm not all positive and Miss Goodie-Two-Shoes. Tell me something. You think people are basically good, don't you?'

Her question surprised me, but I shrugged and nodded. 'Yeah, I guess so.'

'Not me. I think most people, and I'm talking vamp or

human, are shitty. They put on an act. They pretend to be all nicey-nice, but are really just one step away from showing their true asshole-ness.'

'That's a depressing way to go through life,' I said.

'You call it depressing. I call it realistic.'

'How do you ever trust anyone?'

Aphrodite looked away from me. 'I don't. It's easier that way. You'll find out.' She met my eyes again and I couldn't read the weird expression in them. 'Power changes people.'

'I'm not going to change.' I was going to say more, but then I thought about the fact that just a few months ago if someone had told me that I'd be making out with a grown-ass man while I had not one but two boyfriends I would have said no f-ing way. So didn't that mean I'd changed?

Aphrodite smiled like she could read my mind. 'I wasn't talking about you. I was talking about the people around you.'

'Oh,' I said. 'Aphrodite, not to be mean or anything, but I think I pick my friends better than you.'

'We'll see. Speaking of – Shouldn't you be heading to the movies to meet your friends right now?'

I sighed. 'Yeah, but no way can I go. I've got to get the blood for Stevie Rae, get her clothes together, and I also want to stop by Wal-Mart and grab one of those GoPhones. I figured it would be a good idea to give it to Stevie Rae so that she could call me.'

'Fine. Why don't you pick me up outside the trapdoor in the east wall at about two thirty? That gives us plenty of time to get to Philbrook before Stevie Rae.'

'Sounds good. I just need to run up to my room, grab some of Stevie Rae's clothes and my purse, then I'll be out of here.'

'Okay, I'll go into the dorm first.'

'Huh?' I said.

Aphrodite gave me a look that said she thought I was a retard. 'You don't want people to see me with you. They'll think we're friends or something ridiculous like that.'

'Aphrodite, I do not care what people think.'

She rolled her eyes. 'I do.' Then she hurried ahead of me to the dorm.

'Hey!' I called. She looked over her shoulder. 'Thanks for helping me.'

Aphrodite frowned. 'Don't mention it. And I mean it. Don't. Mention. It. Jeesh.' Shaking her head, she hurried into the dorm.

CHAPTER ELEVEN

I FOUND THE HEART LOCKET WHEN I WAS GOING THROUGH the drawer getting Stevie Rae's clothes. I was with her the night she died, and by the time I got back to our room the vamp cleanup squad (or whatever they're called) had already been there and had taken Stevie Rae's stuff. I got pissed. Really pissed. And I'd insisted they put some of her stuff back because I wanted to keep things to remember her by. So Anastasia, the professor who teaches spells and rituals (she's really nice and married to Dragon Lankford, the fencing instructor) took me to a creepy storage room where I shoved some of Stevie Rae's stuff into a bag and then dumped it back in what used to be her dresser. I remember Anastasia was kind to me, but she also clearly disapproved of me having keep-sakes of Stevie Rae.

When a fledgling dies, the vamps expect us to forget them and go on. Period.

Well, I just don't think that's right. I wasn't going to forget my best friend, even before I found out she was really undead.

Anyway, I had grabbed her jeans when something fell out of the pocket. It was a kinda crunched-up envelope that had ZOEY printed on the outside of it in Stevie Rae's messy hand-writing. My stomach hurt as I opened it. Inside was a birthday card – one of those silly ones with a picture of a cat (who looked a lot like Nala) on the front wearing one of those pointy birthday hats and a frown. Inside it said HAPPY BIRTHDAY. OR WHATEVER. LIKE I CARE. I'M A CAT. Stevie Rae had drawn a big heart and written LOVE YOU! STEVIE RAE AND GRUMPY NALA. Sliding around in the bottom of the envelope was a silver chain. I lifted it up to find a delicate silver heart locket dangling from it. My fingers were shaking as I opened the locket. A many-times-folded picture fell out. I smoothed it carefully and, with a little sob, recognized it as a cutout part of a picture I had taken of the two of us (by holding the camera out, smooshing our faces together, and pressing the flash button). Wiping my eyes, I folded the picture back into the locket and clasped the chain around my neck. It was a short chain, so the heart fit just below the hollow of my throat.

Somehow, finding the necklace made me feel stronger, and also taking the blood from the kitchen was way easier than

I'd thought it was going to be. Instead of my normal purse – the little designer one I'd found at a boutique at Utica Square last year (it's made of fake pink fur, totally cool), I took my ginormic bag – the one I used to use as a book bag when I went to South Intermediate High School in Broken Arrow, before I was Marked and my life exploded. Anyway, the bag was big enough to carry a fat kid in (if he was short), so it was simple to cram Stevie Rae's dorky Roper jeans, a T-shirt, her black cowboy boots (ugh), and some under things in it and still have room for five bags of blood. Yes, they were gross. Yes, I wanted to stick a straw in one and suck it down like a juice box. Yes, I'm disgusting.

The cafeteria was closed, as was the kitchen, and completely deserted. But like everything else at the school, not locked. I got into and out of the kitchen easily, holding my blood-filled purse carefully while I tried to look nonchalant and not guilty. (I'm really not good at theft.)

I was worried about seeing Loren (who I was really *really* trying to forget about, not so hard that I took off his diamond earrings, but still), but the only person I saw was a third-former kid named Ian Bowser. He's dorky and scrawny, but also kinda funny. I had drama class with him and he was hilariously in love with our drama teacher, Professor Nolan. Actually, it was Professor Nolan he was looking for when he literally ran into me on my way out of the cafeteria.

'Oh, Zoey, sorry! Sorry!' Ian gave me a nervous little vampyre salute of respect, hand fisted over his heart. 'I – I didn't mean to run over you.'

121

'No problem,' I said. I hated it when kids got all nervous and scared around me like they think I might turn them into something vile. Please. It's the House of Night, not Hogwarts. (Yes, I read the Potter books and love the movies. Yes, that's more proof of my geekness.)

'You haven't seen Professor Nolan, have you?'

'Nope. I didn't even know she was back from break,' I said.

'Yeah, she got back yesterday. We had an appointment to meet about thirty minutes ago.' He grinned and blushed bright pink. 'I really want to make the finals of the Shakespeare monologue contest next year, so I asked her to tutor me.'

'Oh, that's nice.' Poor kid. He'd never final in the kick-ass Shakespeare contest if his voice didn't stop cracking.

'If you see Professor Nolan would you tell her I'm looking for her?'

'Will do,' I said. Ian hurried off. I clutched my bag and headed straight for the parking lot and then on to Wal-Mart.

Buying the GoPhone (and some soap, a toothbrush, and a Kenny Chesney CD) was easy. What hadn't been easy was dealing with the phone call from Erik.

'Zoey? Where are you?'

'Still at school,' I said. Which wasn't a literal lie. By that time I was pulling off the side of the road just outside the place in the east wall where there was a secret trapdoor that led out the back side of school. I say 'secret' because tons of fledglings and probably all of the vamps knew about it. It was an unspoken school tradition that fledglings would sneak off campus for a ritual and some vaguely bad behavior now and then.

'Still at school?' he sounded annoyed. 'But the movie's almost over.'

'I know. I'm sorry.'

'Are you okay? You know you should ignore the crap Aphrodite says.'

'Yeah, I know. But she didn't say stuff about you.' Or at least not much stuff. 'It's just that I'm majorly stressed out right now and I just need to think through some stuff.'

'Stuff again.' He didn't sound happy.

'I'm really sorry, Erik.' **GALWAY COUNTY LIBRARIES**

'Okay, yeah. No problem. I'll see you tomorrow or whenever. Bye.' And he hung up.

'Crap,' I said into the dead phone.

Aphrodite tapping on the passenger's side window made me jump and let out a little squeak. I put away the phone and leaned over to unlock the door for her.

'Bet he's pissed,' she said.

'Do you have freakishly good hearing?'

'Nah, just freakishly good guessing ability. Plus I know our boy Erik. You stood him up tonight. He's pissed.'

'Okay, first, he's not *our* boy. He's *my* boy. Second, I did not stand him up. Third, I'm *so* not talking about Erik with you, Miss Blow Job.'

Instead of hissing and spitting at me like I thought she would, Aphrodite laughed. 'Okay. Whatever. And don't knock something before you try it, Miss Goody-Goody.'

'Okay, eew,' I said. 'Changing the subject. I have an idea about how to handle the Stevie Rae thing. I don't think you should hide, either. So show me how to get to your parents' place. I'll drop you off there and then go get Stevie Rae.'

'Want me to be gone before you get back with her?'

I'd already thought about this. It was tempting, but the truth was that it was looking more and more like Aphrodite and I were going to have to work *together* on fixing Stevie Rae. So my undead best friend was just going to have to get used to having Aphrodite around. Plus, I was already having to do too much sneaking. I just couldn't deal with sneaking around the kid I was sneaking around everyone else for. If that makes any sense.

'No. Stevie Rae's gonna have to learn to deal with you.' I glanced at Aphrodite as I came to a stop sign and added cheerfully, 'Or maybe she'll do us all a favor and eat you.'

'It's so nice that you always look on the positive side of things,' Aphrodite said sarcastically. 'Okay, turn right here. Then when you get to Peoria, take a left and go down a few blocks until you see that big brick sign that points to the turnoff to the Philbrook.'

I did as she said. We didn't make small talk, but it didn't feel all awkward and uncomfortable between us. It was weird how easy it actually was to be around Aphrodite. I mean, not that she wasn't still a bitch, but I was kinda liking her. Or maybe this was just another sign that I needed to give some serious consideration to therapy, and I wondered abstractly if

Prozac or Lexapro or some other lovely antidepressant worked on fledglings.

At the Philbrook sign I turned left and Aphrodite said, 'Okay, we're almost there. It's the fifth house on the right. Don't take the first driveway, take the second one. That one goes around behind the house to the garage apartment.'

We came to it and all I could do was shake my head. '*This* is where you live?'

'Used to live,' she said.

'It's an f-ing mansion!' And I meant a cool one. It looked like something I'd imagine rich folks in Italy would live in.

'It was a fucking prison. It still is.' I was going to say something semi-profound about her being free now that she'd been Marked and was a legally emancipated minor and that she could actually tell her 'rentals to get lost (kinda like I had), but her next smart-alecky comment made me forget the kinda nice thing I meant to say. 'And it's really annoying that you're too damn pure to cuss. Saying fuck won't kill you. It won't even mean you're not all virginal.'

'I cuss. I say hell and crap and even damn. A lot.' And why did I feel the sudden need to defend my non-cussing preference?

'Whatever,' she said, clearly laughing at me.

'And there's nothing wrong with being a virgin. It's better than being a skank.'

Aphrodite was still laughing. 'You have a lot to learn, Z.' She pointed at a building that looked like a miniature version of the mansion. 'Go around behind there. There's a back way

125

into the apartment and your car will be blocked from the street.'

I pulled up behind the totally cool garage and we got out of my Bug. Aphrodite used her key to unlock the door, which opened to a stairway. I followed her up to the apartment.

'Jeesh, servants must have lived pretty well back in the day,' I mumbled, looking around at the dark, shiny wood floors, the leather furniture, and the gleaming kitchen. There weren't a bunch of cheesy knickknacks polluting the decor, but there were candles and some vases that looked totally expensive. I could see that the bedroom and bathroom were at the other end of the apartment, and could just peek in to see a big bed with puffy down comforters and pillows. My guess was the bathroom was nicer than my parents' master bathroom.

'Do you think it'll work?' Aphrodite asked.

I went to one of the windows. 'Thick curtains – that's good.'

'Shutters, too. See, we can close them from in here.' Aphrodite demonstrated.

I nodded at the flat-screen TV. 'Cable?'

'Of course,' she said. 'There's a bunch of DVDs around here somewhere, too.'

'Perfect,' I said, moving to the kitchen. 'I'll just stick all but one of the blood packs in here, and then go get Stevie Rae.'

'Fine. I'll watch *Real World* reruns,' Aphrodite said.

'Fine,' I said. But instead of leaving, I cleared my throat uneasily. Aphrodite looked up from messing with the TV. 'What?'

'Stevie Rae doesn't look or act like she used to.'

'Really? I wouldn't have had a clue about that if you hadn't enlightened me. I mean, most people who die and then come back to life as bloodsucking monsters look and act totally the same.'

'I'm serious.'

'Zoey, I saw Stevie Rae and some of the other creatures in my visions. They're gross. Period, the end.'

'It's worse when you see them in person.'

'No big surprise there,' she said.

'I don't want you to say anything to Stevie Rae,' I said.

'You mean about her being dead and all? Or about her being gross?'

'Either. I don't want her scared off. I also don't particularly want her to jump on you and rip out your throat. I mean, I think I could probably stop her but I'm not one hundred percent sure. And besides the fact that it would be disgusting and hard to explain, I really hate thinking about what all that blood would do to this cool apartment.'

'How sweet of you.'

'Hey, Aphrodite, how about you try something new. Try being nice,' I said.

'How about I just don't say anything.'

'That would work, too.' I headed for the door. 'I'll try to get her here soon.'

'Hey,' Aphrodite called after me. 'Could she really rip out my throat?'

'Absolutely,' I said, and closed the door behind me.

127

CHAPTER TWELVE

I KNEW STEVIE RAE HAD GOTTEN TO THE GAZEBO BEFORE me. I couldn't see her, but I could smell her. Eesh. Seriously, eesh. I hoped a bath and some shampoo would help that stench, but I kinda doubted it. After all, she was, well, dead.

'Stevie Rae, I know you're here somewhere.' I called as quietly as I could. Okay, vamps have the ability to move silently and to create a kind of bubble of invisibility around them. Fledglings also have this ability. It's just not as complete. Being as I'm a weirdly gifted fledgling, I can move around fairly well and not be seen by anyone who might be gawking out a window at 3:00 A.M., like a museum security guard. So I was pretty confident about my ability to be unseen in the semi-dark, fairyland grounds of the museum, but I had no idea if I could extend that ability to covering Stevie Rae. In other words, I needed to get her, and get out of there. 'Come on out. I have your clothes and some blood and the latest Kenny Chesney CD.' I added that last part as a blatant bribe. Stevie Rae had been ridiculously in lurve with Kenny Chesney. No, I don't understand it either.

'The blood!' A voice that might have been Stevie Rae's if she had a really bad cold and had lost every last bit of her mind hissed from the bushes at the rear of the gazebo's base.

I walked around behind the gazebo peeking into the thick (yet well-trimmed) foliage. 'Stevie Rae?'

Eyes glowing a horrible rust red, she stumbled out of the bushes and lurched toward me. 'Give me the blood!'

Ohmygod, she looked like an absolutely crazy person. Hurriedly I reached into my bag, jerked out the bag of blood, and handed it to her. 'Hang on a sec, I have a pair of scissors in here somewhere and I'll—'

With a really disgusting snarl, Stevie Rae tore open the little lip of the bag with her teeth (uh, fangs is more like it), upended the bag, and gulped down the blood. When she'd squeezed the bag dry she dropped it on the ground. She was breathing like she'd just run a race when she finally looked up at me.

'Ain't pretty, is it?'

I smiled and tried my best to ignore how horrified I really

was. 'Well, my grandma always says that correct grammar and good manners make one more attractive, so you might want to drop the "ain't" and try saying "please" next time.'

'I need more blood.'

'I got you four more packets. They're in the refrigerator at the place you're going to be staying. Do you want to change your clothes here, or wait till we get there and take a shower? It's just down the street.'

'What are you talking about? Just give me my clothes and the blood.'

Her eyes weren't such a bright red, but she still looked mean and mad. She was even thinner and paler than she had been the night before. I drew a deep breath. 'This has to stop, Stevie Rae.'

'*This* is how it is with me now. *This* isn't going to change. *I'm* not going to change.' She pointed to the outline of the crescent moon on her forehead. 'It'll never be filled in and I'll always be dead.'

I stared at the outline of her crescent moon. Was it fading? I thought it definitely looked lighter, or at least less distinct, which couldn't be good. That did shake me up. 'You're not dead' was all I could think to say.

'I feel dead.'

'Okay, well, you kinda look dead. I know when I look like crap I usually feel like crap, too. Maybe that's part of why you feel so bad.' I reached into my bag and pulled out one of her cowboy boots. 'Check out what I brought you.'

'Shoes cannot fix the world.' This was a subject Stevie Rae

130

and the Twins had argued about before, and her voice held a hint of the old exasperation.

'That's not what the Twins would say.'

The familiar tone in her voice flattened out to expressionless and cold. 'What would the Twins say if they could see me now?'

I met Stevie Rae's red eyes. 'They'd say you need a bath and an attitude check, but they'd also be unbelievably happy that you're alive.'

'I'm not alive. That's what I keep trying to get you to understand.'

'Stevie Rae, I am not going to understand that because you're walking and talking. I don't think you're anything like dead – I think you're changed. Not like I'm Changing, as in becoming what we're used to recognizing as an adult vampyre. You've made a different kind of Change, and I think it's harder than the one that's happening to me. That's why you're going through all of this. Would you please give me a chance to help you? Can't you just try to believe everything might turn out okay?'

'I don't know how you can be so sure about that,' she said.

I gave her the answer I felt deep in my soul, and knew the moment I'd said it that it was the right thing to say. 'I'm sure about you being okay because I'm sure that Nyx still loves you and she let this happen for a reason.'

The hope that flashed in Stevie Rae's red eyes was almost painful to look at. 'You really believe Nyx hasn't given up on me?'

'Nyx hasn't and I haven't.' I ignored her smell and gave her a firm hug, which she didn't return, but she also didn't jerk away from me or take a bite out of my neck, so I figured we were making progress. 'Come on. The place I found for you to stay is just down the street.'

I started walking, believing she would follow me, which she did after only a slight hesitation. We cut around the grounds of the museum and came out on Rockford, the street that runs in front of it. Twenty-seventh, the street Aphrodite's mansion (well, it's really her crazy parents' mansion) sits off of runs right into Rockford. Feeling more than a little dream-like, I walked down the middle of the road in the darkness, concentrating on shrouding us in silence and invisibility, with Stevie Rae following only a couple of feet behind me. It was dark and seemed preternaturally silent. I glanced up through the winter branches of the huge old trees that lined the street. I should have been able to see an almost full moon, but clouds had rolled in, obscuring all but an indistinct glow of white where the moon should be. It had turned cold, and I was glad that my changing metabolism protected me from the whipping wind. I wondered if weather changes bothered Stevie Rae, and I was going to ask her about it when she suddenly spoke.

'Neferet won't like this.'

'This?'

'Me being with you instead of with the others.' Stevie Rae seemed really agitated and was plucking nervously at one hand with the other.

'Relax, Neferet won't know you're with me, at least not until we're ready for her to know,' I said.

'She'll know as soon as she gets back and sees that I'm not with the rest of them.'

'No, she'll just know you're gone. Anything could have happened to you.' Then a thought hit me that was so incredible I stopped like I'd run into a tree. 'Stevie Rae! You don't have to be around adult vamps to be okay!'

'Huh?'

'It proves you've Changed! You're not coughing and dying!'

'Zoey, I've already done that.'

'No no no! That's not what I mean.' I grabbed her arm, ignoring the fact that she immediately pulled it from my grasp and took a step away from me. 'You can exist without the vamps. Only another adult vampyre can do that. So it is just like I said. You have Changed, it's just a different kind of Change!'

'And that's a good thing?'

'Yep!' I wasn't as sure as I sounded, but I was determined to keep a positive front for Stevie Rae. Plus, she was looking not-so-good. I mean, even more not-so-good than her usual yucky look. 'What's wrong with you?'

'I need blood!' She wiped a shaky hand across her dirty face. 'That little bag wasn't enough. You stopped me from feeding yesterday, so I haven't fed since the day before. It — it's *bad* when I don't feed.' She tilted her head weirdly, like she was listening to a voice in the wind. 'I can hear the blood whispering through their veins.'

'Whose veins?' I was as intrigued as I was grossed out.

She made a sweeping gesture with her arm that was feral and graceful. 'The humans sleeping around us.' Her voice had dropped to a husky murmur. There was something in the tone of it that made me want to move closer to her, even though her eyes had flushed a bright scarlet again and she smelled so bad it made me want to gag. 'One of them is awake.' She pointed to the huge mansion to the right of where we'd stopped. 'It's a girl . . . a teenager . . . she's by herself in her room . . .'

Stevie Rae's voice was an alluring singsong. My heart had started to beat hard against my chest. 'How do you know that?' I whispered.

She turned her burning eyes on me. 'There's so much I know. I know about your bloodlust. I can smell it. There's no reason you shouldn't give in to it. We could enter the house. Go to the girl's room and take her together. I'd share her with you, Zoey.'

For a moment I was lost in the obsession that heated Stevie Rae's eyes, and in my own need. I hadn't had human blood since the taste Heath had given me more than a month ago. The memory of that one exquisite drink lingered in my body like a tantalizing secret. Completely mesmerized, I listened to Stevie Rae spin a web of darkness that was catching me in its beautiful, sticky depths.

'I can show you how to get in the house. I can sense secret ways. You could get the girl to invite me in – I can't go into a person's home now unless they invite me first. But once I'm in . . .' Stevie Rae laughed.

It was her laugh that snapped me out of it. Stevie Rae used to have the best laugh ever. It was happy and young and innocently in love with life. Now what came out of her mouth was a mean, twisted echo of that old joy.

'The apartment is two houses down. There's blood in the fridge.' I turned and started walking quickly down the street.

'It's not warm and it's not fresh.' She sounded pissed, but she was following me again.

'It's fresh enough, and there's a microwave. You can nuke it.'

She didn't say anything else, and we came to the mansion in just a few minutes. I led her around to the garage apartment, opened the outside door, and stepped in. I was halfway up the stairs when I realized Stevie Rae wasn't behind me. Hurrying back down to the door I saw her standing outside in the darkness. All that was clearly visible of her was the red of her eyes.

'You have to invite me in,' she said.

'Oh, sorry.' What she'd said before hadn't really registered with me, and now I felt a jolt of shock at this further proof of Stevie Rae's soul-deep difference. 'Uh, come on in,' I said quickly.

Stevie Rae stepped forward and ran smack into an invisible barrier. She gave a painful yelp, which turned into a snarl. Her eyes glowed up at me. 'Guess your plan won't work. I can't get in there.'

'I thought you said you just had to be invited in.'

'By someone who lives at the house. You don't live here.'

Above me, Aphrodite's coldly polite voice (sounding uncomfortably like her mother) called out. 'I live here. Come in.'

Stevie Rae stepped over the threshold with no problem at all. She started up the stairs and had almost reached me when Aphrodite's voice must have registered on her. I saw her face change from expressionless to slit-eyed and dangerous.

'You brought me to *her* house!' Stevie Rae was talking to me, but staring at Aphrodite.

'Yes, and why is actually easy to explain.' I considered grabbing her in case she started to bolt, and then I remembered how weirdly strong she'd become, so I started to center myself instead, wondering if my affinity with wind could be used to have a breeze slam the door shut before she could escape.

'How could you explain it! You know I hate Aphrodite.' Then she did look at me. 'I die and now she's your friend?'

I was opening my mouth to assure Stevie Rae that Aphrodite and I hadn't exactly buddied up when Aphrodite's haughty voice interrupted me.

'Get real. Zoey and I are *not* friends. Your little nerd herd is still intact. The only reason I'm involved at all is because Nyx has a totally bizarre sense of humor. So come in or go the hell away. Like I care . . .' Her voice trailed off as she stomped back into the apartment.

'Do you trust me?' I asked Stevie Rae.

She looked at me for what seemed like a long time before she answered. 'Yes.'

'Then come on.' I continued up the stairs with Stevie Rae following reluctantly behind.

Aphrodite was lounging on the couch pretending to watch *MTV*. When we entered the room she wrinkled up her nose and said, 'What is that disgusting smell? It's like something died and—' She looked up and caught sight of Stevie Rae. Her eyes widened. 'Never mind.' She pointed to the rear of the apartment. 'Bathroom's back there.'

I handed Stevie Rae my bag. 'Here ya go. We'll talk when you come out.'

'Blood first,' Stevie Rae said.

'Go on back and I'll bring a bag to you.'

Stevie Rae was glaring at Aphrodite, who was staring at the TV. 'Bring two,' she practically hissed.

'Fine. I'll bring two.'

Without another word, Stevie Rae left the room. I watched her move down the short hall with a weird, feral stride.

'Hello! Gross, nasty, and totally disturbing,' Aphrodite whispered. 'Like you couldn't have warned me?'

'I tried. You thought you knew everything. Remember?' I whispered back. Then I hurried into the little kitchen and got the bags of blood. 'You also said you'd be nice.'

I knocked on the closed bathroom door. Stevie Rae didn't say anything, so I opened it slowly and peeked in. She was holding her jeans, T-shirt, and boots, and was just standing there, in the middle of the very nice bathroom, staring at the clothes. She was partially turned away from me, so I couldn't be sure, but I thought she might have been crying.

'I brought the blood,' I said softly.

Stevie Rae shook herself, rubbed a hand across her face, and then tossed the clothes and boots onto the top of the marble counter by the sink. She held out her hand for the bags.

I gave them to her, along with the pair of scissors I'd grabbed from the kitchen.

'Do you need help finding anything?' I asked.

Stevie Rae shook her head. Without looking at me she said, 'Are you waiting around because you're curious about how I look naked or because you want a sip of the blood?'

'Neither.' I kept my voice perfectly normal, refusing to get pissed at her when she was so clearly baiting me. 'I'll be out in the living room. You can pitch your old clothes out in the hall and I'll throw them away for you.' I shut the bathroom door firmly behind me.

Aphrodite was shaking her head at me when I rejoined her. 'You think you can fix *that*?'

'Keep your voice down!' I whispered. Then I sat heavily on the opposite end of the couch. 'And, no, I don't think *I* can fix her. I think you and Nyx and I can fix her.'

Aphrodite shuddered. 'She smells as bad as she looks.'

'I'm as aware of that as she is.'

'I'm just sayin', *ugh*.'

'Say whatever, just don't say it to Stevie Rae.'

'Then for the record I just want to say that the girl doesn't feel safe to me,' Aphrodite said, holding up her hand like she was taking an oath. 'I have two words for her: time bomb. I think she'd even freak out your nerd herd.'

'I really wish you'd stop calling them that,' I said. God, I was exhausted.

'You have geek-ends,' she said.

'Huh?' I had no clue what she was talking about.

'There are weekends where your whole gang gets together to watch marathons of *Star Wars* and *Lord of the Rings* movies.'

'Yeah, so?'

Aphrodite gave a melodramatic eye roll. 'You not getting how geeky that is proves my point. You guys are definitely a nerd herd.'

I heard the bathroom door open and close, so I didn't bother to tell Aphrodite that, yes, indeed, I knew exactly how geeky those movies were but that geeky could also be fun, especially when you're dorking out with all your friends and eating popcorn and talking about how totally hot Anakin and Aragorn are (I kinda like Legolas, too, but the Twins say he's way too gay. Damien, of course, adores him.). I grabbed a garbage bag from under the sink in the kitchen and crammed Stevie Rae's disgusting clothes in it, tying it up and then opening the apartment door and tossing it down the stairs.

'Vile,' Aphrodite said.

I plopped down on the couch, ignored her and stared, unseeing, at the TV screen.

'Are we not going to talk about *it*.' Aphrodite jerked her chin in the direction of the bathroom.

'Stevie Rae is a *her*, not an *it*.'

'She smells like an it.'

'And no. We're not going to talk about *her* until *she* joins us,' I said firmly.

139

CHAPTER THIRTEEN

REFUSING TO GOSSIP WITH APHRODITE ABOUT STEVIE RAE, I went back to staring at the TV, but after a while I could not sit still, so I got up and went from window to window closing the shutters and the thick drapes. That didn't take long, so I headed into the kitchen and started to dig though the cupboards. I'd already noticed that the fridge had a six-pack of Perrier, a couple of bottles of white wine, and a few bricks of that expensive imported cheese that smells like feet. There were some packages of butcher-paper-wrapped meat and fish in the freezer and ice cubes, but that was it. The cupboards had a bunch of stuff in them, but it was all rich-people food.

You know, imported tins of fish that still have their heads on, smoked oysters (eesh), other strange meat and pickled stuff, and long boxes of something called water crackers. There was not one can of decent pop.

'We're gonna have to go to the grocery store,' I said.

'If you can keep Stinky locked back in the bedroom, all you have to do is get into my parents' on-line account with Petty's Foods. Click what you want from the store. They'll deliver and charge it to my parents.'

'Won't they freak when they see the bill?'

'They won't even notice,' she said. 'The bank pays it directly. It's no big deal.'

'Really?' I was amazed people actually lived like that. 'You guys are *rich*.'

Aphrodite shrugged. 'Yeah. Whatever.'

Stevie Rae cleared her throat and Aphrodite and I jumped. The sight of her made my heart squeeze hard. Her short blond hair was wet, and it hung around her face in familiar curls. Her eyes were still tinted red and her face was thin and pale, but it was clean. Her cloths were baggy, but she looked like Stevie Rae again.

'Hi,' I said softly. 'Feel Better?'

She looked uncomfortable, but nodded.

'You smell better,' Aphrodite said.

I glared at her.

'What? That was nice.'

I sighed and shot her an obvious *you're not helping* look. 'Okay, how about we talk about coming up with a plan?'

I meant it to be a rhetorical question, but Aphrodite spoke up right away.

'What exactly are we planning about? I mean, I know Stevie Rae has, uh, unique issues, but I'm not sure what you think can be done about them. She's dead. Or undead dead.' She glanced a Stevie Rae. 'Okay, I'm not actually trying to be mean, but—'

'It's not mean. It's just the truth.' Stevie Rae interrupted her. 'But don't pretend that you care about my feelings now any more than you did before I died.'

'I was trying to be nice,' Aphrodite snapped, sounding the opposite of nice.

'Try harder,' I said. Then, 'Sit down Stevie Rae.' She sat in the puffy leather chair beside the couch. I ignored my headache and sat on the couch. 'Okay, here's what I know.' I ticked the points off on my fingers. 'First, Stevie Rae doesn't have to live around adult vamps anymore, so that means that she has completed a Change.' Aphrodite started to open her mouth and I hurried on. 'Second, she has to have blood, even more often than normal adult vamps.' I looked from Stevie Rae to Aphrodite. 'Do either of the two of you know if adult vamps go crazy if they don't drink blood regularly?'

'In Advanced Vampyre Soc we've learned that adults need to drink blood regularly to stay healthy. That's mind and body.' Aphrodite shrugged. 'Neferet is the prof for the class, and she's never said anything about vamps going crazy if they don't drink. But that might be one of the things they tell us only after we've made the Change.'

'I didn't know anything about it till I died,' Stevie Rae said.

'Can it be blood from any mammal, or does it have to be human blood?'

'Human.'

I'd asked Stevie Rae, but she and Aphrodite answered at the same time.

'Okay, well, besides having to drink blood and *not* having to be around adult vamps, Stevie Rae can't come in someone's house unless she's invited.'

'By someone who lives there,' Stevie Rae added. 'But that's not such a big deal.'

'What do you mean?' I asked.

Stevie Rae turned her red-tinged gaze on me. 'I can get humans to do things they don't want to do.'

With an effort, I didn't shiver.

'That's not a shocker,' Aphrodite said. 'Lots of adult vamps have such strong personalities that they can be very persuasive to humans. That's one of the reasons they're so damn scared of us. You should know about that, Zoey.'

'Huh?'

Aphrodite raised an eyebrow. 'You've Imprinted with your human boyfriend. How tough was it for you to persuade him to let you have a little suck.' She paused, smiling wickedly. 'Of his blood, I mean.'

I ignored her stankness. 'Okay, Stevie Rae has that in common with Changed vamps, too. But vamps don't have to be invited in to someone's house, do they?'

'Never heard of anything like that,' Aphrodite said.

'It's because I'm soulless,' Stevie Rae said in a voice totally washed of all emotion.

'You are not soulless,' I said automatically.

'You're wrong. I died and Neferet figured out a way to bring my body back, but she didn't bring my humanity back, too. My soul's still dead.'

I couldn't even stand to think that what she was saying might be possible, and I opened my mouth to argue with her, but Aphrodite was quicker.

'That makes sense. It's why you can't come inside a living person's home without being invited. It's also probably why you'll burn up if the sun hits you. No soul – no standing against the light.'

'How did you know about that?' Stevie Rae asked.

'I'm vision girl, remember?'

'Thought Nyx abandoned you and took the visions away, too,' Stevie Rae said cruelly.

'That's what Neferet wants people to believe because Aphrodite had visions about her – and about you,' I said pointedly. 'But Nyx has no more abandoned her than she's abandoned you.'

'So why are you helping Zoey?' Stevie Rae shot the question at Aphrodite. 'And don't give me that crap about Nyx having a sense of humor. What's the real reason?'

Aphrodite sneered. 'Why I'm helping is my own damn business.'

Stevie Rae sprang to her feet and moved across the room so fast that her movements were one big blur. Before I could blink she had her hands around Aphrodite's throat and her face pressed close to hers. 'You're wrong. It's my business, too, because I'm here. Remember, you invited me in?'

'Stevie Rae, let her go.' I kept my voice calm, but my pulse was pounding like crazy. Stevie Rae looked and sounded dangerous and more than a little crazy.

'I've never liked her, Zoey. You know that. I told you a zillion times she was no damn good and you should stay far away from her. I don't know why I shouldn't snap her neck.'

I was beginning to worry about how bugged Aphrodite's eyes looked and how bright red her face was turning. She struggled against Stevie Rae, but it was like a little kid trying to break the hold of a big, mean adult. *Help me to get through to Stevie Rae.* I sent up a silent prayer to the Goddess as I began to center myself so I could call the power of the elements to me. Then words whispered into my mind and I quickly repeated them.

'You shouldn't snap her neck because you're not a monster.'

She didn't let go of Aphrodite, but Stevie Rae turned her head so she could look at me. 'How do you know that?'

I didn't hesitate, 'Because I believe in our Goddess, and because I believe in the part of you that is still my best friend.'

Stevie Rae released Aphrodite, who started coughing and rubbing her neck.

'Say you're sorry,' I told Stevie Rae. Her red eyes pierced me, but I lifted my chin and stared right back at her. 'Say you're sorry to Aphrodite,' I repeated.

'I'm *not* sorry,' Stevie Rae said as she walked (at a normal speed) back to the chair.

'Nyx has given Aphrodite an affinity for earth,' I said abruptly. Stevie Rae's body jerked like I'd slapped her. 'So by attacking her you're really attacking Nyx.'

'Nyx is letting her take my place!'

'No. Nyx is letting her help you. I cannot figure this out on my own, Stevie Rae. I can't tell any of our friends about you because if I do it's only a matter of time before Neferet knows everything they know, and even though I'm not sure about much, I do absolutely believe Neferet has gone bad. So basically it's us against a powerful High Priestess. Aphrodite is the only fledgling besides me who Neferet can't read. We need her help.'

Stevie Rae narrowed her eyes at Aphrodite, who was still rubbing her neck and sucking air. 'I still want to know why she'd bother to help us. She's never liked any of us. She's a liar and a user and a total bitch.'

'Atonement,' Aphrodite managed to gasp.

'What?' Stevie Rae said.

Aphrodite glared at her. Her voice was raspy, but she was definitely regaining her breath and had gone from being scared to being pissed. 'What's wrong? Is the word too big for you? A-T-O-N-E-M-E-N-T.' She spelled it. 'It means I have to make up for something I've done. A lot of somethings, actually. So I have to do what I didn't do before – which is to follow Nyx's will.' She paused and cleared her throat, grimacing in pain. 'No, I don't like it any better than you do.

146

And, just by the by, you still smell bad and your country-ass clothes are stupid.'

'Aphrodite answered your question,' I told Stevie Rae. 'She could have been nicer about it, but you did just try to choke her to death. Now apologize to her.' I stared hard at Stevie Rae while I silently called spirit energy to me. I saw Stevie Rae flinch, and she finally looked away.

'Sorry,' she muttered.

'I can't hear her,' Aphrodite said.

'And I can't deal with the two of you acting like big ol' babies!' I snapped. 'Stevie Rae, apologize to her like a normal person instead of spoiled brat.'

'I'm sorry,' Stevie Rae said, frowning at Aphrodite.

'Okay, look,' I said. 'We need to have some kind of truce between the three of us. I cannot be afraid if I turn my head the two of you are going to be trying to kill each other.'

'She couldn't kill me,' Stevie Rae said, curling her lip unattractively.

'Because you're already dead or because I don't want to get close enough to your stinkiness to kick your bony ass?' Aphrodite asked in a sickeningly sweet voice.

'This is exactly what I mean!' I shouted. 'Stop it! If we can't get along, how in the hell can we expect to figure out a way to stand up to Neferet and fix what's happened to Stevie Rae?'

'We have to stand up to Neferet?' Aphrodite said.

'Why do we have to stand up to her?' Stevie Rae said.

'Because she's fucking evil!' I yelled.

'You said fuck,' Stevie Rae said.

'Yeah, and you didn't get struck by lightning or melt or anyfuckingthing like that,' Aphrodite said gleefully.

'That didn't even look right coming out of your mouth, Z,' Stevie Rae said.

I couldn't help smiling at Stevie Rae. She suddenly looked and sounded so much like herself that I felt a huge rush of hope. She was still in there. I just had to figure out a way to get her to be in touch with—

'That's it!' I sat forward excitedly.

'You cussing is it? I don't think so, Z. It's really just not you,' Stevie Rae said.

'I think you were right when you said your soul was missing, Stevie Rae. Or at least part of it's missing.'

'You're sounding like that's a good thing, which I totally don't get,' Aphrodite said.

'I hate to agree with her, but yeah, why is my missing soul a good thing?' Stevie Rae said.

'Because *that's* how we fix you!' They just stared at me with blank, dopey looks. I rolled my eyes. 'All we have to do is figure out how to get your soul back into you all in one piece and you'll be whole. You might not be exactly like you used to be. Clearly, you've completed a Change that's not exactly normal.'

'Clearly,' Aphrodite mumbled.

'But with a healed soul you get your humanity back – you get yourself back. And that's really what's most important. All this other stuff,' I made an abstract gesture at her.

'You know, your weird eyes and the whole drink-blood-or-you-go-crazy issue, all that stuff can be dealt with if you're really *you* again.'

'Is this more of that what's-inside-is-more-important-than-what's-outside shit?' Aphrodite said.

'It is, and Aphrodite you are getting on my last nerve with your negative attitude,' I said.

'I think your group needs a pessimist,' she said, looking kinda pouty.

'You aren't part of her group,' Stevie Rae said.

'Neither are you right now, Stinky,' Aphrodite shot back.

'Hateful hag! Don't you ever—'

'*Enough!*' I flung my hands out at both of them while I concentrated on the fact that both of them needed a good spanking. Wind obeyed me and they were knocked back in their seats as a small, concentrated gale surged around them. 'Okay, stop now,' I said quickly. The wind instantly died. 'Uh, sorry. Lost my temper.'

Aphrodite immediately began to run her fingers through her completely messed up hair. 'I think you lost your damn mind,' Aphrodite grumbled.

Personally, I thought that she might have been right, but I didn't want to say so. I glanced at the clock and was shocked to see that it was seven o'clock. No wonder I was exhausted. 'Look, you two. We're all tired. Let's get some sleep and meet back here after the Full Moon Ritual. I'll do some more research and see if I can come up with anything about missing or broken souls and how to fix them.' At least I had something I could focus on now, versus flailing around aimlessly in the library. Well, that is when I wasn't making out with Loren. Ah, hell. I'd forgotten about him.

'Sounds like a plan to me. I'm ready to get out of here.' Aphrodite stood up. 'My parents are going to be gone for three weeks, so you don't need to worry about them coming home. There's yard boys who come twice a week, but that's during the day and – oh, yeah – you'll burst into flames if you go out during the day, so them seeing you shouldn't be a problem, either. The maid service usually comes once a week when my parents are gone, to keep the house all perfect, but they only come out here when my grandma's visiting, so no problem with them, either.'

'Wow, she's really rich,' Stevie Rae said to me.

'Apparently,' I said.

'Do you have cable?' Stevie Rae asked Aphrodite.

'Of course,' she said.

'Cool,' Stevie Rae said, looking happier than she had since she died.

'Okay, so, we're out of here,' I said, joining Aphrodite at the door. 'Oh, Stevie Rae, I got you one of those GoPhones. It's in my bag. If you need anything, just call my cell. I'll remember to keep it with me and actually turned on.' I paused, feeling weirdly uncertain about leaving her.

'Go on. I'll see you later,' Stevie Rae said. 'You don't need to worry about me. I'm already dead. What more can go wrong?'

'She has a point,' Aphrodite said.

'Okay, well. See ya,' I said. I didn't want to say I thought she had a point, too. That seemed to be asking for trouble. I mean, she was undead, and that was pretty awful. But there were other things that could go wrong, too. The thought made a creepy chill go up my spine, which, sadly, I ignored and kept blundering on into my future. Too bad I didn't have any idea of the horror I was blundering blindly into.

CHAPTER FOURTEEN

'DROP ME BACK BY THE TRAPDOOR IN THE WALL. I STILL don't think it's a good idea if people think we're hanging out,' Aphrodite said.

I turned right on Peoria Street and headed back to the school. 'I'm surprised you care so much what other people think.'

'I don't. I care what Neferet finds out. If she thinks the two of us are friends, or even just not enemies, she's going to figure that we've shared info about her.'

'And that would be majorly bad,' I finished for her.

'Definitely,' she said.

'But she's going to see us together once in a while because you're going to be evoking earth in my circles.'

Aphrodite gave me a startled look. 'No, I'm not.'

'Of course you are.'

'No, I am not.'

'Aphrodite, Nyx has given you an affinity for earth. You belong in the circle. Unless you want to ignore Nyx's will.' I didn't add the word 'again,' but it seemed to hang in the air between us.

'I already said I'd do Nyx's will,' she said through clenched teeth.

'Which means you're going to be part of the Full Moon Ritual tonight,' I said.

'That's going to be a little difficult, seeing as I'm not a member of the Dark Daughters anymore.'

Crap. I'd forgotten about that.

'Well, then, you'll just have to rejoin the Dark Daughters.' She started to say something. I raised my voice and talked over the top of her. 'Which means you're going to have to swear to uphold the new rules.'

'Lame,' she muttered.

'You're doing that attitude thing again,' I said. 'So, will you swear to it?'

I could see her chewing her lip. I waited without saying anything else and just kept driving. This was something Aphrodite was going to have to decide for herself. She said she wanted to atone for her screw-ups and wanted to do the Goddess's will. But wanting something and actually doing it was totally not the same thing. Aphrodite had been selfish and mean for a really long time. Sometimes I could see a spark of a change in her, but mostly I just saw the girl the Twins called the Hag from Hell.

'Yeah, whatever.'

'What was that?'

'I said, yeah. I'll swear to your new lame-ass rules.'

'Aphrodite, part of the swearing means that you don't believe the rules are lame.'

'No, there's nothing in the swearing that says I can't think they're lame. I just have to say that I'll be authentic for air, faithful for fire, wise for water, empathetic for earth, and sincere for spirit. So I'm authentically saying I think your new rules are lame.'

'If that's what you think, then why did you memorize them?'

'Know thy enemy,' she quoted.

'Who said that, anyway?'

She shrugged. 'Someone back in the day. The "thy" gives it away as from the olden back in the day.'

I thought she was full of poopy, but didn't want to say anything (especially since she'd make fun of me saying 'poopy' instead of the s word).

'Okay, here you go.' I pulled over to the side of the road. Thankfully, the clouds that had rolled in during the late night hours had multiplied, and the morning was dark and gloomy. All Aphrodite would have to do was cross the little grassy area that sat between the road and the wall that surrounded the school, go through the trapdoor, and then follow the sidewalk a short way to the dorm. As the Twins would say, easy-peasy. I squinted up at the sky, considering whether I should try asking the wind to blow in more clouds to make it even darker, but a glance at Aphrodite's sullen face made me decide, nah, she could deal with the sunlight. 'So, you'll be at the ritual tonight, right?' I prompted, wondering why it was taking her so long to get out of my car.

'Yeah, I'll be there.'

She sounded distracted. Whatever. The girl was just plain weird sometimes.

'Okay, see ya,' I said.

'Yeah, see ya,' she mumbled, opening the door and (finally) getting out of the car. But before she closed it, she bent down and said, 'Something feels wrong. Do you feel it, too?'

I thought about it. 'I dunno. I'm feeling kinda restless and stressed, but that could be because my best friend's dead – I mean undead.' Then I looked more closely at her. 'Are you getting ready to have a vision?'

'I don't know. I can never tell when one will come on. I do get feelings about things sometimes and don't have a full-blown vision, though.'

She looked really pale and even a little sweaty (which was definitely out of the norm for Aphrodite). 'Maybe you should get back in the car. There's probably no one awake to see us come in together anyway.' Aphrodite was a pain in the ass, but I'd seen how visions made her helpless and sick and I really didn't like the thought of her getting stuck outside in the daylight alone when one hit her.

She shook herself, reminding me of a cat coming in out of the rain. 'I'll be okay. I'm probably just imaging things. See you tonight.'

I watched her hurry toward the thick brick and stone wall that ringed the school grounds. Huge ancient oaks lined the wall, throwing it into shadow so that suddenly it looked unusually sinister. Jeesh, now who was imagining things? I had my hand on the gear and was just shifting into first so I could pull away when Aphrodite screamed.

Sometimes I don't think. My body takes over and I just act. This was one of those times. I was out of my car and running toward Aphrodite before I even thought about it. When I got to her, I knew two things at once. One was that something smelled wonderful, kinda familiar, yet not. Whatever it was, the scent had settled in the area like a delicious fog and I automatically inhaled deeply. The second thing I saw was Aphrodite bent over at the waist, puking her guts out and crying at the same time, which is not a very pleasant thing to do or to watch. I was too busy looking at her and trying to figure out what was going on and too distracted by the lovely smell to notice *it*. At first.

'Zoey!' Aphrodite sobbed, still retching. 'Get someone! Fast!'

'What is it – a vision? What's wrong?' I grabbed her by the shoulders and tried to steady her while she continued to puke her guts up.

'No! Behind me! Against the wall...' She gagged, but didn't have anything else to puke up. 'It's so awful.'

I didn't want to, but my eyes automatically looked up and behind her to the school's shadowy wall.

It was the most horrible thing I'd ever seen. At first my mind wouldn't even register what it was. Later I thought that must have been some kind of instant defense mechanism. Unfortunately, it didn't last long. I blinked and peered into the darkness. Something looked slick and wet and—

And I knew what the sweet, seductive smell was. I fought against falling to my knees and puking my guts up beside Aphrodite. I smelled blood. Not ordinary human blood, which is delicious enough. What I was smelling was a lethal shedding of a full-grown vampyre's lifeblood.

Her body was nailed grotesquely to a crude wooden cross that was resting against the wall. They'd not just nailed her wrists and ankles. They'd also driven a thick wooden stake through her heart. There was some kind of paper over her heart, held in place by the grotesque stake. I could see that it had something written on it, but my eyes wouldn't focus well enough to read the words.

They'd also cut off her head. Professor Nolan's head. I knew it was her because they'd mounted her head on a wooden stake next to her body. Her long dark hair lifted softly in the breeze, looking obscenely graceful. Her mouth was open in a terrible grimace, but her eyes were closed.

I grabbed Aphrodite's elbow and hauled her to her feet. 'Come on! We have to get help.'

Leaning on each other, we stumbled to my car. I don't

know how I managed to start the Bug and pull away from the curb.

'I – I – I think I'm gonna be sick again.' Aphrodite's teeth were chattering so bad she could hardly talk.

'No, you're not.' I couldn't believe how calm I sounded. 'Breathe. Center yourself. Draw strength from the earth.' I realized I was automatically doing what I was telling her to do, only in my case I was drawing strength from the five elements. 'You're okay,' I told her as I channeled energy from wind, fire, water, earth, and spirit to keep back the hysterics and shock I wanted to give in to. 'We're okay.'

'We're okay . . . we're okay . . . ,' Aphrodite kept repeating.

She was shivering so hard that I reached behind me and grabbed the hoodie I kept in my backseat. 'Wrap this around you. We're almost there.'

'But everyone's gone! Who are we going to tell?'

'Everyone's not gone.' My mind flailed around. 'Lenobia never leaves her horses for long. She's probably here.' And then I grasped at a dark, alluring straw. 'And I saw Loren Blake yesterday. He'll know what to do.'

'Okay . . . okay . . . ,' Aphrodite murmured.

'Listen to me Aphrodite,' I said sternly. She turned wide, shock-filled eyes on me. 'They're going to want to know why we were together, and especially why I was dropping you off so you could sneak back.'

'What do we say?'

'I wasn't with you and I wasn't dropping you off. I'd been to visit my grandma. You were . . .' I paused, trying to force my numb mind to think. 'You were at home. I saw you walking back to the school and I gave you a ride. When we passed the wall you felt something was wrong and we stopped to check it out. That's how we found her.'

'Okay. Okay. I can say that.'

'You'll remember?'

She took a deep, shaky breath. 'I'll remember.'

I didn't bother with parking in a regular space. I screeched to a stop as close as possible to the section of the main building that held the in-residence professors' rooms. I waited only long enough to grab hold of Aphrodite again, and together we ran up the sidewalk to the old castle-like wooden front doors. Silently thanking my Goddess for the non-lock school policy, I wrenched open the door and stumbled inside just ahead of Aphrodite.

And I ran right into Neferet.

'Neferet! You have to come! Please! It's horrible!' I sobbed and threw myself into her arms. I couldn't help it. My mind knew that she had done terrible things, but up until just a month ago Neferet had been a mother to me. No, actually, she'd become *the* mother I wished I'd had, and in my panic seeing her sent a rush of incredible relief pouring through my body.

'Zoey? Aphrodite?'

Aphrodite had collapsed against the wall beside us and I could hear her sobbing brokenly. I realized I'd started to shake so hard that if it hadn't been for Neferet's strong arms around me I would probably have not been able to stand. The High

Priestess held me gently, but firmly away from her so that she could look into my face. 'Talk to me, Zoey. What has happened?'

My trembling got worse. I bowed my head and gritted my teeth, trying to find my center again and draw enough strength from the elements to speak.

'I heard something and—' I recognized our equestrian professor, Lenobia's, clear strong voice getting closer as she strode purposefully down the hall to us. 'By the Goddess!' From the corner of my graying vision I could see that she had rushed to Aphrodite and was trying to support her weeping body.

'Neferet? What's wrong?'

My head snapped up at the familiar voice and I saw Loren, hair all messed up as if he'd been asleep, coming out of the stairwell that led to his loft as he pulled on an old House of Night sweatshirt. My gaze locked on his and I somehow managed to find the strength to speak.

'It's Professor Nolan,' I said, and wondered at how clear and strong my voice sounded when I felt like my body was being shaken into little pieces. 'She's out by the trapdoor in the eastern wall. Someone killed her.'

CHAPTER FIFTEEN

Everything happened fast after that, but it seemed to me like it was happening to someone else who had temporarily taken up residence in my body. Neferet immediately took charge. She assessed Aphrodite and me and decided (unfortunately) that I was the only one still together enough to return with them to the body. She called for Dragon Lankford, who showed up armed. I heard Neferet checking with Dragon about which warriors had already come back from winter break. It seemed like seconds later that two tall, muscular male vamps appeared. I vaguely recognized them. There was always an assortment of adult vamps coming and going from the school. I'd learned early that vampyre society was heavily matriarchal, which just means women run things. It doesn't mean that male vamps aren't respected, though. They are. It's just that their gifts are usually more in the physical realm and women's gifts are more intellectual and intuitive. Bottom line is, male vampyres are amazing warriors and protectors. These two plus Dragon and Loren made me feel about a zillion times safer.

That doesn't mean I was thrilled about leading them to Professor Nolan's body. We got in one of the school SUVs and retraced the path I'd taken to the school. With a shaking hand I pointed to the spot where I'd pulled to the side of the road. Dragon parked the SUV.

'I was driving by and here's where Aphrodite said she felt like something was wrong,' I launched into our Big Lie. 'We couldn't see much from here.' My eyes skittered over to the dark area by the trapdoor in the wall. 'I felt weird, too, so we decided to check out what was wrong.' I drew a shaky breath. 'I guess I thought there might be a kid who was trying to sneak back to the dorm, but she couldn't find the trapdoor.' I swallowed to clear the thickness in my throat. 'As we got closer to the wall we could tell there was something there. Something terrible. And – and I smelled the blood. When we realized what it was – that it was Professor Nolan – we came straight to you.'

'Can you go over there again, or would you rather stay here and wait for us?' Neferet's voice was kind and understanding, and I wished with everything inside me that she was still one of the good guys.

'I don't want to be alone,' I said.

'Then you'll come with me,' she said. 'The warriors will protect us. You have nothing to fear now, Zoey.'

I nodded and got out of the SUV. The two warriors, Dragon and Loren, flanked Neferet and me. It seemed to take only a couple of seconds to cross the grassy area and get within smelling – and seeing – distance of the crucified body. I felt my knees go all shaky as the fresh horror of what had been done to her registered on my already shocked senses.

'Oh, gracious Goddess!' Neferet gasped. She moved forward slowly until she reached the terrible staked head. I watched as she stroked Professor Nolan's hair back and then rested her hand on the dead woman's forehead. 'Find peace, my friend. Rest in the green meadows of our Goddess. It is there we will, one day, meet again.'

Just as I felt my knees give way a strong hand was under my elbow holding me steady.

'You're okay. You'll make it through this.'

I looked up at Loren and had to blink hard to focus on him. He kept his hold on me, but pulled from his pocket one of those old-fashioned linen handkerchiefs. It was only then that I noticed that I was crying.

'Loren, take Zoey back to the dorm. There's nothing more she can do here. As soon as we're properly protected, I'm going to call the human police,' Neferet said, and turned her sharp gaze on Dragon. 'Get the other warriors back here now.' Dragon flipped open his cell phone and started making calls.

Then Neferet turned her attention to me. 'I know this was a terrible thing for you to see, but I'm proud that you managed to stay strong through it.'

I couldn't make my voice work, so I just nodded.

'Let's get you home, Zoey,' Loren murmured.

As Loren helped me back to the SUV a cold rain started to fall softly all around us. I looked back over my shoulder and saw that it was washing the blood from Professor Nolan's body as if the Goddess herself was weeping her loss.

All the way back to the school Loren kept talking to me. I don't really remember what he was saying. I just know that he was telling me everything was going to be okay in that beautiful, rich voice of his. I could feel it wrapping around me and trying to keep me warm. He parked and led me through the school, still keeping a strong hold on my arm. When he took a turn that brought us to the dining hall instead of the dorm I looked at him questioningly.

'You need something to drink and something to eat. Then you need sleep. I'm going to make sure you get the first two before the second.' He paused and smiled sadly. 'Even though you look ready to pass out on your feet.'

'I'm not really hungry,' I said.

'I know, but eating will make you feel better.' His hand slid down from my elbow to hold mine. 'Let me cook for you, Zoey.'

I let him pull me into the kitchen. His hand was warm and strong, and I could feel it starting to unthaw the frozen numbness that had settled into me.

'Can you cook?' I asked him, grabbing at any subject that wasn't death and horror.

'Yes, but not well,' he grinned, looking like a handsome little boy.

'That doesn't sound promising,' I said. I felt my face smile, but it seemed stiff and awkward, like I'd forgotten how.

'Don't worry, I'll be gentle with you.' He pulled a stool out from the corner of the room and put it next to the long butcher block counter that sat in the middle of the enormous kitchen. 'Sit,' he ordered.

I did as he said, relieved I didn't have to stand up anymore. He turned to the cabinets and started pulling things from them and one of the walk-in refrigerators (not that one they kept the blood in, though).

'Here, drink this. Slowly.'

I blinked in surprise at the large goblet of red wine. 'I don't really like—'

'You'll like this wine.' His dark eyes held mine. 'Trust me and drink it.'

I did as he told me. The taste exploded on my tongue, sending sparks of heat throughout my body. 'It has blood in it!' I gasped.

'It does.' He was making a sandwich and he didn't even look up at me. 'It's how vampyres drink their wine – laced with blood.' He did glance up to meet my eyes then. 'If the taste is disagreeable to you, I'll get you something else to drink.'

'No, it's fine. I'll drink it like this.' I took another sip, forcing myself not to chug it all down in one huge swallow.

'I had a feeling you wouldn't have a problem with it.'

My eyes shot back to his. 'Why would you say that?' I could feel my strength as well as my wits returning to me as the wonderful blood settled into my body.

He kept making the sandwich and shrugged. 'You Imprinted that human boy, didn't you? That's how you were able to find and rescue him from the serial killer.'

'Yeah.'

When I didn't say anything else he glanced up at me and smiled. 'I thought so. It happens. Sometimes we accidentally Imprint.'

'Fledglings don't. We're not even supposed to be drinking human blood,' I said.

Loren's smile was warm and filled with appreciation. 'You're not a normal fledgling, so the *normal* rules don't apply to you.' His gaze held mine and it seemed he was talking about much more than accidentally drinking a little human blood.

He made me feel hot and cold – scared but totally grown-up and sexy – all at once.

I kept my mouth shut and went back to sipping the blood-spiked wine. (I know it sounds completely gross, but it was delicious.)

'Here, eat this.' He passed the plate to me that held the ham and cheese sandwich he'd just made me. 'Wait, you'll need some of these, too.' He rummaged around in a cabinet until he made a little 'ahha!' noise and turned around to pour a big ol' pile of nacho cheese-flavored Doritos on my plate.

I smiled. This time my mouth felt more natural doing it. 'Doritos! That's perfect.' I took a big bite as I realized I really was starving. 'You know, they don't like fledglings to eat junk food like this.'

'As I said' – Loren smiled his slow, sexy smile at me again – 'you're not like the rest of those fledgling children. And I happen to adhere to the belief that some rules were meant to be broken.' His eyes went from my eyes to the diamond earrings that nestled in my earlobes.

I felt my face getting hot, so I refocused on eating, glancing up only once in a while at him. Loren hadn't made himself a sandwich, but he had poured himself a glass of wine and was drinking it slowly while he watched me eat. I was just getting ready to tell him that he was making me nervous when he finally said something.

'Since when are you and Aphrodite friends?'

'We're not,' I said around a bite of sandwich (which actually was very good – so he's ridiculously handsome, sexy, smart, *and* he can cook!). 'I was driving back to school and I saw her walking.' I lifted one shoulder like I couldn't give a good poop about her. 'I figure it's part of my job as leader of the Dark Daughters to be nice, even to her. So I gave her a ride.'

'I'm a little surprised she accepted a ride from you. Aren't you two sworn enemies?'

'Whatever! Sworn enemies? I don't think much about her at all.' I wished I could tell Loren the truth about Aphrodite. Actually, I hated lying (and I'm really not very good at it, although I seemed to be getting better with practice). But even as I thought about liking to unload to Loren, I was slammed in the gut with a feeling that plainly said *no way do you tell him*. So I smiled and chewed my sandwich and basically just tried to focus on the fact that I was feeling less *Night of the Living Dead*.

Which reminded me of Professor Nolan. I put down the half-eaten sandwich and took another gulp of wine.

'Loren, who could have done something like that to Professor Nolan?'

The expression on his handsome face darkened. 'I think the quote made it pretty obvious.'

'Quote?'

'Didn't you see what was written on the paper they staked to her?'

I shook my head, feeling a little queasy again. 'I know there was something written on the paper, but I couldn't look long enough to read it.'

'It said, "Thou shalt not suffer a witch to live. Exodus 22:18." And REPENT written and underlined several times.'

Something tickled at my memory and I felt a burning begin inside of me that had nothing to do with the blood in my wine. 'The People of Faith.'

'That's what it looks like.' Loren shook his head. 'I wondered what the priestesses were thinking when they decided to buy this place and set up a House of Night here. Seemed to be asking for trouble. There are few parts of the country more narrow-minded and rabid about what they call their *religious* beliefs.' He shook his head and looked truly angry. 'Although I don't understand worshipping a god who denigrates women and whose "true believers" feel it's their right to look down on anyone who doesn't think exactly as they do.'

'That's not how everyone is in Oklahoma,' I said firmly. 'There's also a strong Native American belief system, and lots of regular people who don't buy into the stupid People of Faith prejudices.'

'Regardless, it's the People of Faith who are most vocal.'

'Just because they have the biggest mouths that doesn't make them right.'

He laughed and his face relaxed. 'You're feeling better.'

'Yeah, I guess I am.' I yawned.

'Better but exhausted, I bet,' he said. 'Time to head to your dorm and your bed. You'll need to rest and regain your strength for what is to come.'

I felt an icy prick of fear in my stomach, and I wished I hadn't eaten so many chips. 'What's going to happen?'

'It's been decades since there's been an open attack by humans on vampyres. It will change things.'

The cold fear expanded in my gut. 'Change things? How?'

Loren met my gaze. 'We will not suffer insult without giving insult in return.' His expression went hard, and all of a sudden he looked more warrior than poet, more vampyre than human. He looked powerful and dangerous and exotic and more than a little scary. Okay, he was honestly the hottest thing I'd ever seen.

Then, as if realizing he'd said too much, he smiled and walked around the counter to stand close to me. 'But you don't need to worry about any of that. Within twenty-four hours the school will be flooded with our elite vampyre warriors, the Sons of Erebus. No human fanatic will be able to touch any of us.'

I frowned, worrying about the ramifications of increased security. How the hell was I supposed to sneak myself and squishy bags of blood out to Stevie Rae with a zillion testosterone-filled warriors banging their chests and being all superprotective?

'Hey, you'll be safe. I promise.' Loren took my chin in his hands and tilted my face up.

Nervous anticipation made my breath go all quick and my stomach feel all fluttery. I'd tried to put him out of my mind, tried not to think about his kisses and the way he made my blood pound when he looked at me, but the truth was that even knowing how much my being with Loren would hurt Erik, and with the stress of Stevie Rae and Aphrodite and the horror of what had happened to Professor Nolan, I could still feel the imprint of his lips on mine. I wanted him to kiss me again and again and again.

'I believe you,' I whispered. Right then I swear I would have believed anything he said to me.

'It pleases me to see you wearing my earrings.'

Before I could say anything, he bent and kissed me, long and deep. His tongue met mine and I could taste wine and a seductive hint of blood in his mouth. After what seemed like a long time he lifted his mouth from mine. His eyes were dark and he was breathing deeply.

'I need to get you back to your dorm before I'm tempted to keep you beside me forever,' he said.

I used all the brilliance of my wit and managed to breath-lessly say, 'Okay.'

He took my arm again, like he had supported me on the way in. This time the touch felt hot and intimate. Our bodies brushed against each other as we walked through the gloomy morning to the girls' dorm. He led me up the front stairs and opened the door. The big dayroom was deserted. I glanced at the clock and could hardly believe it was a little after 9:00 A.M.

Loren lifted my hand quickly to his mouth, kissing it warmly before he dropped it. 'A thousand times good night. A thousand times the worse, to want thy light. Love goes toward love as schoolboys from their books, but love from love, toward school with heavy looks.'

I vaguely recognized the lines from *Romeo and Juliet*. Was he telling me he loved me? My face flushed with nerves and excitement.

'Good-bye,' I said softly. 'Thank you for taking care of me.'

'It was my pleasure, my lady,' he said. 'Adieu.' He bowed to me, closing his fist over his heart in a respectful vampyre salute from a warrior to his High Priestess, and then he was gone.

In a haze of leftover shock and the lightheadedness Loren's kisses made me feel, I practically stumbled up the stairs and

171

to my room. I thought about going to see Aphrodite, but I was on the edge of total exhaustion and there was only one thing I had enough energy to do before I passed out. First, I dug into my wastepaper basket and found the two halves of the horrid birthmas card Mom and the step-loser had sent me.

I felt a sick jolt in my stomach as I held the edges together and saw that I'd remembered right. It had been a cross with a note staked to the middle of it. Yes. It did remind me eerily of what had been done to Professor Nolan.

Before I could change my mind, I took out my cell phone, drew a deep breath, and dialed the number. Mom answered on the third ring.

'Hello! It's a blessed morning!' she said perkily. Clearly she hadn't checked the caller I.D.

'Mom, it's me.'

As I expected, her tone instantly changed. 'Zoey? What's happened now?'

I was too tired to play our usual mother-daughter games. 'Where was John late last night?'

'What ever do you mean, Zoey?'

'Mom, I don't have time for this crap. Just tell me. After you two left Utica Square, what did you do?'

'I don't think I like your tone, young lady.'

I stifled an urge to scream in frustration. 'Mom, this is important. Very important. As in life and death.'

'You're always so dramatic,' she said. Then she gave a nervous little fake laugh. 'Your father came home with me, of course. We watched a football game on TV and then we went to bed.'

'What time did he leave for work this morning?'

'What a silly question! He left about an hour and a half ago, as usual. Zoey, what is this about?'

I hesitated. Could I tell her? What had Neferet said about calling the police? Surely what had happened to Professor Nolan would be plastered all over the news later today. But not yet. Not now. And I knew darn well my mother couldn't be trusted to keep anything quiet.

'Zoey? Are you going to answer me?'

'Just watch the news. You'll see what it's about,' I said.

'What have you done?' I realized she didn't sound worried or upset, only resigned.

'Nothing. It's not me. You better look closer to home for who did what. And remember, I don't live at your home anymore.'

Her voice turned brittle. 'That's right. You most certainly do not. I don't know why you're even calling here. Didn't you and your hateful grandmother say you weren't going to talk to me anymore?'

'*Your* mother is not hateful,' I said automatically.

'She is to me!' my mother snapped.

'Never mind. You're right. I shouldn't have called. Have a good life, Mom.' I said, and hung up on her.

Mom had been right about one thing. I should never have called her. The card was probably just a coincidence anyway. I mean, there are only about a gazillion religious specialty stores in Tulsa and Broken Arrow. They all carry those crappy cards. And they all tend to look the same – either doves and waves washing over footprints in the sand, or crosses and blood and nails. It didn't necessarily mean anything. Did it?

My head felt as woozy as my stomach felt sick. I needed to think, and I couldn't think while I was so tired. I'd sleep and then try to figure out what I should do. Instead of throwing the card away, I put the two halves in the top drawer of my desk. Then I yanked off my clothes and pulled on my most comfortable pair of sweats. Nala was already snoring on my pillow. I snuggled next to her, closed my eyes, forced my mind to clear of terrible images and unspeakable questions, and instead concentrated on my cat's purring until I finally drifted off into an exhausted sleep.

CHAPTER SIXTEEN

I KNEW THE SECOND HEATH GOT BACK IN TOWN BECAUSE he interrupted my dream. I had been lying out in the sun (see, clearly a dream) on a big, heart-shaped floatie in the middle of a lake made of Sprite (who knows?), when all of a sudden everything disappeared and Heath's familiar voice burst into my skull.

'Zo!'

My eyes fluttered open. Nala was staring at me with grumpy green cat eyes.

'Nala? Did you hear something?'

The cat 'mee-uf-owed,' sneezed, stood up long enough to

pad around and around in a circle several times, then she plopped down and went right back to sleep.

'You're really no help at all,' I said.

She ignored me.

I looked at the clock and groaned. It was seven o'clock. P.M. Jeesh, I'd slept for about eight hours but my eyelids were like sandpaper. Ugh. What did I have to do today?

Then I remembered Professor Nolan and the conversation with my mom and my stomach clenched.

Should I tell someone about my suspicions? As Loren had said, the People of Faith had already been implicated in the murder by the awful note that was left behind. So, did I really need to say anything about the fact that I wouldn't be surprised if the step-loser was involved? Mom had made it clear to me that he'd been home all last night, and this morning. At least, that's what she was saying.

Could she be lying?

A shiver went through my body. Of course she could be. She'd do anything for that disgusting man. She'd already proven that by turning her back on me. But if she was lying, and I told on her, then I'd be responsible for what happened to her. I hated John Heffer, but did I hate him enough to cause my mom to go down with him?

I felt like puking.

'If the step-loser is tied up in the murder, the police will figure it out. If that happens, nothing that comes of it will be my fault.' I said the words out loud, letting my voice calm me. 'I'll wait and see what happens.' I couldn't do it. I just couldn't.

She was awful, but she was my mom, and I still remembered when she used to love me.

So I wasn't going to do anything except try and put my mom and the step-loser out of my mind. Period. I mean it.

While I was attempting to continue to convince myself I'd made the right choice, I remembered what else was going on today. The Dark Daughters' Full Moon Ritual. My heart sank into my clenching stomach. Normally, I'd be excited and a little nervous. Today I was just stressed. On top of everything else, having Aphrodite join our circle wasn't going to be a popular move. Whatever. My friends were just going to have to deal with it. I sighed. My life seriously sucked. Plus, I was probably depressed. Didn't depressed people sleep for, like, ever? I closed my bristly eyes, giving in to my self-diagnosis and was almost asleep when '*Zoey baby!*' screamed through my mind just as my alarm started bleating. Alarm? It was the weekend. I hadn't set my alarm.

My cell phone was chiming with the little noise it made when I had a text message. Groggily, I flipped open the phone. Instead of finding one text message I found four.

Zo! Im bak!
Zoey I have to see u
Still luv you Zo
Zo? Call me.

'Heath.' I sighed and sat back on my bed. 'Crap. This just keeps getting worse and worse.' What in the hell was I going to do about him?

He and I had Imprinted more than a month ago. He'd also been snatched by Stevie Rae's gross undead dead kids' gang and almost killed. I'd played like I was the calvary (or at the very least Storm from *X-Men*) and rescued him, but before we could get totally away Neferet had showed up and zapped our memories. Because of my gifts from Nyx, I'd regained my memories. I didn't have a clue if Heath remembered anything at all.

Okay, clearly he remembered that we Imprinted. Or that we're still dating. Although we really weren't. I sighed again. How did I feel about Heath? He'd been my on-again, off-again boyfriend since I was in third grade and he was a fourth-grader. Truthfully, we'd mostly been on-again until he decided to have a deep and meaningful relationship with Budweiser. I so don't want my young lad to be a drunk, so I dumped him, even though he hadn't really seemed to understand he'd been dumped. Not even my being Marked and moving to the House of Night had made him understand we were through.

I guess my sucking his blood and making out with him probably hadn't helped him realize we were supposed to be broken up, either.

Jeesh, I was turning into such a ho.

For about the zillionth time I wished I had someone I could talk to about all of my boy issues. Actually, counting Loren I should call them my boy-man issues. I rubbed my forehead and then tried to smooth my hair back into place.

Okay, I really needed to make a decision and get some of myself straightened out.

1. I liked Heath. I might actually love him. And the blood-lust thing with him was majorly hot, even though I'm not supposed to be drinking his blood. Did I want to break up with him? No. Should I break up with him? Definitely.
2. I liked Erik. I liked him a lot. He's smart and funny and an honestly nice guy. His being the cutest, most popular fledgling at school didn't hurt, either. And, like he'd reminded me more than once, he and I had a lot in common. Did I want to break up with him? No. Should I break up with him? Well, only if I kept cheating on him with guy number one and man number three.
3. I liked Loren. He existed in a whole other universe than Erik and Heath. He. Was. A. Man. An adult vampyre, with all the power and wealth and position that came along with it. He knew stuff that I was only beginning to guess at. He made me feel like no one had ever made me feel before; he made me feel like a real woman. Did I want to break up with him? No. Should I break up with him. Not just yes, but hell yes.

So it was obvious what I should do. I needed to break up with Heath (for real this time), keep dating Erik, and (like I had some sense) never, ever be alone with Loren Blake again.

Plus, with all the other crap going on in my life – as in my undead best friend, trying to deal with Aphrodite, who *all* my friends can't stand, and the horror that had happened with Professor Nolan – I really didn't have the time or energy it took for dating drama.

Not to mention the fact that I'm really not used to feeling ho-ish. It wasn't a feeling I particularly liked. (Although the lifestyle did seem to come with good jewelry.)

So I made a decision, and this time it was one that called for action. Immediate action. I flipped open my phone and text messaged Heath.

We need to talk

His reply was almost instant. I could practically see his cute grin.

Yes! 2day?

I chewed my lip while I thought about it. Before I made my decision I pushed the thick curtain aside and peeked out the window. The day had stayed cloudy and cold. Good. That meant there would be less chance of people hanging around outside, especially since it was already dark. I was just trying to figure out where we should meet when my phone chimed again.

I can come 2 u

NO

I texted back quickly. The last thing I needed was for cute, clueless, and totally Imprinted Heath to show up at the House of Night. But where could I meet him? Getting away probably wouldn't be easy, what with one of our professors having been killed. My phone chimed. I sighed.

Where?

Crap. Where? Then it hit me and I knew the perfect place. I smiled and texted Heath back.

Starbucks in 1 hr

OK!

Now all I had to do was figure out how to *really* break up with Heath. Or at least figure out a way I could keep him at a distance until the Imprint between us faded. If it faded. Surely it would fade.

I made my way blurrily to the bathroom and washed my face with cold water, trying to shock some awake into me. Not feeling like answering a barrage of questions about where I was headed, I tossed into my purse the jar of concealer that fledglings were required to wear whenever they went off school grounds to mingle with the local populace (which kinda made us sound like scientists doing field studies while they tried to blend in with the alien population). I suppose I real'y hadn't needed to look out the window to see what the weather was like. My long dark hair was being extra crazy today, which could only mean rain and humidity. On purpose I picked out very unsexy clothes, deciding on a black tank top, my dorky *Borg Invasion 4D* hoodie, and my most comfortable pair of jeans. Keeping in mind that I needed to detour through the kitchen and grab a can of brown pop – fully leaded *with* sugar and caffeine – I opened my door to see Aphrodite standing there with her hand raised to knock.

'Hi,' I said.

'Hey.' She looked furtively up and down the empty hall.

'Come on in.' I stepped aside and shut the door behind us. 'I gotta hurry, though. I'm meeting someone off campus.'

'That's part of why I'm here. They're not letting anyone off campus.'

'They?'

'The vamps and their warriors.'

'The warriors are here already?'

Aphrodite nodded. 'A bunch of the Sons of Erebus. They're damn nice to look at – I mean truly, seriously hot – but they're definitely going to be cramping our style.'

And then I realized what she was saying. 'Ah, crap. Stevie Rae.'

'She'll be out of blood by tomorrow. That is, if she's not already. She was really pigging down those blood bags,' Aphrodite said with a little curl of her lip.

'I'll call her and tell her to make them last, but we're going to have to get more to her. Soon. Crap!' I said again. 'I really need to not put off this, uh, appointment.'

'So Heath's back in town?'

I frowned at her. 'Maybe.'

'Oh, please. Your face is totally easy to read.' Then she lifted one of her perfectly plucked blond brows. 'Bet Erik doesn't know about this *appointment*.'

Keeping in mind that Aphrodite was Erik's ex-girlfriend, and no matter how friendly she and I appeared to be getting I knew she would jump at the chance to latch back onto Erik, I shrugged nonchalantly. 'Erik will know as soon as I get back. I happen to be going to break up with Heath. As if that's any of your business.'

'I hear breaking an Imprint bond is next to impossible,' she said.

'That's an Imprint with an adult vamp. It's different for fledglings.' At least I hoped it was. 'Plus, still not your business.'

'Okay. No problem. If it's not my business that you need to get off campus, then there's no reason for me to tell you how to sneak out of here.'

'Aphrodite. I do not have time for games.'

'Fine,' she started to turn to go and I stepped in front of her. 'You're being a bitch. Again,' I said.

'And you're almost cussing. Again,' she said.

I crossed my arms and tapped my foot.

Aphrodite rolled her eyes. 'Okay, whatever. You can sneak out if you go to the part of the school wall closest to the stables – the section that's near the edge of the little pasture. There's a grove at the end of it and a tree there was split by lightning a couple years ago. It's leaning against the wall. The split makes it easy to climb. Jumping from the top of the wall isn't really that big a deal.'

'How do you get back on campus? Is there a tree on the other side, too?'

She gave me an evil smile. 'No, but *someone* just *happened* to *conveniently* leave a rope tied to the branch. Climbing back over the wall isn't hard, but it's hell on your manicure.'

'Okay. I got it. Now all I have to do is figure out how to get some more blood from the kitchen.' I was speaking to myself more to Aphrodite. 'I have just enough time to meet Heath, run by and see Stevie Rae, and get back here for the ritual.'

'You have less time than that. Neferet is having a Full Moon Ritual of her own and she wants everyone to be there,' Aphrodite said.

'Dang it! I thought Neferet wasn't performing a school-wide ritual this month because of winter break.'

'Winter break has been officially called off. All vamps and fledglings have been ordered to return to campus immediately. And *dang it* isn't actually a word.'

I ignored her commentary on my non-cuss cuss words. 'Break is called off because of what happened to Professor Nolan?'

Aphrodite nodded. 'It was really horrible, wasn't it?'

'Yeah.'

'Why didn't you puke?'

I shrugged uncomfortably. 'I think I was too freaked to puke.'

'I wish I had been,' Aphrodite said.

I glanced at my watch. It was almost eight. I was going to have to rush to get out of here and get back in time. 'I gotta go.' I was already feeling sick about having to figure out a way to sneak blood out of what was probably a busy kitchen.

'Here.' Aphrodite handed me the canvas bag she'd been carrying over her shoulder. 'Take this to Stevie Rae.'

The bag was full of pouches of blood. I blinked in surprise. 'How did you get these?'

'I couldn't sleep, and I figured the vamps would call in major backup after what happened to Professor Nolan, which means the kitchen was going to be busy again. So I thought I better make a quick trip to clean out the supply of blood before we couldn't get to it anymore. I kept it in the mini-fridge in my room.'

'You have a mini-fridge.' Dang. I'd really like to have a mini-fridge.

She gave me a very Aphrodite-like sneer while she looked down her nose at me. 'It's one of the privileges of being an upperclassman.'

'Well, thanks. It was really nice of you to get this for Stevie Rae.'

Her sneer deepened. 'Look, I wasn't being nice. I just didn't want Stevie Rae foaming at the mouth and eating my parents' help. As Mother says, dependable illegals are really hard to find.'

'You're all heart, Aphrodite.'

'Don't mention it.' She walked around me and cracked

open the door, peeking out into the hall to be sure no one was out there. Then she looked back at me. 'And I mean it: Don't mention it.'

'I'll see you at the Dark Daughters ritual. Don't forget.'

'Sadly, I haven't forgotten. Even more sadly, I'll be there.' Then she hurried out of my room and disappeared down the hall.

'Issues,' I muttered as I left my room and went the opposite way down the hall. 'The girl has such issues.'

CHAPTER SEVENTEEN

ERIK WAS GOING TO BE SO DANG PISSED AT ME. THE TWINS had been perched on their favorite chairs staring at a *Spider-Man 3* DVD as I hurried out of the kitchen clutching my can of brown pop and the canvas bag full of blood.

'Holy shit, Z, are you okay?' Shaunee asked, looking kinda wide-eyed and freaked.

'We heard about you and the hag—' Erin paused and then reluctantly corrected herself, 'I mean you and *Aphrodite* finding Professor Nolan. It must have been totally awful.'

'Yeah, it was pretty bad.' I made myself smile reassuringly at them and not act like I was dying to bolt from the room.

'I can't believe it really happened,' Erin said.

'I know. It just doesn't seem real,' Shaunee said.

'It's real. She's dead,' I said solemnly.

'You're sure you're okay?' Shaunee asked.

'We're all really worried about you,' Erin added.

'I'm fine. Promise.' My gut twisted. Shaunee, Erin, Damien, and Erik were my best friends, and I hated lying to them, even if most of the lies I was telling were by omission. In the two months I'd been at the House of Night we had become a family, so they weren't faking. They were genuinely worried about me. And as I stood there trying to sift through what I could and couldn't say to them, a horrible premonition shivered over my skin. What if they found out about all the stuff I had been keeping from them and they turned away from me? What if they stopped being my family? Just thinking about that terrible possibility made me all fluttery and panicky inside. Before I could chicken out, confess everything, and fling myself at their feet while I begged them to understand and not be mad at me, I blurted, 'I have to go see Heath.'

'Heath?' Shaunee looked utterly confused.

'Her human ex-boyfriend, Twin. Remember?' Erin supplied.

'Oh yeah, the blond hottie who almost got eaten by the vamp ghosts two months ago, and then almost got killed by that nasty street-person-turned-serial-killer last month,' Shaunee said.

'You know, Z, you're hard on your ex-boyfriends,' Erin said.

'Yeah, sucks to be him,' I inserted, moving casually toward the door. 'I gotta go, guys.'

'They're not letting anyone leave campus,' Erin said.

'I know, but I, um, well ...' I hesitated, and then I felt ridiculous for the hesitation. I couldn't tell the Twins about Stevie Rae or Loren, but I sure as hell could tell them something as typically teenage as sneaking out of school. 'I know a secret way off campus.'

'Well done, Z!' Shaunee said happily. 'We'll totally use your superior sneaking-out-of-school skills during finals this spring when we're supposed to be studying.'

'Please.' Erin rolled her eyes. 'As if *we* have to study. Especially when there are end-of-season shoe sales to pillage.' Then she raised her very blond brows and added, 'Uh, Z. What do we tell boyfriend?'

'Boyfriend?'

'*Your* boyfriend, Erik I'm-So-Damn-*Fiiiine* Night.' Erin gave me a look that said she thought I'd lost my mind.

'Hello. Earth to Zoey. Are you sure you're okay?' Shaunee said.

'Yeah, yeah. I'm okay. Sorry. Why do you have to tell Erik anything?'

'Because he said for us to tell you to call him the instant you woke the hell up. He's majorly worried about you, too,' Shaunee said.

'No doubt if he doesn't hear from you pretty soon he'll be camped out here,' Erin said. 'Ooooh, Twin!' Her eyes widened and her lips curled into a sexy smile. 'Do you think boyfriend will bring along the two hotties?'

Shaunee tossed back her thick dark hair. 'It's a definite possibility, Twin. T. J. and Cole *are* friends of his and this *is* a very stressful time.'

'Right you are, Twin. And we all know that during stressful times *friends* should stick together.'

In perfect agreement the Twins turned to me. 'Go ahead and go do whatever with ex-boyfriend,' Erin said.

'Yeah, we have your back here. We'll wait around for Erik to show up and then tell him it's just too scary for little ol' us to be all alone,' Shaunee said.

'We definitely need protection,' Erin said. 'Which means he'll have to go get his friends and all of us will curl up and wait for you to get back from your *meeting*.'

'Sounds like a plan. Oh, but don't tell him I went off campus. He might freak. Just be vague, like I might be talking to Neferet or whatnot.'

'Whatever. We'll cover for you. But, speaking of going off campus, are you sure it's safe?' Shaunee said. 'We're not completely making up the fact that it's scary around here right now.'

'Yeah, can't you break up with human boyfriend later, like *after* they catch the psycho who beheaded and crucified Professor Nolan?' Erin asked.

'It's something I have to do now. You know, what with the Imprint it's not exactly a normal breakup.'

'Drama,' Erin said.

'Serious drama.' Shaunee nodded in solemn agreement.

'Yeah, and the longer I put it off, the worse it's gonna be.

I mean, Heath just got back in town and he's already text messaging me to death.' The Twins gave me sympathetic looks. 'So, later. I'll be back in time to change before Neferet's ritual.' I retreated fast while the Twins called 'see ya' after me.

I'd rushed out the door and had run right into what felt like a large male mountain. Impossibly strong hands steadied me before I could fall off the steps. I looked up (and up and up) into a stonelike, starkly handsome face. And then blinked in surprise. He was definitely a full-grown vampyre (complete with cool tattoo), even though he didn't look much older than me. But, dang, he was big!

'Careful, fledgling,' the mountain who was dressed all in black said. Then his nonexpression shifted. 'You're Zoey Redbird.'

'Yeah, I'm Zoey.'

Releasing me, he took a step back and pressed his fist over his heart in a snappy salute. 'Merry meet. It is a pleasure to know the fledgling Nyx has so greatly gifted.'

Feeling awkward and silly, I returned his salute. 'Nice to meet you, too. And you are?'

'Darius, of the Sons of Erebus,' he said, bowing formally and making it a title and not just a description.

'You're one of the guys called in because of what happened with Professor Nolan?' My voice cracked a little, which he clearly noticed.

'Hey,' he said, looking even younger, yet also somehow incredibly powerful, 'You shouldn't worry, Zoey. The Sons of Erebus will protect Nyx's school with our last breath.'

The way he said it made my skin prickle. He was huge and muscular and very, very serious. I couldn't imagine anything or anyone who could get past him, let alone make him breathe his last breath. 'Th-thank you,' I stammered.

'My brother warriors are posted all over the school grounds. You may rest safely, little priestess,' he smiled at me. Little priestess? Please. The kid had to have just Changed recently.

'Oh, good. Uh, I will.' I started down the steps. 'I'm just going to the, uh, stable to visit my mare, Persephone. It was nice to meet you. I'm glad you're here,' I added, giving him a ridiculous wave and then hurrying down the sidewalk toward the stables. I could feel his eyes following me.

Crap. That was so not good. I wondered what the hell I was going to do. How was I going to sneak out of there with warrior mountains (no matter how young and cute) all over the place? Not that it mattered how young and cute he was. Like I had time for another possible boyfriend? Absolutely no way. Not to mention his hotness didn't make him any less mountainous. Jeesh, I was a mess and I had such a dang headache.

And then the soft voice was in my head, telling me to *think . . . be calm . . .*

The words swirled soothingly through my frantic mind. Automatically I began to slow down. I breathed deeply, willing myself to relax and think. I needed to be calm . . . be still . . . think and—

And just like that it came to me. I knew what I had to do. In the shadows between the next two gaslights I stepped quietly off the sidewalk as if I'd decided to take a walk among the huge old oaks, only when I came to the first tree I paused in its shadow, closed my eyes, and centered myself. Then, as I had before, I called silence and invisibility to me, shrouding myself in the stillness of the grave (I briefly hoped that that metaphor was just me being overly imaginative and wasn't any kind of creepy, foretelling omen).

I'm perfectly silent . . . no one can see me . . . no one can hear me . . .
I'm like mist . . . dreams . . . spirit . . .

I could sense the presence of the Sons of Erebus, but I didn't look around. I didn't allow my concentration to falter. Instead I kept up my internal prayer turned spell turned magic. I moved like the wisp of a thought or a secret, undetectable and hidden in layers of silence and fog, mist and magic. My body shivered. It seemed I actually floated, and when I glanced down at myself I saw only a shadow within fog within shadow. *This must have been what Bram Stoker described in Dracula.* Instead of startling me, the thought strengthened my concentration and I felt myself become even less substantial. Moving like a dream, I found the lightning-damaged tree and climbed up its broken trunk and out onto the thick branch that rested against the wall as if I was weightless.

Just like Aphrodite had said, there was a rope tied securely around a fork in the branch and coiled like a waiting snake. Still moving in silent, dreamlike motions I tossed the end over the wall. Then, following an instinct that rippled up from the core of my soul through my body, I lifted my arms and whispered, 'Come to me air and spirit. Like midnight mist, carry me to earth.'

I didn't have to jump from the wall. The wind swirled around me in an airy caress, lifting my body, which had turned as insubstantial as spirit, and floating me the twenty feet to the grass on the other side of the wall. For a moment the sense of wonder that filled me made me forget about murdered teachers, boyfriend issues, and the stress of my life in general. Arms still upraised, I twirled around, loving the feel of wind and power against my dewy, transparent skin. It was like I had become part of the night. Barely touching the ground I moved along the grassy path until I came to the sidewalk that led down Utica Street the short distance to Utica Square. I was feeling so amazing that I almost forgot to stop and dab the concealer over my facial tattoos. Reluctantly, I paused to fish the concealer and a mirror out of the canvas bag. My reflection made my breath catch in my throat. I looked iridescent. My skin shimmered with pearlized colors like a mirage. My dark hair lifted softly around me, floating in a breeze that blew for me alone. I didn't look human and I didn't look vampyre. I looked like a new kind of being, born of the night and blessed by the elements.

What was it Loren had said about me in the library? Something like me being a goddess among demigods. The way I looked right then made me think that he might be on to something. Power shivered through me, and my hair lifted from my shoulder. I swear I could feel the tattoos burning deliciously down my neck and back. Maybe Loren had been right about a lot of things – like about the two of us being star-crossed lovers. Maybe after I told Heath I couldn't see him again I should back away from Erik, too. The thought of leaving Erik made me feel a little breathless, but that was to be expected. I wasn't heartless – I really did like him. But hadn't Professor Nolan's death proved that you never knew what could happen? That life, even for vampyres, could be way too short. Maybe I should be with Loren – maybe *that* was the right thing to do. I kept staring at my magical reflection.

After all, I really wasn't like other fledglings.

That was something I should accept and stop fighting against or feeling freaky about.

And if I wasn't like other fledglings, then wasn't it only logical that I needed to be with something special – someone other fledglings wouldn't be able to be with?

But Erik cares about me, and I care about him, too. I'm not being fair to Erik . . . or to Heath . . . Loren is a grown man . . . he's supposed to be a teacher . . . so maybe we shouldn't be sneaking around together . . .

I ignored the guilty thoughts that my conscience whispered to me. And silently ordered the wind and mist and concealing darkness to lift so that I could materialize fully and cover my intricate tattoos. And then, lifting my chin and straightening my back, I headed down the sidewalk to Utica Square,

Starbucks, and Heath, still not one hundred percent sure about what the hell I was doing.

I stayed on the dark side of the street where there were very few streetlights and walked slowly, trying to figure out what I would say to Heath to get him to understand he and I couldn't keep seeing each other. I'd gone less than half the distance to the square when I saw him coming toward me. Actually, I felt him first. Like an itch beneath my skin that I couldn't quite reach to scratch. Or an abstract compulsion to move forward, looking for something I knew I wanted, but didn't know how to find. And then the compulsion went from abstract to defined – from subconsciously insistent to demanding. *Then* I saw him. Heath. He was coming to meet me. We saw each other at the same instant. He was walking on the opposite side of the street and was right under a street-light. I could see his eyes sparkle and his smile blaze. Instantly, he kicked into a jog and crossed the street (I noticed he didn't look either way and was glad the crappy weather was keeping traffic to a minimum – the kid could have gotten smushed by a car).

His arms were around me and his breath tickled my ear as he hugged me. 'Zoey! Oh, baby, I've really missed you!'

I hated that my body instantly responded to him. He smelled like home – a sexy, yummy version of home – but home nonetheless. Before I could melt helplessly in his arms I pushed back from him, suddenly aware of just how dark and secluded, intimate even, it was on this shadowy sidewalk.

'Heath, you were supposed to wait for me at Starbucks.' Yeah, on their little patio sidewalk area that would be busy with caffeine-aholics and definitely *not* intimate.

He shrugged and grinned. 'I was, but then I felt you coming and no way could I just sit there anymore.' His brown eyes sparkled adorably and his hand caressed the side of my cheek as he added, 'We're Imprinted, remember? It's you and me, baby.'

I made myself take a little half step back so that he wasn't in my personal space anymore. 'That's what I have to talk to you about. So let's go back to Starbucks and get a couple drinks and talk.' In public. Where I wouldn't be so tempted to pull him off the sidewalk into an alley and sink my teeth in his sweet neck and . . .

'Can't,' he said, grinning again.

'Can't?' I shook my head, trying to get rid of the semi-nasty (okay, it probably wasn't *semi*) scene that had started to play around in my (ho-ish) imagination.

'Can't, 'cause Kayla and the bitch squad picked tonight to go to Starbucks.'

'Bitch squad?'

'Yeah, that's what me and Josh and Travis call Kayla and Whitney and Lindsey and Chelsea and Paige.'

'Oh, ugh. Since when did Kayla start hanging around with those hateful sluts?'

'Since you got Marked.'

Then my eyes narrowed at him. 'And why would Kayla and her new friends just happen to pick this particular night to go to Starbucks? And why *this* Starbucks instead of the one in Broken Arrow that's way closer to where they all live?'

Heath held up his hands like he was surrendering. 'I didn't do it on purpose!'

'Do *what*, Heath?' Jeesh, the kid was such a moron sometimes.

'I didn't know they'd be coming out of the Gap just when I was pulling up in front of Starbucks. I didn't see them till after they saw me. It was too late then.'

'Well that explains their sudden desire for caffeine. I'm surprised they didn't follow you down the sidewalk.' Okay, yes. I did remember that I was supposed to be breaking up with him, but it still annoyed the crap outta me to think that Kayla was sniffing around him.

'So you don't want to see them, do you?'

'Not no, but hell no,' I said.

'Didn't think so. Well, how about I walk you back to your school then.' He stepped closer to me. 'I remember when we *talked* on the wall a couple months ago. That was nice.'

I remembered, too. I especially remembered that had been the first time I had tasted his blood. I shivered. And then caught myself. I really needed to get a handle on this bloodlust thing. 'Heath,' I said firmly. 'You can't go with me to my school. Haven't you been watching the news? Some idiot human killed a vampyre. Now the place is like an army camp. I had to sneak out to see you, and I can't be gone long.'

198

'Oh, yeah, I did hear about that.' He took my hand in his. 'Are you okay? Did you know the vamp that was killed?'

'Yes, I knew her. She was my drama professor. And no, I'm not okay. That's one reason I needed to talk to you.' I made up my mind. 'Come on. Let's cut down this street and go to Woodward Park. We can talk there.' Plus, it was a public park smack in the center of midtown Tulsa, it couldn't be too private. At least I hoped it couldn't.

'Cool with me,' Heath said happily.

He refused to let loose of my hand, so we started down the side street joined together like we'd been since grade school. We'd only gone a few feet when his voice broke in to me trying not to think about the fact that his wrist was pressed against mine and I could feel that our pulses were beating in time with one another.

'Zo, what happened in the tunnels?'

I gave him a sharp, sideways glance. 'What do you remember?'

'Mostly darkness and you.'

'What do you mean?'

'I don't remember how I got there, but I do remember teeth and red eyes that glowed.' He squeezed my hand. 'And I don't mean your teeth, Zo. Plus, your eyes don't glow. They shine.'

'They do?'

'Totally. Especially when you're drinking my blood.' He'd slowed down so that we were almost standing still when he lifted my hand to his lips and kissed it. 'You know it feels so damn good when you drink me, don't you?'

Heath's voice had gotten deep and husky, and his lips felt like fire against my skin. I wanted to lean into him and get lost in him and sink my teeth into him and . . .

CHAPTER EIGHTEEN

'HEATH, FOCUS.' I CHANNELED THE HEAT THAT WAS SHIM-mering through my body into annoyance. 'The tunnels. You're supposed to be telling me what you remember.'

'Oh, yeah.' He grinned his cute, bad-boy smile. 'I really don't remember much, that's why I was asking you about it. Just teeth and claws and eyes and such, and then you. It's all kinda like a bad dream. Well, except for the part about you. That part's cool. Hey, Z, did you rescue me?'

I rolled my eyes at him and started walking again, drag-ging him with me. 'Yes, I rescued you, dork.'

'From what?'

'Jeesh, do you not read the papers? The story was on page two.' It had been a lovely, but fictionalized article where they quoted Detective Marx and his very brief and mostly untrue statement.

'Yeah, but it didn't say much. So what really happened?'

I chewed my lip while my mind raced. He didn't remember hardly anything about Stevie Rae and her pack of undead dead thingies. Neferet's mind block was obviously still firmly in place with him. And, I suddenly realized, it needed to stay that way. The less Heath knew about what had happened, the less chance that Neferet would give him a second thought and what would amount to a third mind screwing, which couldn't be good for him. Plus, the kid needed to get on with his life. His *human* life. And stop obsessing about me and vamp stuff.

'There wasn't much more than the papers said. I dunno who the guy was, just some crazed street person. The same guy who killed Chris and Brad. I found you and used my power over the elements to get you away from him, but you were pretty messed up. He'd, uh, cut you up and stuff. That's probably why you have such weird memories, when you remember anything at all.' It was my turn to shrug. 'I wouldn't worry about it, or even think about it much if I were you. No big deal, really.' He started to say something else, but we'd come to the rear entrance to the park and I pointed to a bench under the first big tree. 'How about sitting over there?'

'Whatever you say, Zo.' He slung his arm around me and we walked to the bench.

As we sat down I managed to slide out from under his arm and angle my body toward him so that my knees were a kind of barrier against him getting too close to me. I took a deep breath and made myself meet Heath's eyes. *I can do this. I can do this.*

'Heath, you and I can't see each other again.'

His forehead wrinkled. He looked like he was trying to figure out a complex math word problem. 'Why would you say something like that, Zo? Of course we can see each other again.'

'No. It's not good for you. This has to be over between us.' I hurried on when he started to protest. 'I know it seems hard to not see me, but that's because of our Imprint, Heath. Really. I've been reading up on it. If we don't see each other the Imprint will fade.' That wasn't exactly true. The text said *sometimes* an Imprint will fade due to nonexposure. Well, I was counting on sometimes being this time. 'It'll be okay. You'll forget about me and go back to being normal.'

As I'd been talking Heath's expression had become more and more serious and his body had gotten very still. I knew because I could feel his heartbeat, and even that had slowed. When he spoke he sounded old. Really old. Like he'd lived a thousand years and knew things I could only guess at.

'I won't forget about you. Not even after I'm dead. And this *is* normal for me. Loving you is my normal.'

'You don't love me. You're just Imprinted with me,' I said.

'Bullshit!' he shouted. 'Don't tell me I don't love you. I've loved you since I was nine years old. This Imprint thing is just another part of what's been going on between us since we were kids.'

'This Imprint thing has to end,' I said calmly, meeting his gaze.

'Why? I've told you it's good for me. And you know we belong together, Zo. You have to believe in us.'

His eyes pleaded with me and I felt my gut twist. He was right about so much. It had been the two of us for so long – and if I hadn't been Marked, we probably would have gone to college together and then gotten married after we graduated. We would have had kids and lived in the suburbs and gotten a dog. We would have had fights once in a while, mostly over him being too obsessed with sports, and then we would have made up when he brought me flowers and teddy bears, like he'd been doing since we were teenagers.

But I had been Marked and my old life had died the day the new Zoey was born. The more I thought about it, the more I knew breaking up with Heath was the right thing to do. With me he could never be more than my Renfield, and sweet Heath, the love of my childhood, deserved better than that. I realized what I had to do and how I had to do it.

'Heath, the truth is it's not as good for me as it is for you.' My voice was cold and emotionless. 'It's not you and me anymore. I have a boyfriend. A *real* boyfriend. He's like me. He's not a human. He's the one I want now.' I wasn't sure if I was talking about Erik or Loren, but I was sure of the pain that clouded Heath's eyes.

'If I have to share you, I will.' His voice had dropped almost to a whisper, and he looked away from me like he was too embarrassed to meet my eyes. 'I'll do whatever it takes not to lose you.'

It made something inside me break, but I laughed at Heath. 'Listen to you! You sound pathetic. Do you know what vampyre men are like?'

'No.' His voice had gotten stronger and he met my eyes again. 'No, I don't know what they're like. I'm sure they can do all sorts of cool stuff. They're probably big and bad and all that. But I know one thing they *can't* do that I can. They can't do this.'

In a motion so fast I didn't understand what he was doing until it was too late, Heath pulled a razorblade from the pocket of his jeans and slashed a long, deep line down the side of his neck. I knew right away that he hadn't hit an artery or anything like that. The cut wouldn't kill him, but it was pouring blood – hot, sweet, fresh trails of blood down his neck and shoulder. And it was Heath's blood! A scent that I'd been Imprinted to desire above all others. The sweetness of it covered me, brushing against my skin with hot insistence.

I couldn't help myself. I leaned forward. Heath tilted his head to the side, stretching his neck so that all of the beautiful, glistening cut was exposed.

'Make the pain go away, Zoey, for both of us. Drink from me and stop the burning before I can't stand it anymore.'

His pain. I was causing him pain. I'd read about it in the Advanced Vampyre Sociology book. It warned about the danger of Imprinting and how the blood bond can become so close that not drinking from the human can actually cause him pain.

So I'd drink from him . . . just this once more . . . just to stop his pain . . .

I leaned farther forward and rested my hand on his shoulder. By the time my tongue reached out and licked the slick line of red from his neck, my body was trembling.

'Oh, Zoey, yes!' Heath moaned. 'You're cooling it. Yes, come closer baby. Take more.'

He fisted his hand in my hair and pressed my mouth against his neck and I drank from him. His blood was an explosion. Not just in my mouth, but throughout my body. I'd read all of the whys and how-comes about the physiological reaction that takes place between a human and a vampyre when blood-lust consumes them. It was simple. Something Nyx had gifted us with so that both could feel pleasure in an act that could otherwise be brutal and deadly. But flat words on the page of a passionless textbook didn't begin to describe what was happening inside our bodies as I drank from Heath's bleeding neck. I straddled him, pressing the most private part of myself against his hardness. His hands left my hair to hold my hips and he rocked me against him rhythmically as he moaned and panted and whispered for me not to stop. And I didn't want to stop. I didn't ever want to stop. My body was burning, just as his had been. Only my pain was sweet, hot, delicious. I knew Heath was right. Erik was like me and I cared about him. Loren was a real man and powerful and incredibly mysterious. But neither of them could do this for me. Neither of them could make me feel like this... want like this... desire to take like this...

'Yeah, bitch! Ride him! Make him hurt so *gooood!*'

'That little white boy don't have nothin' for you. I'll give ya somethin' you can really feel!'

Heath's grip on my hips changed and he was in the middle of trying to turn my body away from the jeering voices so he could shield me, but the anger that spiked through me was blinding. My fury was impossible to ignore and my response was immediate. I lifted my face from his neck. Two black guys were just a few feet away and getting closer to us. They were wearing the stereotypical ridiculous sagging pants and stupid, oversized down coats and when I bared my teeth at them and hissed, their expressions changed from sneers to shocked disbelief.

'Get away from us or I will kill you.' I snarled at them in a voice so powerful I didn't recognize it as my own.

'She's a fucking bloodsucker bitch!' the shorter of the two said.

The other guy snorted. 'Nah, bitch got no tattoo. But if she wants somethin' to suck, I'll give it to her.'

'Yeah, first you and then me. Her little punk boyfriend can watch and see how it's done.' With a mean laugh, they started walking toward us again.

Still straddling Heath, I lifted my one arm over my head. With the other I dragged the back of my hand across my forehead and down my face, wiping off the concealer that hid my identity. That made them stumble to a stop. Then both of my arms were over my head. It was easy to center myself. Filled with Heath's fresh blood, I felt powerful and strong and very, very pissed.

'Wind come to me,' I commanded. My hair began lifting in the breeze that swirled restlessly around me. 'Blow them the hell outta here!' I flung my hands out toward the two men, letting my anger explode with my words. The wind obeyed instantly, crashing into them with such force that they were swept, yelling and cussing, off their feet and hurled away from me. I watched with a kind of detached fascination as the wind dropped the two men down in the middle of Twenty-first Street.

I didn't even flinch when the truck hit them.

'Zoey, what did you do!'

I looked down at Heath. His neck was still bleeding and his face was pale, his eyes wide and shocked.

'They were going to hurt you.' Now that I'd flung the anger out of me I was feeling weird, kinda numb and confused.

'Did you kill them?' His voice sounded all wrong, scared and accusing.

I frowned at him. 'No. All I did was get them away from us. The truck did the rest. And anyway, they might not be dead.' I glanced back at the road. The truck had come to a skidding, tire-squealing halt. Other cars had stopped, too, and I could hear people shouting. 'And Saint John's Hospital is like less than a mile down the street.' Sirens started wailing not far away. 'See, the ambulance is coming already. They'll probably be okay.'

Heath pushed me off his lap and scooted away from me, pressing the sleeve of his sweater against the cut on his neck. 'You have to leave. There will be cops all over here pretty soon. They shouldn't find you here.'

'Heath?' I lifted my hand toward him, but dropped it when he flinched away from me. The numbness was fading and I had started to shake. My god, what had I just done? 'Are you afraid of me?'

Slowly, he reached out, taking my hand and pulling me to him so he could wrap his arm around me. 'I'm not afraid of you. I'm afraid *for* you. If people find out all the stuff you can do, I – I don't know what might happen.' He leaned back a little, not taking his arm from around me, but looking into my eyes. 'You're changing, Zoey. And I'm not sure what you're changing into.'

My eyes filled with tears. 'I'm becoming a vampyre, Heath. That's what I'm Changing into.'

He touched my cheek, and then he used his thumb to wipe away the rest of the concealer so that my Mark was completely visible. Heath bent to kiss the crescent moon in the middle of my forehead. 'I'm okay with you being a vampyre, Zo. But I want you to remember that you're still Zoey, too. My Zoey. And my Zoey isn't mean.'

'I couldn't let them hurt you,' I whispered, really shaking now as I realized how cold and horrible I'd just been. *I might have just caused the deaths of two men.*

'Hey, look at me Zo.' Heath took my chin in his hand and forced me to meet his eyes. 'I'm almost six one. I'm a kick-ass starting quarterback for a 6A school. OU is offering me a full-ride football scholarship. Would you please remember that I can take care of myself?' He let loose of my chin and touched my cheek again. His voice was so serious and grown-up that he suddenly reminded me weirdly of his dad. 'When I was away with my parents, I did some reading up on your vampyre goddess, Nyx. Zo, there's a lot of stuff written about vampyres, but I didn't find anything that said your goddess is mean. I think you should keep that in mind. Nyx has given you a bunch of powers, and I don't think she'd like it if you used them in the wrong way.' His eyes glanced over my shoulder to the distant road and the awful scene that was playing out there. 'You shouldn't be mean, Zo. No matter what.'

'When did you get so old?'

He smiled. 'Two months ago.' Heath kissed my lips softly, and then stood up, pulling me to my feet. 'You gotta get out of here. I'm gonna go back the way we came. You should probably cut through the rose gardens and get back to school. If those guys aren't dead they're gonna talk, and that's not gonna be good for the House of Night.'

I nodded. 'Okay, yeah. I'll get back to the school.' Then I sighed. 'I was supposed to break up with you.'

His smile turned into a full grin. 'Not happening, Zo. It's you and me, baby!' He kissed me good and hard, and gave me a little shove in the direction of the Tulsa Rose Garden, which bordered Woodward Park. 'Call me and we'll meet next week. 'Kay?'

''Kay,' I mumbled.

He started to back away so that he could watch me leave. I turned and walked toward the rose garden. Automatically, like I'd been doing it for decades, I called mist and night, magic and darkness, to cover me.

'Wow! Cool, Zo!' I heard him yell from behind me. 'I love you, baby!'

'I love you, too, Heath.' I didn't turn around, but whispered into the wind and willed it to carry my voice to him.

CHAPTER NINETEEN

YEP, I WAS SERIOUSLY MESSED UP. NOT ONLY HAD I NOT broken up with Heath, but I had probably made our Imprint even stronger. Plus, I may have caused two men to be killed. I shivered, feeling more than a little sick. What in the hell had happened to me? I'd been drinking Heath's blood and having a horny old good time (jeesh, I was becoming such a ho-bag), and then those men had started messing with us and it was like something inside of me freaked and changed from Regular Zoey to Psycho Killer Vampyre Zoey. Was that what happened? Did vamps freak when the human they'd Imprinted was threatened?

I remembered in the tunnels how pissed I'd been when Stevie Rae's 'friends' (not that she was actually buddies with those disgusting undead dead kids) had attacked Heath. Okay, I'd even gotten violent, but I hadn't felt such a powerful urge to wipe them off the face of the earth! Just remembering the anger that had rushed through me as the two men had started toward us (Heath) to give us (Heath) a hard time was enough to make my hands start to shake again.

Clearly there was just too much vampyre stuff that I didn't know about. Hell, I'd even taken notes and memorized some of the chapter on Imprinting and bloodlust, but I was starting to see that there was lots of stuff the oh-so-educational text-book had left out. What I needed was an adult vamp. Fortunately, I knew one I was sure would be very happy to volunteer to be my teacher.

I'm sure there were lots of things he'd be ever so pleased to teach me.

I thought about those *things*, which was easy to do when I was filled with Heath's delicious, sexy blood. My body still tingled with heat and power and sensations I knew I didn't have a clue about, but I craved more of. A lot more of.

There was no denying that Loren and I had a thing. It was different than the thing Heath and I had, and even different than the thing Erik and I had. Crap. I had too many things going on in my life.

Basically, I floated to Aphrodite's parent's garage apartment in a kind of horny, power-filled, yet confused haze and was so distracted by, well, sex that I didn't think about the fact that I appeared to be nothing more than mist and darkness until I was actually standing in the living room of the apartment watching Stevie Rae stare with wet, red-tinged eyes at the TV screen and sniffle. I glanced at the TV and realized she was watching a Lifetime Movie of the Week. It looked like the one about the mom who knew she was dying of some horrid disease and she had to race against time (and commercial breaks) to find a new family for her zillions of overly perky children.

'Talk about depressing,' I said.

Stevie Rae's head whipped around as she crouched in a feral, defensive pose after leaping behind the couch where she hissed and snarled at me.

'Ah, crap!' I instantly shooed away darkness and whatnot, so that I was solid, visible me again. 'Sorry, Stevie Rae. I forgot I'd gone all Bram Stoker.'

She peered over the couch at me, eyes glowing and fangs bared, but she'd stopped hissing.

'Uh, relax. It's just me.' I lifted the canvas bag and shook it so the blood sloshed nastily. 'Your meals on wheels.'

She stood up and narrowed her eyes. 'You shouldn't do that.'

I raised my eyebrows at her. 'Shouldn't do what? Bring you blood or turn into mist and darkness.'

Stevie Rae snatched the canvas bag I was dangling in her direction. 'Sneak up on me. It could be dangerous.'

I sighed and sat on the couch, trying to ignore the fact that she was already gulping down the first bag of blood. 'If you

214

ate me the way my life sucks right now, you'd be doing me a favor.'

'Yeah, I'll bet. I remember how tough it was to be alive. All filled with dating drama and ohmygoodness, what should I wear to school. Real awful, unlike the stress of being dead and then undead but still feeling mostly dead.' Stevie Rae spoke in the cold, sarcastic voice that was totally different from the way she used to sound, which suddenly annoyed the crap right outta me. Like I didn't have stress in my life just because I wasn't dead? Or undead? Or whatever.

'Professor Nola was killed last night. It looks like some of the People of Faith crucified her and chopped her head off and left her out by the trapdoor on the east wall with a lovely note about not suffering a witch to live. I think that my step-loser might be involved, but I can't say anything about it because my mom is covering for him, and if I rat him out she'll probably go to jail forever. I just sucked Heath's blood and got interrupted by some gang wannabes who I think I might have kinda sorta accidentally killed, and Loren Blake and I have been making out. So, how was your day?'

The old Stevie Rae flickered inside this one's red eyes. 'Ohmygood*ness*,' she said.

'Yeah.'

'You've been making out with Loren Blake?' As usual, Stevie Rae got to the heart of the juiciest gossip. 'What was it like?'

I sighed and watched her start on her second bag of blood. 'It was amazing. I know this is going to sound totally ridiculous, but I think we might really have something together.'

'Just like Romeo and Juliet,' she said between swallows.

'Uh, Stevie Rae, let's use a different analogy, shall we? R&J didn't end so well.'

'I'll bet he tastes good,' she said.

'Huh?'

'I mean his blood.'

'I wouldn't know.'

'Yet,' she said, and reached for another bag o' blood.

'Speaking of. You'd better slow down on the blood drinking. Neferet called in the Vamp's Sons of Erebus warriors and it's pretty hard to sneak out of school right now. I'm not sure when I'll be able to get back here with more tasty bloody goodness.'

A shiver passed through Stevie Rae's body. She had been looking almost normal, but at my words her expression flattened out and her eyes reddened.

'I can't stand it much longer.'

She'd spoken in such a low, strained voice that I almost didn't hear her.

'Is it that big of a deal, Stevie Rae? I mean, can't you just ration yourself or something?'

'It's not like that! I can feel it slipping away . . . more and more each day . . . each hour.'

'What's slipping away?'

'My humanity!' she practically sobbed.

'But, honey,' I scooted over and put my arm around her,

ignoring the weird way she smelled and the fact that her body was so rocklike. 'You're better. I'm here now. We'll figure this out.'

Stevie Rae looked into my eyes. 'Right now, I can feel your pulse. I know every time your heart beats. There's something inside of me that is screaming at me to rip your throat open and drink your blood. And that something is growing stronger.' She pulled away from me, moving to press herself against the end of the couch. 'I can put on the old Stevie Rae's face, but it's only part of the monster in me. I just do it so that I can hunt you.'

I took a deep breath and refused to look away from her. 'Okay, I know some of that is true. But I don't believe all of it, and I don't want you to believe all of it either. Your humanity is still there, inside you. Yeah, it might be getting buried, but it's still there. And that means we're still best friends. Plus, think about it. You don't have to hunt me. Hello – I'm right here. Not exactly hiding.'

'I think you might be in danger from me,' she whispered.

I smiled. 'I'm tougher than you think, Stevie Rae.' Moving slowly so I didn't startle her, I reached out and put my hand over hers. 'Draw on the power of earth. I believe you're different than the rest of the, uh—' I paused, trying to figure out what to call them.

'Gross undead dead kids?' Stevie Rae supplied.

'Yeah. You're different from the rest of the gross undead dead kids because of your affinity with the earth. Draw on that and it will help you fight whatever is going on inside you.'

'Darkness . . . it's all darkness inside me,' she said.

'It's not *all* darkness. The earth is in there, too.'

'Okay . . . okay . . . ,' she panted. 'The earth. I'll remember. I'll really try.'

'You can beat this, Stevie Rae. *We* can beat this.'

'Help me,' she said, suddenly squeezing my hand so hard I almost cried out. 'Please, Zoey, help me.'

'I will. I promise.'

'Soon. It has to be soon.'

'It will be. I promise,' I repeated, not having a clue how I was going to keep my promise.

'What are you going to do?' Stevie Rae asked, eyes desperately locked with mine.

I blurted the only thing that came into my brain. 'I'm going to cast a circle and ask for Nyx's help.'

Stevie Rae blinked. 'That's it?'

'Well, our circle is powerful and Nyx is a goddess. What more do we need?' I sounded way surer than I felt.

'You want me to represent earth again?' Her voice quivered.

'No. Yes.' I paused guiltily, wondering what I was supposed to do about Aphrodite. It had been clear when she manifested earth that she was supposed to join our circle. But would it freak Stevie Rae out to see her place filled by someone she definitely considered an enemy? Plus, no one except Aphrodite knew about Stevie Rae, which is how I needed to keep it until I was ready for Neferet to know I knew about her. Issues. I definitely had issues. 'Uh, I'm not sure. Let me think about it, okay?'

Stevie Rae's expression shifted again. Now she looked broken, utterly defeated. 'You don't want me to be part of your circle anymore.'

'It's not that! It's just that you're the one who needs to be healed, so it might be best if you're in the center of the circle with me instead of standing in your normal place.' I sighed and shook my head. 'I need to do some more research.'

'Do it fast, okay?'

'I will. And you have to promise me that you'll go easy on the blood and stay here and focus on your connection with earth,' I said.

'Okay. I'll try.'

I squeezed her hand and then pried mine from her grip. 'I'm sorry, but I gotta go. Neferet is having a special ritual for Professor Nolan, and then I have to do the Full Moon Ritual thing.' And I was going to have to hit the library again and come up with some kind of ritual that might help Stevie Rae. And I didn't have a clue what to do about Loren. And Erik was probably going to be mad at me for taking off. *And* I hadn't broken up with Heath. Jeesh, my head hurt. Again.

'It's been a month.'

'Huh?' I was standing, and already distracted with thinking about all the ands I had to deal with.

'I died during the last full moon, and that was one month ago.'

That got all of my attention. 'That's right. It has been a month. I wonder . . .'

'If that might mean something? If tonight might be the right time to try to fix whatever happened with me?'

I almost flinched at the sound of her hope-filled voice. 'I don't know. Maybe.'

'Should I try to get on campus tonight?'

'No! The place is crawling with warriors. They'd grab you for sure.'

'Maybe they should,' she said slowly. 'Maybe everyone should know about me.'

I rubbed my head, trying to understand what my gut was telling me. It'd been shouting to keep Stevie Rae a secret for so long that I couldn't tell if I was still supposed to keep her hidden, or whether what I was feeling were just echoes and confusion (and probably some desperation and depression thrown in there, too).

'I don't know about that. I – I need a little more time, okay?'

Stevie Rae's shoulders slumped. 'Okay. But I don't think there's enough of me left to last another month.'

'I know. I'll hurry,' I said inanely. I bent and hugged her quickly. 'Bye. Don't worry. I'll be back soon. Promise.'

'If you figure it out, just text me or something and I'll come. Okay?'

'Okay.' I turned at the door. 'I love you, Stevie Rae. Don't forget that. We're still best friends.'

She didn't say anything, but nodded, looking bleak. I called night and mist and magic to me and hurried out into the darkness.

CHAPTER TWENTY

NATURALLY, I GOT CAUGHT SNEAKING BACK ON CAMPUS. I'd already floated back over the wall. (Yes, I literally floated, which was too cool for words.) I was making my way back to the dorm with what I considered excellent speed and stealth when I practically ran into them – a group of vamps and upperclassmen ringed by at least a dozen of the warrior mountains (I did see the Twins and Damien in the group, so Aphrodite had been right, Neferet was including my Prefect Council). I froze, stepped back into the shadow of a big oak, and held my breath, hoping that my newfound cool power of invisibility (or maybe mist-ability was a better way of describing it) would let me remain unseen. Unfortunately, as I watched, Neferet paused, which caused the entire dang group to pause. She cocked her head and I swear she sniffed the breeze like a bloodhound. Then her eyes went to my tree – my hidey place – and seemed to bore into me. And just like that I lost concentration. My skin shivered and I knew I was completely visible again.

'Oh, Zoey! There you are. I was just asking your friends' – she paused long enough to give the Twins, Damien, and (eek!) Erik one of her amazing one-hundred-twenty-five-watt smiles – 'where you could have gotten off to.' She dimmed the smile and exchanged it for a perfect look of motherly concern. 'Now is not the time to wander about by yourself.'

'Sorry. I, uh, I needed . . .' I trailed off, majorly aware that all eyes were on me.

'She needed to be alone before the rituals,' Shaunee said, stepping up to put an arm through mine.

'Yeah, she always needs to be alone before rituals. It's a Zoey thing,' Erin said, moving to my other side and taking my other arm.

'Yep, we call it Z.A.T. – Zoey Alone Time,' Damien said, joining the three of us.

'It's kinda annoying, but what can you do?' Erik said, moving around behind me to rest his warm hands on my shoulders.

'That's our Z.'

I had to struggle not to burst into tears. My friends were the best. Of course, Neferet probably knew they were lying,

but they'd done it in a way that made it look like I was probably only up to little teenage mischief (i.e., sneaking out to
break up with a boyfriend) versus big, scary mischief (i.e.,
hiding my undead dead best friend).

'Well, I want you to be sure you limit your *alone* time in
the near future,' Neferet told me in a mildly chastising tone.

'I will. Sorry,' I mumbled.

'And now, on to the ritual.' Regally, Neferet strode out
from the group, causing the warriors to scramble to keep up
with her and leaving me and my little cluster of friends in
the figurative dust.

Of course, we followed her. What else could we do?

'So, did you get the dirty done?' Shaunee whispered.

'Huh?' I blinked in shock at her. How did she know I'd
been ho-ishly grinding against Heath. Did it show? God, I
was going to die if it showed!

Erin rolled her eyes. 'Heath. Breakup. You with him,' she
whispered.

'Oh, that. Well, I, uh—'

'I was worried about you today.' Erik had moved up and
neatly nudged Shaunee from her place beside me. I expected
the Twins to hiss and spit at him, but instead they waggled their
brows at us and fell back to walk with Damien. I heard Shaunee
murmur, 'So damn *fiiiine*.' Jeesh, they could face Neferet, but
Erik's hotness totally did them in.

'Sorry,' I said hastily, feeling guilty about how nice it felt
when he took my hand. 'I didn't mean to worry you. I just
had, well, stuff.'

223

Erik grinned and laced his fingers through mine. 'I hope you got rid of him – I mean, that particular *stuff* this time.'

I sent daggerlike looks over my shoulder at the Twins, who tried to look innocent. 'Traitors!' I muttered.

'Don't be pissed at them. I used my unfair advantage and bribed them with their weakness.'

'Shoes?'

'Something they like better, at least for a moment in time. T.J. and Cole.'

'That was very sly of you,' I said.

'And not very tough to manage. T.J. and Cole think the Twins are *dead sexy*,' Erik said, using an excellent Scottish accent and proving, again, what an old movie dork he was (hello – Austin Powers).

'T. J. and Cole called the Twins dead sexy in that awful accent?'

He squeezed my hand playfully. 'My accent isn't awful.'

'You're right. It's not.' I smiled up into his clear blue eyes and wondered how I could have gotten myself into a position where I was double cheating on him.

'How are you today, Zoey?'

I knew through our joined hands Erik could feel the shock that went through my body at the sound of Loren's voice.

'I'm fine. Thanks,' I said.

'You slept well last night? I wondered how you'd managed after I left you at the dorm.' Loren gave Erik what was obviously a patronizing, I'm-way-older-than-you smile and explained, 'Zoey had quite a shock yesterday.'

'Yeah, I know.' Erik clipped the words out. I could feel the tension between them and wondered a little frantically if anyone else had noticed. When I heard Shaunee's whispered, *'Damn, girl!'* and Erin's *'Um-hum!'* I had to force myself not to groan. Clearly everyone else (translation: the Twins) noticed.

By then we'd caught up to the group of adults that were now standing around what I realized was the trapdoor in the east wall. Ignoring the potentially explosive boyfriend situation I'd put myself right smack in the middle of, I said, 'Hey! Why are we stopped here?'

'Neferet is offering prayers for Professor Nolan's spirit, as well as invoking a protective spell around the school grounds,' Loren said. His voice sounded way too friendly and his gaze felt way too warm as our eyes met and locked. God, he was utterly gorgeous. I remembered how his lips had felt against mine and . . .

And then I realized what he'd just said.

'But isn't her blood and stuff still . . .' I trailed off help-lessly, making a vague gesture out at the grassy area on the other side of the wall, the horrible grassy area that had been drenched with Professor Nolan's blood just yesterday.

'No, don't worry, Neferet has had it cleansed,' Loren said gently.

For a second I thought he was going to touch me right there in front of everyone. I even felt Erik tense, like he expected it, too, then Neferet's solemn but powerful voice broke through our little drama, calling everyone's attention to her.

'We are going to move through the trapdoor to the site of the atrocity. Make a crescent around the statue of our beloved Goddess, which I placed in the exact spot Professor Nolan's ravaged body was discovered. I ask that you concentrate your hearts and minds on sending positive energy to our fallen sister as her spirit flies free to the wondrous realm of Nyx. Fledglings,' her gaze swooped over us, 'I want you each to take your position by the candle which represents your element.' Neferet's eyes were kind, her voice gentle. 'I know it is unusual to use fledglings in an adult ritual, but never before has a House of Night been gifted with so many extraordinary young people at one time, and today I believe it is only right that I tap into your affinities to add power to what we ask of Nyx.' I could practically feel Damien and the Twins vibrating with excitement. 'Can you do this for me, for us, fledglings?'

Damien and the Twins nodded like crazed bobble-heads. Neferet's green eyes moved to me. I nodded once. The High Priestess smiled, and I wondered if anyone else could see past her beautiful exterior to the cold, calculating person within.

Looking pleased with herself, Neferet turned and ducked through the open trapdoor followed closely by the rest of us. I'd readied myself for something terrible, or at the very least for something bloody, but Loren had been right. The area that had been so gruesome just yesterday had been completely cleansed of any nastiness, and I wondered briefly how the Tulsa cops had gathered their evidence, and then shook myself.

Surely Neferet had waited for them to do their job before she'd cleaned everything. Hadn't she?

In the spot where Professor Nolan's body had been there was now a beautiful statue of Nyx that looked like it had been carved from a single slab of onyx. Her hands were upraised, and within them she held a thick green candle symbolizing earth. Without speaking, the vamps formed a semicircle around the statue. Damien and the Twins moved to stand behind the oversized candles that represented each of their elements. I didn't really want to, but I took my place by the purple candle that symbolized spirit. I could see the warriors had spread out and were surrounding us. With their backs to our group they stared out into the night, bristling with alertness.

Without any of her usual theatrics (which were always cool to watch), Neferet walked to Damien, who was nervously holding the yellow wind candle, and raised the ceremonial lighter.

'It fills us and breathes life into us. I call wind to our circle.' Neferet's voice was strong and clear, obviously augmented by the power of a High Priestess. She touched the lighter to the candle's wick and instantly wind whipped around Damien and her. Neferet's back was to me, so I couldn't see her face, but Damien's smile was wide and joyous. I tried not to scowl. The sacred circle was not the right place for me to be pissed off, but I couldn't help feeling annoyed. Why was I the only one who could see Neferet's fakeness?

She moved to Shaunee. 'It warms and succors us. I call fire

to our circle.' As I'd experienced several times before, Shaunee's red candle burst into flame before the lighter touched it. Shaunee's smile was almost as bright as her element.

Neferet followed the circle around to Erin. 'It soothes and washes us. I call water to our circle.' As the candle lit I heard waves crashing on a distant beach and smelled salt and sea in the night breeze.

I watched carefully as Neferet moved to stand before the statue of Nyx and the green candle. The High Priestess bowed her head. 'The fledgling who personified this element perished, and it is fitting that the position of earth remain empty tonight, and that it rests upon the spot our beloved Patricia Nolan's body has so recently rested upon. It sustains us. From it we are born, and to it we all shall return. I call earth to our circle.' Neferet lit the green candle, and though it burned brightly I didn't smell even a hint of green meadows or wildflowers.

Then Neferet was standing in front of me. I don't know what kind of expression she'd showed Damien and the Twins, but to me her face was strong and stern, and amazingly beautiful. She reminded me of one of the ancient vampyre Amazon warriors, and I almost forgot that she was actually dangerous.

'It is our essence. I call spirit to our circle.' Neferet lit my purple candle and I felt my soul lift with the tickle-tummy feeling a roller coaster gives me. The High Priestess didn't pause to share any kind of special look with me, instead she began to work the crowd. Walking around inside the circle, making eye contact with the vampyres who surrounded us, she got right to the point. 'It hasn't happened for more than one hundred years – not so openly – not so brutally. Humans have murdered one of us. In this case they have awakened not a sleeping giant, but have provoked a leopard who they believed was tamed.' Neferet's voice rose, powerful with anger. 'She is not tamed!' The little hairs on my arms lifted. Neferet was amazing. How could someone who was so blessed by Nyx have gone as wrong as I knew she'd gone?

'They believe our fangs have been filed flat and our claws removed, like a fat household tabby. Again, they are wrong.' She raised her arms over her head. 'From this sacred circle, cast on the site of a murder, we call on our Goddess, Nyx, the beautiful Personification of Night. We ask that she welcome Patricia Nolan to her bosom, though it is decades too early for her to have departed. We also ask Nyx to rouse her righteous anger, and with the sweetness of her divine fury, to grant us this spell of protection so that we will not be caught in the humans' murderous web.' As she spoke the spell Neferet walked back to Nyx's statue.

'Protect us with the night;
above all it is in darkness we delight.'

When she turned to face the crowd I saw that she was now holding a small, ivory-handled knife with a wickedly-sharp-looking curved blade.

> *'Around this coven we ask*
> *Nyx's curtain to be cast.'*

With one hand she lifted the knife. With the other she wove intricate shapes in the air that around her became glittery and semi-substantial as she continued incanting the spell.

> *'All who enter or leave I shall detect,*
> *vampyre, fledgling, human, all will be checked.*
> *If harm is meant*
> *to my will it shall be bent.'*

Then, in a fast, ferocious gesture, Neferet slashed through her wrist, so deep that her blood instantly began to spurt, red and rich, hot and delicious. The scent washed around me, automatically making my mouth water. With grim determination, the High Priestess walked the circumference of the circle so that her blood fell around us in a scarlet arch, sprinkling grass that had so recently been soaked with Professor Nolan's blood. Finally she reached Nyx's statue again. Neferet lifted her face to the night sky and completed the spell.

> *'My blood binds thee,*
> *so mote it be.'*

I swear the night air rippled all around us, and for a moment I could actually see something settle on the walls of the school, like a black, gauzy curtain. *She's set a spell that will not just tell her when danger enters the school, but when anyone enters or leaves it.* I had to bite the inside of my cheek to keep from groaning. No way was the curtain of a goddess going to be fooled by my little Bram Stoker-ing. How in the hell was I going to sneak Stevie Rae her blood?

Completely preoccupied with my own drama, I hardly noticed when Neferet closed the circle. Woodenly, I let the tide of people carry me back through the trapdoor. I only snapped out of it when Loren's deep voice sounded surprisingly close to my ear.

'I'll meet you in the rec hall in a little while.' I looked up at him. My face must have been a complete question mark because he added, 'Your Full Moon Ritual. I'm your bard tonight for the opening of the circle, remember?'

Before I could say anything Shaunee's voice purred, 'We always look forward to hearing you recite poetry, Professor Blake.'

'Yeah, wouldn't miss it. Not even for a shoe sale at Saks,' Erin added, eyes twinkling.

'Then I'll see you there,' Loren said, his eyes never leaving my face. He smiled, gave me a little bow, and hurried away.

'*Dee-lish-us,*' Erin said.

'Ditto, Twin,' Shaunee said.

'I think he's slimy.'

We all looked up to see Erik glaring at Loren's back.

'Oh, no way!' Shaunee said.

'Luscious Loren Blake is just being friendly,' Erin said, rolling her eyes at Erik like he was insane.

'Hello! Don't go all psycho-jealous boyfriend on Z,' Shaunee said.

'Uh, I gotta go change,' I blurted, not wanting to even comment on Erik's way-too-obvious jealousy. 'Could you guys go on to the rec hall and make sure everything's ready? I'll run to the dorm and be back in just a sec.'

'No problem,' the Twins said together.

'We'll take care of the last-minute stuff,' Damien said.

Erik didn't say anything. I smiled a quick and, I hoped, non-guilty smile at him, and took off down the sidewalk to the dorm. I could feel eyes on me and knew with a terrible sinking feeling that I was going to have to do something about Erik and Loren (and Heath). But what the hell was I going to do?

I was crazy about Heath. And his blood.

Erik was an amazing guy who I really, really liked.

Loren was completely delicious.

Jeesh, I sucked.

CHAPTER TWENTY-ONE

I WAS TRYING TO CONVINCE MYSELF THAT THIS RITUAL WAS going to be a snap. I'd just cast a quick circle, offer up prayers for Professor Nolan, announce that Aphrodite was rejoining the Dark Daughters (which would be obvious after she showed her affinity for earth), and then say that because of the stress that the school has been dealing with I've decided not to Tap any new Prefect Council members till the end of the school year. *It really should be an easy ritual*, I told my knotted stomach over and over again. *Nothing like last month when Stevie Rae died. Nothing that bad could happen tonight*. Dressed and as ready as I was going to be, I opened the door to find Aphrodite standing there.

'Take a breath, will ya?' she said, backing out of my way. 'Hello! They have to wait for you.'

'Aphrodite, has no one ever told you that it's rude to keep people waiting?' I said as I hurried down the hall, practically skipped down the stairs two at a time, and rushed out of the dorm with Aphrodite scrambling to keep up with me. I nodded at Darius, who had taken up his position outside, and he saluted me.

'You know, those warriors really are some totally hot-looking vamps,' Aphrodite said, craning her neck around to get a last view of Darius. Then she shot me a curled lip look and said in her stuck-up, rich-girl's voice, 'And no, no one has ever told me it's rude to keep people waiting. I was raised to keep people waiting. As far as my mother's concerned, the sun waits for her before it rises and sets.'

I rolled my eyes.

'So how did Neferet's ritual go?'

'Fabulous. She set a protective curtain around the school. No one gets in or out without her knowing about it. Couldn't be better. Oh, that is, unless you're us.'

Even though there was no one around us, Aphrodite lowered her voice. 'She's still gulping down the bags of blood?'

'She's barely hanging on. We gotta do something soon.'

'I don't know what the hell you think *we're* gonna do,' Aphrodite said. '*You're* the one with the mega-powers. I'm just along for the ride.' She paused and lowered her voice even more. 'Plus, I don't know what you expect to do. She's *gross* and more than a little bit scary.'

'She's my best friend,' I whispered fiercely.

'No. She used to be your best friend. Now she's a scary undead dead girl who drinks blood like pop.'

'She's still my best friend,' I repeated stubbornly.

'Fine. Whatever. Then heal her.'

'Okay, it's so not that simple.'

'How do you know? Have you tried?'

And I stopped totally dead in my tracks. 'What did you just say?'

Aphrodite raised an eyebrow at me, shrugged, and looked utterly bored. 'Something like, have you tried?'

'Holy crap! Could it be that easy? I mean, I've been spending all this time looking for a spell or a ritual or a . . . a . . . *something* specific and amazing and totally magical, and maybe all I needed to do is just ask Nyx to heal her.' And as I stood there basking in my ohmygod moment, I heard Nyx's voice echo through my mind, repeating what the goddess had told me a month ago right before I used my elemental powers to break the blocks Neferet had put in my memory: *I wish to remind you that the elements can restore as well as destroy.*

'Holy crap? You said holy crap? You know, that's another almost cuss. I'm starting to worry about your terrible potty mouth.'

Feeling suddenly so utterly happy and hopeful that not even Aphrodite could piss me off, I laughed. 'Come on! Worry about my mouth later.' I took off again, almost jogging down the sidewalk.

There was another of the warriors standing outside the rec hall, a huge black vamp who looked like he should have been a professional wrestler. Aphrodite made a little purring sound at him, and he gave her a sexy, yet somehow still warriorlike smile. She hung back to do more flirting.

'Don't be late!' I hissed back at her.

'Relax your panties. I'll be in there in a sec.' She waved me off and shot me a look that reminded me it was better if she and I weren't seen hanging out together. I gave her a tight little nod and went on in.

'Z! There you are.' Jack came scampering over to me with Damien close behind him.

'Sorry. I hurried as fast as I could,' I said.

Damien smiled. 'Not a problem. Everything's ready for you.' His smile faded a little. 'Well, except Aphrodite. She's nowhere to be seen.'

'I've seen her. She's coming. Go ahead and take your place.'

Damien nodded. He went back to the circle and Jack moved over to the audio equipment area (the kid is a genius with any kind of electronic equipment).

'Whenever you're ready, just let me know,' he called.

I smiled at him, then looked back at the circle. The Twins waved at me from their places in the south and west. Erik was standing near the empty spot behind the earth candle. He caught my eyes and winked at me. I smiled back, but wondered why he was standing so close to where he knew Aphrodite was going to be.

Speaking of . . . Annoyed that she had managed to make *me* wait for *her*, I glanced at the door in time to see Aphrodite twitch into the room. I watched her hesitate, and thought her face went kinda pale as she looked over at the circle of waiting Dark Daughters and Sons. Then she lifted her chin and tossed back her blond mane, and ignoring everyone, she strutted straight over to the northernmost part of the circle to stand behind the green candle. As kids caught sight of her, the easy talking was cut off like someone had pressed a mute button. No one said anything for a couple seconds, and then low whispering started. Aphrodite just stood there behind the candle, looking calm and beautiful and very stuck-up.

'Better get this thing started before you have a mutiny.'

This time I didn't jump at the sound of Loren's deep, sexy voice coming from close behind me. I did turn around, though, mostly so that people (Erik) couldn't see what I'm sure was an inappropriate-for-public-consumption look on my face as I smiled up at him.

'I'm as ready as I'll ever be,' I said.

'And she's supposed to be here?' Loren jerked his chin in the direction of Aphrodite.

'Sadly, yes,' I said.

'This should be interesting.'

'That's me and my life – interesting. As in a isn't-that-car-wreck-interesting kind of a way.'

Loren laughed. 'Break a leg.'

'To me that would happen literally.' I sighed, settled my face, and turned back around to face the circle. 'I'm ready,' I said.

'I'll cue the music. You start your dance to the center as I recite the poem,' Loren said.

I nodded and concentrated on my breathing and settling myself. When the music started, the whispering circle went completely still. All eyes were on me. I didn't recognize the song, but the beat was steady, rhythmic, sonorous, reminding me of a pulse. My body automatically picked it up and I began to move around the outside of the circle.

Loren's voice complemented the music perfectly.

> *'I have been one acquainted with the night.*
> *I have walked out in rain – and back in rain . . .'*

The words of the old poem set the mood perfectly, somehow conjuring images of the otherworldliness that I'd begun to be comfortable with during my solitary trips away from campus.

> *'I have looked down the saddest city lane.*
> *I have passed by the watchman on his beat*
> *And dropped my eyes, unwilling to explain.'*

I could almost feel the darkness of last night and how it seemed to seep into my skin. And I knew again the sense that I belonged more to it than to the human world that surrounded me. As I moved into the circle, I shivered and heard Damien's small gasp of surprise, and I knew that mist and magic had taken over my body.

'And further still at an unearthly height,
A luminary clock against the sky
Proclaimed the time was neither wrong nor right.
I have been one acquainted with the night.'

Loren's voice faded away and I twirled around one last time, willing away the sense of mist and magic, so that I was now fully visible. Still filled with night magic, I picked up the ritual lighter from the riches-laden table in the center of the circle and realized that maybe for the first time I felt like a true High Priestess of Nyx, drenched in the Goddess's magic and complete with her power. All the stress I'd been dealing with was washed away by a wave of happiness. I walked lightly over to stand in front of Damien.

He smiled and whispered, 'That was really cool!'

I smiled back at him and lifted the lighter. The words that came instinctively to my mind had to have come from Nyx. I'd definitely never been so poetic. 'Soft and whispering winds from afar, greetings be unto thee. In the name of Nyx I call you to blow clear and fresh and free, and call you here to me!' I touched the flame to the wick on Damien's yellow candle and was instantly surrounded by a sweet, caressing wind.

I hurried to Shaunee and her red candle. Deciding to go with the special sense of priestess magic I was feeling, I began the invocation without lifting the lighter. 'Warming and quickening fire from afar, with the warmth that brings forth life, and in the name of Nyx, I send greetings unto thee, and call you here to me!' I flicked my fingers at the candlewick, and it burst into a beautiful flame. Shaunee and I grinned at each other before I followed the circle around to Erin.

'Cool waters of lake and of stream from afar, I offer greetings to thee. Flow clear and pure and swift in magical presence here. In the name of Nyx manifest so that we shall see, as I call you here to me!' I touched the lighter to Erin's blue candle and loved how the kids standing closest to her gasped and laughed as water that was visible, but that didn't actually touch them, lapped all around Erin's feet.

'Easy-peasy,' Erin whispered.

I grinned and moved clockwise to stand in front of Aphrodite and her green candle. The gentle laughter and happy whispering that had been traveling through the group with me quieted. Aphrodite's face was an emotionless mask. It was only in her eyes that I could see her nervous fear, and I wondered for a second how long she'd been hiding her emotions. Knowing her nightmare parents, I figured it had been a long time.

'It's going to be okay,' I whispered almost without moving my lips at all.

'I may puke,' she whispered back.

'Nah!' I grinned. And then lifted my voice and spoke the beautiful words that were floating through my mind. 'Lands afar and wild places of the earth, greetings I say unto thee. Awaken from your mossy sleep to bring forth bounty and beauty and stability. In Nyx's name I call earth here to me!' I lit Aphrodite's candle and the fresh, rich scent of a newly mown hay field completely filled the rec hall. The sound of chirping birds surrounded us. Lilacs made the air so sweet that it was like we'd been spritzed with the lightest and most perfect perfume ever. I met Aphrodite's shining eyes, and then turned to glance around the rest of the circle. Everyone was staring at Aphrodite, shocked into absolute silence.

'Yes,' I said simply, cutting through all the questions I knew were milling around in their heads, and (hopefully) putting an end to their doubts. They might not like her – they might not trust her – but they had to accept the fact that Nyx had blessed her. 'Aphrodite has been blessed with an affinity for the element earth.' Then I went to the center of the circle and picked up my purple candle. 'Spirit filled with magic and night, whispering soul of the Goddess, friend and stranger, mystery and knowledge, in Nyx's name I call thee here to me!' My candle lit, and I stood very still while the familiar cacophony of all five elements filled me, body and soul.

It was so amazing I almost forgot to breathe.

When I settled myself again, I lit the braided rope of dried eucalyptus and sage, and then blew them out, breathing deeply of the herbs and concentrating on the properties my grand-mother's people had prized them for – eucalyptus for healing, protection, and purification, and white sage for its ability to drive out negative spirits, energies, and influences. With the spicy smoke swirling around me, I faced outward and began speaking, as conscious of all the eyes on me as I was of the glistening silver thread that so visibly tied together my circle. 'Merry meet!' I cried, and the group responded with, 'Merry meet!' I could feel my tension start to relax as I addressed them. 'You all know by now that yesterday Professor Nolan was killed. It was as horrible and true as the rumors have made it out to be. Right now I'd like to ask you to join me in asking Nyx to soothe her spirit and also to soothe us.' I paused and found Erik. 'I haven't been here very long, but I know a lot of you were really close to Professor Nolan.' Erik tried to smile, but his obvious sadness wouldn't let his lips turn up, and he blinked hard to keep the tears that were making his blue eyes sparkly and liquid from falling down his cheeks. 'She was a good teacher, and a nice person. We're going to miss her. Let's send her spirit a final blessed be.' The kids responded automatically with a heartfelt shout of 'Blessed be!'

I paused to let them get quiet again, and then I continued. 'I know I was supposed to announce who has been chosen to be Tapped for the Prefect Council, but because of everything that has happened in the past month I've decided to wait until the end of this school year, and then the Council and I will get together and have several names to pass along to you for your vote. Until then I have decided to automatically add one more fledgling to our Council.' I was careful to speak matter-of-factly, as if I wasn't saying anything that most of them would think was a completely insane idea. 'As you've already seen, Aphrodite has been given an affinity for earth. Like Stevie Rae, that gives her a position on our Council. Also like Stevie Rae, she has agreed to abide by my new rules for the Dark Daughters.' I turned then so that I could meet Aphrodite's eyes, and was relieved when she gave me a tight, nervous smile, and then nodded her head once. Then, not giving them time to start to babble among themselves, I took the goblet of sweet red wine from Nyx's table and began the official invocation of the Full Moon Prayer.

'Again this month we find that with the full moon we have to face many new beginnings. Last month it was a new order of the Dark Daughters and Sons. This month it is a new member of the Prefect Council, and the sadness of a professor's death. I've only been your leader for one month, but already I know that I—' I paused and then corrected myself. 'I mean that *we* can trust Nyx to love us and be with us, even when really awful things happen.' I lifted the goblet and worked my way around the circle, reciting the beautiful old poem I'd memorized the month before.

> *'Airy light of the moon*
> *Mystery of the deep earth*
> *Power of the flowing water*
> *Warmth of the burning flame*
> *In Nyx's name we call to thee!'*

I offered each fledgling a taste of wine, nodding as they smiled at me. I concentrated on trying to look like someone they could count on – someone they could trust.

> *'Healing of ills*
> *Righting of wrongs*

Cleansing of impurity
Desiring of truths
In Nyx's name we call to thee!'

I was glad that they all murmured 'blessed be' after they drank, and that they didn't look particularly mutinous.

'*Sight of the cat*
Hearing of the dolphin
Speed of the snake
Mystery of the phoenix
In Nyx's name we call to thee
and ask that with us you will blessed be!'

I offered Aphrodite the last drink before me, and almost didn't hear her whispered, 'Good job, Zoey,' before she sipped from the goblet and handed it back to me, saying the standard 'Blessed be' loud enough for everyone else to hear.

Feeling relieved and pretty darn proud of myself, I drank the last of the wine and put the goblet back on the table. In reverse order, I thanked each element and sent them away in turn, as Aphrodite, Erin, Shaunee, and Damien blew out their candles. Then I completed the ritual by saying, 'This Full Moon Rite is ended. Merry meet and merry part and merry meet again!'

The fledglings echoed, 'Merry meet and merry part and merry meet again!'

I remember that I was grinning like a clueless moron when Erik cried out in pain and fell to his knees.

CHAPTER TWENTY-TWO

UNLIKE WHEN STEVIE RAE HAD BEEN DYING, I DIDN'T HAVE even an instant of numbness or hesitation.

'No!' I screamed, running over to Erik and falling to my knees beside him. He was on his hands and knees, groaning in pain, with his head almost touching the floor. I couldn't see his face, but I could see that sweat – or maybe even blood, though I didn't smell it yet – was already soaking his shirt. I knew what would follow: Blood would gush from his eyes, nose, mouth, and he would literally drown in his own fluids. And, yes, it would be as horrible as it sounded. Nothing could stop it. Nothing could change it. All I could do was be there for him and hope that somehow he became like Stevie Rae and managed to retain some kind of hold on his humanity.

I put my hand on his trembling shoulder. Heat radiated through his shirt, as if his body was burning from the inside. I looked around frantically for help. As always, Damien was there when I needed him. 'Get towels and Neferet,' I said. Damien took off with Jack on his heels.

I turned back to Erik, but before I could pull him into my arms Aphrodite's voice cut through the noise of his moans and the sounds of the frightened, watching crowd of kids.

'Zoey, he's not dying.' I looked up at her, not really getting what she was saying. She grabbed my arm and pulled me away from Erik. I started to struggle, but her next words got through to me and made me freeze. 'Listen to me! He's not dying. He's Changing.'

Suddenly Erik screamed, his body curling in on itself as if something inside his chest was trying to claw its way free. His hands were pressed against his face. He was still trembling violently. Clearly, he was in pain and something big was happening to him. But there was absolutely no blood.

Aphrodite was right. Erik was Changing into an adult vampyre.

Jack rushed up to me and thrust several towels into my hands. I looked up at him. The kid was bawling so hard he was snotting on himself. I stood up and hugged him.

'He's not dying. He's Changing.' My voice sounded weird – hoarse and strained – as I repeated Aphrodite's words.

Then Neferet burst into the room with Damien and several

of the warriors following close behind her. She ran over to Erik. I watched her face closely, and felt a dizzying rush of relief as her tense, worried expression changed instantly to one of joy. Neferet dropped gracefully to the floor beside him. Murmuring something so softly that I couldn't catch the words, she gently touched his shoulder. His body jerked violently once, and then he began to relax. His awful trembling stopped, and so did his scary, painful moaning. Slowly Erik's body unwrapped from around itself and he pulled himself to his hands and knees. His head was still bent down toward the floor, so I couldn't see his face.

Neferet whispered something else to him and he nodded in response. Then she stood and turned to us. Her smile was amazing, completely filled with joy and almost blindingly beautiful. 'Rejoice fledglings! Erik Night has completed the Change. Arise, Erik, and follow me for your purification ritual and the beginning of your new life!'

Erik stood up and raised his head. I gasped along with everyone else. His face was luminous. It seemed someone had turned a switch on inside him. He'd been handsome before, but now everything was intensified. His eyes were bluer, his thick hair was wild and black and dangerous, he even appeared taller. And his Mark had been completed. The sapphire crescent was filled in. And framing his eyes, along his brows and over his well-defined cheekbones, was a stunning pattern of interlocking knots that formed the shape of a mask, reminding me instantly of Professor Nolan's beautiful Mark. I felt dizzy with the rightness of it.

Erik's gaze touched mine for a moment. His full lips tilted up and he smiled a special smile just for me. I thought my heart would burst. Then he raised his arms over his head and cried out in a voice filled with power and pure joy, 'I've Changed!'

All the kids started to cheer, though no one except Neferet and the vamps actually approached him. Then he left the rec hall with them on a tide of excitement and noise.

I just stood there. I felt numb and shocked and more than a little sick.

'They'll take him to be anointed into the service of the Goddess,' Aphrodite said. She was still standing beside me and her voice sounded as bleak as I suddenly felt. 'Fledglings don't know exactly what happens during the anointing. It's a big vamp secret, and they're not allowed to tell.' She shrugged. 'Whatever. Guess we'll find out some day.'

'Or we die,' I said through numb lips.

'Or we die,' she agreed. Then she looked at me. 'Are you okay?'

'Yeah. Fine,' I said automatically.

'Hey, Z! Was that cool or what?' Jack said.

'Man, it was incredible. I'm still reeling!' Damien fanned himself and his large vocabulary.

'Oh, baby! Now Erik Night joins the other vamp hotties like Brandon Routh, Josh Hartnett, and Jake Gyllenhaal.'

'And Loren Blake, Twin. Do not leave his hotness out,' Erin said.

'Wouldn't think of it, Twin,' Shaunee said.

'It is totally cool that Z's boyfriend is a vamp. I mean a real one,' Jack said.

Damien took a breath to say something and then shut his mouth and looked uncomfortable.

'What?' I said.

'Well, it's just that . . . uh . . . well . . .' He hesitated.

'God, what it is? Just spit it out!' I snapped.

He flinched at my tone, making me feel like a jerk, but answered me. 'Well, I don't know much about it, but once a fledgling goes through the Change he leaves the House of Night and starts his life as a full-grown vampyre.'

'Zoey's boyfriend is gonna leave?' Jack said.

'Long-distance relationship, Z,' Erin said quickly.

'Yeah, you two will work it out. Easy-peasy,' Shaunee said.

I looked from the Twins to Damien and Jack, and finally at Aphrodite.

'Sucks,' she said. 'At least for you.' Aphrodite raised her brows and shrugged. 'Makes me glad he dumped me.' Then she tossed back her hair and headed toward the food that was set out in the other room.

'If we can't call her a hag from hell, can we call her a bitch?' Shaunee asked.

'Hateful bitch would be my choice, Twin,' Erin said.

'Well, she's wrong,' Damien said stubbornly. 'Erik's still your boyfriend, even if he's off doing vamp stuff.'

They were all staring at me, so I tried to smile at them. 'Yeah, I know. It's okay. It's just – just a lot to take in, that's all. Let's get something to eat.' Before they could do any more comforting, I strode off toward the food with them trailing after me like baby ducks.

It seemed like it took forever for the Dark Daughters and Sons to eat and then clear out, but when I looked at the clock I realized that they had actually eaten quickly and were leaving early. There had been a lot of excited talk about Erik, and I'd nodded and made noises in semi-appropriate response, trying to hide how numb and wrong I felt. I suppose everyone taking off early was proof of what a crappy job I did of it. Finally I realized the only kids left were Jack and Damien and the Twins. They were quietly throwing away the leftovers and bagging up the trash.

'Uh, guys, I'll get that,' I said.

'We're just about done, Z,' Damien said. 'Really all that's left is to put away the stuff on Nyx's table in the middle of the circle.'

'I'll do that,' I said, trying (unsuccessfully by the looks on their faces) to be nonchalant.

'Z, is everything—'

I held up my hand to cut off Damien. 'I'm tired. I'm kinda freaked about Erik. And, honestly, I need some alone time.' I hadn't wanted to sound so totally bitchy, but I was getting beyond the point where I could keep the happy look plastered on my face and continue pretending that I wasn't shaking all over inside. And I absolutely would rather have my friends think I was PMS-ing than that I was ready to totally fall apart. High Priestesses in training didn't fall apart. They handled things. I really really *really* didn't want them to know that I was *so not handling things*. 'Guys, could you just give me awhile. Please?'

'No problem,' the Twins said together. 'Later, Z.'

'All right. I'll, uh, see you later, too,' Damien said.

'Bye, Z,' Jack said.

I waited till the door closed behind them before I walked slowly into the side room that was used as a dance studio and yoga room. It had a bunch of soft mats stacked in the corner and I sank down on them. My hands were shaking when I pulled my cell phone out of the pocket of my dress.

Are U ok?

I keyed in the short text message and then sent it to the disposable cell phone I'd bought Stevie Rae. It felt like an eternity before she answered.

Im ok

Hang on I replied.

Hurry she texted back.

Will do

I closed my phone, leaned against the wall, and, feeling like the entire world was pressing down on my shoulders, I burst into sobbing, snotty tears.

I cried and shook and shook and cried while I hugged my

legs hard to my chest and rocked back and forth. I knew what was wrong with me. It surprised me that no one else, not one of my friends, had figured it out.

I'd thought Erik was dying, and it had brought back the night Stevie Rae had died in my arms. It was as if it was happening all over again – the blood, the sadness, the horror. It had completely blindsided me. I mean, I'd thought I was over what had happened to Stevie Rae. After all, she wasn't really dead.

I'd just been fooling myself.

I'd been bawling so hard that I didn't know he was there until he touched my shoulder. I looked up, wiping tears from my eyes, trying to think of something reassuring to say to whatever friend had come back for me.

'I could feel that you needed me,' Loren said.

With a sob I hurled myself into his arms. He sat beside me, pulling me onto his lap. Holding me tight, he murmured sweet words, telling me that everything would be okay now and that he'd never let me go. When I finally got myself under control and hiccupped instead of sobbed, Loren handed me one of his old-time linen hankies.

'Thanks,' I muttered as I blew my nose and wiped my face. I tried not to look at myself in the wall of mirrors across from us, but I couldn't avoid catching a glimpse of my puffy eyes and red nose. 'Oh, great. I look like utter crap.'

Loren chuckled and shifted me on his lap so that I was facing him. He gently smoothed back my hair. 'You look like a goddess who has been saddened by stress and hardship.'

I felt a little hysterical laughter bubble up from somewhere inside my chest. 'I don't think goddesses snot on themselves.'

He smiled. 'Oh, I wouldn't be too sure about that.' Then his expression sobered. 'When Erik Changed you thought he was dying, didn't you?'

I nodded, scared that if I said anything I'd start bawling again.

Loren's jaw clenched and unclenched. 'I've told Aphrodite over and over that *all* fledglings, and not just fifth and sixth formers, should be aware of how the Change manifests in the final stage so that they're not frightened if they witness it.'

'Does it hurt as bad as it looks like it does?'

'It is painful, but it's a good pain – if that makes sense. Think of it like sore muscles after you've worked out. They hurt, but it's not a bad hurt.'

'Looked like a lot more than sore muscles,' I said.

'It's not that bad – more shocking than painful actually. Sensations rush into your body and everything becomes hyper-sensitive.' His hand caressed the side of my face as his finger lightly followed the line of my Mark. 'You'll experience it yourself some day.'

'I hope so.'

Neither of us said anything for a moment, although he continued to caresses my face and trace the Mark that decorated the side of my neck. His touch was making my body relax and tingle at the same time.

'But something else is upsetting you, isn't it?' Loren spoke gently. His voice was deep and musical and hypnotically beautiful. 'It's more than just Erik's Change bringing back the memory of your friend's death.'

When I didn't say anything, he leaned forward and kissed me on my forehead, touching his lips softly to the crescent-moon tattoo. I shivered.

'You can talk to me, Zoey. There's already so much between us that you must know you can trust me.'

His lips brushed over mine. It would be really nice to tell Loren about Stevie Rae. He could help me, and god knows I needed his help. Especially now that I'd kinda decided that Stevie Rae might be healed by my asking Nyx, which, of course, meant that there was going to be a circle casting involved, and that meant either getting Damien, the Twins, Aphrodite, and me to Stevie Rae or getting Stevie Rae to us. Neferet's protective spell would not be helping that, but maybe Loren knew some adult vampyre secret way around it. I tried to listen to my gut – tried to decide whether my instinct was still screaming at me to keep my mouth shut – but all I could feel were Loren's hands and lips.

'Talk to me,' he whispered against my mouth.

'I – I want to . . .' I whispered back breathlessly. 'It's just so complicated.'

'Let me help you, love. Together there's nothing we can't work though.' He kisses got longer, hotter.

I wanted to tell him, but my head was spinning and it was hard for me to think, let alone talk.

'I'll show you how much we can share . . . how completely we can be together,' he said.

Loren took the hand he was fisting in my hair and pulled at his shirt so that the buttons popped, exposing his chest. Then he drew his thumbnail slowly over his left breast, leaving behind a line of perfect scarlet. The scent of his blood wrapped around me.

'Drink,' he said.

I couldn't stop myself. I lowered my face to his chest and tasted him. His blood surged through me. It was different than Heath's – not as hot, not as rich. But it was more powerful. It pounded through me, along with a desire that was red and urgent. I moved against his body, wanting more and more.

'Now it's my turn. I have to taste you!' Loren said.

Before I realized what he was doing he'd wrenched off my dress. I didn't have a chance to freak about the fact that he was seeing me in nothing but my bra and panties because he took his thumb and this time sliced it across my breast. I gasped at the sharp pain, and then his lips were on me and he was drinking my blood and the pain was replaced by waves of amazing pleasure so intense that all I could do was moan. Loren tore at his clothes while he drank me, and I helped him. All I knew what that I had to have him. Everything was all heat and sensation and desire. His hands and mouth were everywhere and still I couldn't get enough of him.

Then it happened. His heartbeat was under my skin and I could feel my pulse pounding in time with his. I could feel his passion along with mine and hear his desire roaring inside my head.

And then, somewhere in the back of my jumbled mind I heard Heath screaming, '*Zoey! No!*'

My body jerked in Loren's arms. 'Ssh,' he whispered. 'It's okay. It's better this way, love, much better. Being Imprinted with a human is too difficult – it has too many ramifications.'

My breath was coming fast and hard. 'Is it broken? Has my Imprint with Heath been broken?'

'It has. Our Imprint has replaced it.' He rolled so that I was under his body. 'Now let's finish it. Let me make love to you, baby.'

'Yes,' I whispered. My lips found Loren's chest again, and as I drank from him, Loren made love to me until our world exploded in blood and passion.

CHAPTER TWENTY-THREE

I WAS LYING ON TOP OF LOREN IN A DELICIOUS FOG OF sensation. His hand caressed a long sweep down my back, stroking over and over the line of my tattoos.

'Your tattoos are exquisite. Like you,' Loren said.

I sighed happily and nuzzled against him. Turning my head, I was mesmerized by our reflection in the floor-to-ceiling studio mirrors. We were naked and there were smudges of blood on both of our bodies, which were twined together intimately, my long black hair only partially covering us. The filigree of my tattoos looked exotic stretching from my face and neck down along the line of my curving spine to my lower back. The thin film of sweat on my body made them glisten like sapphires.

Loren was right. I was exquisite. And he'd been right about us. It didn't matter that he was older and a full-grown vampyre (and a professor at my school). What we had together went beyond all of that. What we had was really special. More special than what I felt for Erik. Even more special than Heath.

Heath . . .

The sleepy, satisfied feeling left me like someone had splashed cold water on my skin. My gaze went from our reflection to Loren's face. He was watching me with a slight smile curving the corners of his lips. God, he was so dang gorgeous I couldn't believe he was mine. Then I mentally shook myself, and asked the question I had to have answered. 'Loren, is it really true that my Imprint with Heath is broken?'

'Yes, it's really true,' he said. 'You and I have Imprinted, and that severed your link with the human boy.'

'But I read the Vamp Soc book, and it only talked about how painful and hard it is to break an Imprint between a vampyre and a human. I don't understand how it could have happened so easily, and it didn't say anything about one Imprint breaking another.'

His slight smile spread and he gave me a sweet, soft kiss. 'You'll learn that there's a lot the textbooks don't teach about being a vampyre.'

That made me feel young and stupid and more than a little embarrassed, which he instantly picked up on.

'Hey, I didn't mean anything. I remember how confusing

it was not to really understand what it is you're Changing into. It's okay. It happens to all of us. And now you have me to help you.'

'I just don't like not knowing,' I said, relaxing again in his arms.

'I know. So here's the deal with breaking that Imprint. You and the human did have a bond, but you're not a vampyre. You haven't completed your Change.' He paused and then added a firm 'Yet. So it wasn't a full-blown Imprint. When you and I shared our blood, that bonding overwhelmed the lesser one.' His smile turned sexy. 'Because I *am* a vampyre.'

'Did it hurt Heath?'

Loren shrugged. 'Probably, but the pain doesn't last. And in the long run it's better this way. The entire vampyre world will be open to you very soon, Zoey. You will be an extraordinary High Priestess. There won't be a place for a human in that world.'

'I know you're right,' I said, trying to sort through everything in my mind and remembering how sure I'd been earlier that night that I had to break up with Heath. It was really a good thing that my being with Loren had broken the Imprint with Heath. It was easier this way – for both of us. Another thought had me saying, 'It's a good thing that I wasn't Imprinted with you and Heath at the same time.'

'That would be impossible. Nyx had made it so that we Imprint singly. I suppose it's to keep us from making an army of Imprinted human minions.'

I was startled as much by the sarcastic tone of his voice as by what he'd just said. 'I would never have thought about doing that,' I said.

Loren laughed softly. 'There are many vamps who would.'

'Would you?'

'Of course not.' He kissed me again and added, 'Besides, I'm more than happy with our Imprint. I don't need any others.'

His words thrilled me. He was mine and I was his! Then Erik's face swam before my eyes and the thrill faded.

'What is it?' he said.

'Erik,' I whispered.

'You belong to me!' Loren's voice was rough, as were his lips as he kissed me possessively, making my blood pound.

'Yes' was all I could say when the kiss was over. He was like a tidal wave I couldn't stand against, and I let him sweep Erik away from me. 'I do belong to you.'

Loren's arms tightened around me, and then he lifted me gently and shifted his body so that he could look into my eyes. 'Can you tell me now?'

'Tell you what?' Even though I asked the question I thought I knew what it was he wanted to hear.

'Tell me what it is that upset you so badly.'

Ignoring the sudden clenching of my stomach I made my decision. After what had just happened between us, I had to trust Loren.

'Stevie Rae didn't die. At least not like what we think of as dying. She's alive, even though she's different. And she's not the only fledgling to survive a supposed death. There's a bunch of them, but they're not like her. Stevie Rae has managed to keep a hold on her humanity. They haven't.'

I felt his body tense and half expected him to tell me I was nuts, but all he said was, 'What do you mean? Explain everything to me, Zoey.'

So I did. I told Loren everything – from the 'ghosts' I'd seen to the fact that they weren't really ghosts, to the awfulness of the undead dead kids killing the Union football players, and then how I saved Heath. Finally, I told him about Stevie Rae. All about her.

'So she's waiting at Aphrodite's garage apartment right now?' he said.

I nodded. 'Yeah, she needs blood every day. The hold she has on her humanity isn't very good. If she doesn't get blood, I'm afraid she'll become like the rest of them.' I shivered and his arm tightened around me.

'They're that bad?' he said.

'You can't imagine. They're not human and they're not vampyre. It's like they've turned into all the stereotypes that are most horrible about vamps *and* humans. They're soulless, Loren.' I searched his eyes. 'And too far gone to fix, but Stevie Rae's affinity for the earth has made it possible for her to keep some of her soul, even if she's not whole. I really think I can do something for Stevie Rae.'

'You do?'

The thought flitted through my mind that it was kinda weird that he sounded shocked about me healing Stevie Rae but that he'd had no problem accepting the fact that undead dead kids existed.

'Well, yeah. I might be way wrong, but I believe I just need to use the powers of the elements. You know,' I paused and shifted my weight, wondering if I was getting heavy, 'I have that whole special connection with the five elements. I'm guessing that I just need to use it.'

'It might work. But you should keep in mind that you're invoking powerful magic, and there's always a cost associated with that.' He spoke slowly, like he was considering what he said carefully before he said it (unlike how I usually blurted stuff and then was sorry or embarrassed later). 'Zoey, how did this terrible thing happen to Stevie Rae and the other fledglings? Who or what is responsible for it?'

I started to say Neferet when *Don't speak her name* slammed into my gut. Okay, the words themselves didn't hit me, but I knew what was all of a sudden making me feel like I was gonna puke. And then I realized with a small start of surprise that I hadn't actually admitted *everything* to Loren. In my telling of the night when I'd rescued Heath from the undead dead kids and first found Stevie Rae, I'd left out any mention of Neferet. I hadn't thought about it. I hadn't done it on purpose, but there was a whole piece of the story puzzle that I'd failed to put together for him.

Nyx. It had to be the Goddess working through my subconscious. She didn't want Loren to know anything about Neferet. Was she trying to protect him? Probably . . .

'Zoey, what's wrong?'

'Oh, nothing. I'm just thinking. No,' I kinda stuttered, 'I – I don't know how it happened, but I wish I did. I wish I could figure it out,' I added hastily.

'Stevie Rae doesn't know?'

Warning bells rang in my stomach again. 'She's not really communicating very well right now. Why? Have you ever heard of anything like this happening before?'

'No, nothing like this.' He ran a soothing hand down my back. 'I just thought if you knew how it happened, that might help you to fix it.'

I looked into his eyes, wishing the sick feeling in my stomach would go away. 'You can't tell anyone about this, Loren. *Not anyone*, not even Neferet.' I tried to be all High Priestessy and firm, but my voice shook and broke.

'You don't need to worry, love! Of course I won't tell anyone.' Loren held me close and stroked my back. 'But who else knows besides you and me?'

'No one.' The lie was so automatic it shocked me.

'What about Aphrodite? You said you're using her garage apartment to hide Stevie Rae, right?'

'Aphrodite doesn't know. I heard her talking to some kids about her parents being gone for the rest of the winter. She was saying that they should use the garage apartment to party, but, well, everyone's pretty pissed at Aphrodite, so no one took her up on it. That's how I knew the apartment was empty, so I snuck Stevie Rae up there.' I hadn't consciously meant not to tell him about Aphrodite, but it seemed my mouth had already made that decision for me.

I mentally crossed my fingers, hoping that he couldn't tell I was lying.

'Okay, that's probably for the best. Zoey, you said Stevie Rae's not herself, and can't communicate very well. How do you talk to her?'

'Well, she can talk, but she's confused and ... and ...' I floundered around trying to figure out how to explain it without giving more away than I should, 'and sometimes more animal-like than human,' I said inanely. 'I just saw her earlier tonight before Neferet's ritual.'

I could feel him nod. 'That's where you were coming from.'

'Yeah.' I decided not to mention Heath. Just thinking about him made me feel guilty. Our Imprint was gone, but instead of being relieved I was weirdly hollow.

'But how do you know she's still at Aphrodite's apartment and okay right now?'

Distracted, I said, 'Huh? Oh, I gave her a cell phone. I can call or text her. I just checked in with her a little while ago.' I motioned to my cell phone, which had fallen out of the pocket of my dress and was lying beside it on the floor next to our pallet. Then I shook Heath from my mind and focused on my more immediate problem. 'I might need to ask for your help.'

'Ask me anything,' he said, gently brushing my hair back out of my face.

'I'm going to need to either get Stevie Rae in here to the school, or get the gang and me out there to her.'

'The gang?'

'You know, Damien and the Twins and Aphrodite, so we can cast a circle. I have a feeling I'll need the added strength they bring to their elements to help Stevie Rae.'

'But you said they don't know about Stevie Rae,' he said.

'They don't. I'll have to tell them, but I'm going to wait till right before I try the fixing of Stevie Rae thingie.' God, what a moronic thing to call it. I sighed and shook my head. 'I'm definitely not looking forward to telling them, though,' I said miserably, meaning the Stevie Rae thingie *and* how pissed my friends were going to be that I'd been keeping important stuff from them.

'So are you and Aphrodite really friends?'

Loren asked the question in an off-hand way, with a smile and a tug on one long strand of my hair, but like with Heath, our Imprint linked us and I could feel the tension hidden inside him. He cared a lot more about my answer than he was letting on. That worried me, and not just because my gut was cramping up again and warning me to keep my mouth shut.

So I tried to match his 'whatever' tone. 'Nah, Aphrodite is awful. It's just that for some reason – totally *not* understood by Damien and the Twins and me – Nyx has given her an affinity for earth. The circle doesn't work as well without her, so kinda by default she's in. It's not like we're hanging out or anything like that.'

'Good. From what I've heard Aphrodite has some major problems. You shouldn't trust her.'

'I don't.' And as I said it I realized that I actually did trust

Aphrodite. Maybe even more than I trusted Loren, who I'd just lost my virginity to and with whom I'd just Imprinted. Great. Just my luck.

'Hey, relax. I can tell talking about this has upset you.' Loren caressed my cheek and I automatically leaned into his hand. Whenever he touched me it just felt so amazing. 'I'm here now. We'll figure this out. Take it one step at a time.'

I wanted to remind him that Stevie Rae really didn't have much time, but his lips were on mine again and all I could think about was how good he felt against my body . . . that I could feel his pulse speeding up . . . that my heart was beating in time with his. Our kisses deepened and his hands moved down my body. I rocked against him, thinking about heat and blood and nothing but Loren . . . Loren . . . Loren—

A weird choking noise broke through the haze of heat that was engulfing me. Dreamily, I turned my head as Loren trailed kisses down my naked throat, and a jolt of horror shocked through my body.

Erik was standing in the doorway with a look of utter disbelief on his newly Marked face.

'Erik, I—' I lunged forward, grabbing at my dress and trying to cover myself with it. As it turned out, I didn't need to worry about Erik seeing me naked. With one quick motion, Loren moved me behind him, shielding me with his body.

'You're interrupting.' Loren's beautiful voice was dark with barely suppressed violence. The power in it pressed against my bare skin, making me gasp with surprise.

266

'Yeah, I can see that,' Erik said. Without another word he turned and walked out.

'Ohmygod! Ohmygod! I can't believe that just happened!' I put my burning face in my hands.

Loren's arms were back around me and his voice was as soothing as his touch. 'Baby, it's okay. He's was going to have to know about us some time anyway.'

'But not like this,' I cried. 'Erik finding out like this is too awful for words.' I lifted my face to look at him. 'And now everyone will know. That can't be okay, Loren! You're a teacher and I'm a fledgling. Aren't there rules against that? Not to mention that we've Imprinted.' Then another terrible thought hit me and I started to shake. What if I was kicked out of the Dark Daughters for being with Loren?

'Zoey, love, listen to me.' Loren put his hands on my shoulders and shook me gently. 'Erik won't say anything to anyone.'

'Yeah, he will! You saw the look on his face. No way is he going to keep a secret for me.' No way was he going to do anything for me, ever again.

'He'll keep his mouth shut because I'll tell him to keep it shut.'

Loren's concerned expression had shifted, and suddenly he looked as dangerous as he had sounded when he'd told Erik he was interrupting us. I felt a prickle of fear, and I began to wonder if there might be more to Loren than what he was showing me.

'Don't hurt him,' I whispered, ignoring the tears that washed my cheeks.

'Ah, baby, don't worry. I won't hurt him. I'll just have a little talk with him.' He took me into his arms, and even though my body, my heartbeat, the very essence within me wanted to be close to him, I forced myself to pull away. 'I have to go,' I said.

'Yeah, okay. I should go, too.'

As he handed me my clothes and we dressed, I told myself that he was only hurrying away from me because he needed to find Erik, but thinking about being separated from Loren made my stomach feel like a pit with nasty black stuff boiling around in it. The cut over my breast where he'd tasted my blood stung. And besides that, my body was sore in private places it'd never, ever been sore before. I glanced at the wall of mirrors. My eyes were puffy and red. My face was blotchy and my nose was pink. My hair was a nappy mess. I looked like hell, which wasn't surprising, because I felt like hell.

Loren took my hand and we walked through the empty rec hall. At the door he kissed me again before opening it.

'You look tired,' he said.

'I am.' I glanced at the rec hall clock, shocked to see that it was only two thirty in the morning. It seemed like several nights had passed in the space of just a couple hours.

'Go to bed, love,' he said. 'We'll be together again tomorrow.'

'How? When?'

He smiled and caressed my cheek, tracing the path of my tattoo. 'Don't worry. We won't be apart long. I'll come to you after both of us get some sleep.' His touch was warm against my skin. Of its own will, my body leaned toward him as his fingers traced their way intimately down the curve of my neck while he recited:

> *I arise from dreams of thee*
> *In the first sweet sleep of night,*
> *When the winds are breathing low,*
> *And the stars are shining bright*
> *I arise from dreams of thee,*
> *And a spirit in my feet*
> *Has led me – who knows how?—*
> *To thy chamber-window, sweet!'*

His touch made me tremble and his words made my heart speed up and my head dizzy. 'Did you write that?' I whispered as he kissed my neck.

'No, Shelley did. Hard to believe he wasn't a vampyre, isn't it?'

'Uh-huh,' I said, not really listening.

Loren chuckled and hugged me. 'I'll come to you tomorrow. I promise.'

We walked out together, but separated soon as he headed in the direction of the boys' dorm and I walked slowly toward my own dorm. There weren't many fledglings or vamps around, and I was glad. I didn't want to run into anyone just then. It was a dark, cloudy night and the old-time gaslights hardly touched the darkness around me. I didn't mind, though. I wanted to be covered in night. It somehow soothed the rawness in my nerves that being physically separated from Loren caused.

I wasn't a virgin anymore.

The fact hit me with a weird zing. Things had happened so fast I hadn't really had time to think about it, but I'd *done it*. Man, I needed to talk to Stevie Rae – even the undead version of Stevie Rae would want to hear about this. Did I look different? No, that was stupid. Everyone knew you couldn't tell by just looking at someone. Or not usually. Well, I'm not exactly a normal teenager (as if there really is such a thing). I better take a good long look in the mirror when I got back to my room.

I'd just turned up the sidewalk that went to the front of my dorm, and was readying myself for what I was going to say to my friends, who were probably hanging out watching movies or whatnot. I couldn't tell them about Loren and me, of course, but I did need to make up a story about breaking up with Erik. Or maybe I didn't. Loren was going to talk to him, so Erik probably wouldn't say much of anything to anyone. I could just say we had to break up because of his Change, and leave it at that. No one would be surprised that I'd be too upset to talk about it. Yeah, that's what I'd do.

Suddenly one of the shadows under a good-smelling cedar tree shifted and then stepped in front of me.

'Why, Zoey?' Erik said.

CHAPTER TWENTY-FOUR

MY BODY FELT FROZEN AS I LOOKED UP AT ERIK. HIS MARK was still a surprise. It was unique and incredible and made him look even more handsome.

'Why, Zoey?' He repeated when I just stood there staring at him like a speechless moron.

'I'm so sorry Erik!' I managed to blurt. 'I didn't mean to hurt you. I didn't want you to find out like that.'

'Yeah,' he said coldly. 'Finding out my girlfriend, who has been playing oh-so-innocent with me, is really a slut would have been no problem if you'd, I don't know, advertised it in the school paper. Yeah, that would have been way better.'

I flinched at his hateful tone. 'I'm not a slut.'

'Looked like you were doing a good imitation of one. And I knew it!' he yelled. 'I knew there was something going on between you two! But I was so damn stupid I believed you when you said it wasn't true.' His laugh was completely humorless. 'God, I'm an idiot.'

'Erik, we didn't mean for this to happen, but Loren and I are in love. We tried to stay away from each other, but we just couldn't.'

'You have got to be kidding! You actually believe that asshole loves you?'

'He does love me.'

Erik shook his head and laughed humorlessly again. 'If you believe that, then you're stupider than I am. He's using you, Zoey. There's only one thing a guy like him wants from a girl like you, and he got it. When he's had enough of it, he'll dump you and move on.'

'That's not true,' I said.

He kept talking as if I hadn't spoken. 'Damn, I'm glad I'm out of here tomorrow, even though I would like to be here to say told-you-so when Blake dumps you.'

'You don't know what you're talking about, Erik.'

'You know, you might be right,' he said in a cold, hard voice that made him sound like a stranger. 'I sure as hell didn't know what I was talking about the whole time I was saying you and I were going out, and the whole time I was telling everyone how great you are and how happy I was that you were with me. I actually thought I was falling in love with you.'

My stomach twisted. I felt like his words were stabbing me in the heart. 'I thought I was falling in love with you, too,' I said softly, blinking my eyes hard to keep from crying.

'Bullshit!' he yelled. He sounded mean even though I could see tears filling his eyes. 'Stop playing games with me. And you think Aphrodite is a hateful bitch? You make her look like a fucking angel!'

He started to back away from me. 'Erik, wait. I don't want it to end like this between us,' I said, feeling tears spill over and fall down my cheeks.

'Stop crying! This is what you wanted. This is what you and Blake planned.'

'No! I didn't plan this!'

Erik shook his head back and forth, blinking hard. 'Leave me alone. It's over. I never want to see you again.' Then he practically ran away from me.

My chest felt tight and hot and I couldn't seem to stop crying. My feet started moving, carrying me to the only place I could go – to the only person I wanted to see. Somehow on the way to the poet's loft I got myself together. Okay, not really together, but at least I looked normal enough to keep anyone who walked by me (like two vamp warriors and a couple of fledglings) from stopping me and asking what was wrong. I'd managed to quit crying. I'd run my fingers through my hair and pulled it forward over my shoulders so that it partially covered my blotchy face.

I didn't hesitate when I came to the building that held the

on-campus faculty quarters. I just took a big, deep breath and prayed silently that no one would see me.

As soon as I was inside I realized that I shouldn't have worried so much about being seen. It wasn't set up like a dorm. There was no big meeting room as you walked in where vamps hung out and watched TV like fledglings. It was just a big, stone-floored hallway that had closed doors leading off it. The stairs were on my right and I hurried up them. I knew Loren might not be back at his room yet. He might still be looking for Erik. But that was okay. I'd curl up in his bed and wait for him. At least that way I would kinda be close to him again. My body felt stiff and unfamiliar as I walked out of the stairwell on the top floor and headed to the one large wooden door not far away from me.

As I approached it I could see that the door was cracked and I heard Loren's voice trickle out from inside. He was laughing. The sound brushed against my skin, washing through the pain and sadness the scene with Erik had caused. I'd been right to come to him. I could already almost feel his arms around me. Loren would hold me and call me 'love' and 'baby' and tell me that everything would be all right. His touch would wipe away Erik's hurt and the terrible things he'd said and make me stop feeling so broken. I put my hand flat against the door so that I could push it all the way open and go in to him.

Then she laughed, low and musical and seductive, and my world stopped.

It was Neferet. She was in there with Loren. There was

no mistaking that sound – that beautiful, alluring laughter. Neferet's voice was as distinctive as Loren's. When the laughter stopped, her words came to me, sliding through the crack between door and frame like a poisonous mist.

'You've done well, my darling. Now I know what she knows, and everything is coming together perfectly. It will be a simple thing to continue to isolate her. I just hope the part you have to play isn't too unpleasant for you.' Neferet's voice was teasing, but there was an edge of hardness to it.

'She's easy to lead around. A shiny present here, a pretty compliment there, and you have true love and a popped cherry sacrificed to the god of deception and hormones.' Loren laughed again. 'Young girls are so ridiculous – so predictably easy.'

I felt like his words were piercing my skin in one hundred different places, but I made myself move silently forward so that I could peek in through the cracked door. I got a glimpse of a big room filled with rich leather furniture and lit by lots of pillar candles. My eyes were drawn instantly to the center-piece of the loft – the huge iron bed in the middle of the room. Loren was lying back on it, propped up by zillions of fat pillows. He was completely naked.

Neferet was wearing a long red dress that hugged her perfect body and dipped low to show the top of her boobs. She paced back and forth as she spoke, letting her long, mani-cured fingers trail over the iron railing of Loren's bed.

'Keep her busy. I'll make sure that little gang of friends deserts her. She's powerful, but she'll never be able to tap into her gifts if she doesn't have her friends to help keep her head on straight while she's chasing around after you.' Neferet paused and tapped a slender finger against her chin. 'You know, I was surprised by the Imprint, though.' I saw Loren's body jerk. Neferet smiled. 'You didn't think I'd be able to smell it on you? You reek of her blood, and her blood reeks of you.'

'I don't know how it happened,' Loren said quickly, the obvious irritation in his voice driving daggers into my heart so that I could feel it shattering into tiny pieces. 'I guess I underestimated my acting abilities. I'm just relieved that there's nothing real between us – saves me from the messy emotions and bond that would go with a true Imprinting.' He laughed. 'Like the one she had with that human boy. He must have experienced some nasty pain when that was broken. Weird that she was able to Imprint so fully with him before she's Changed.'

'More proof of her power!' Neferet snapped. 'Even though she has been ridiculously easy to lead astray for a Chosen One. And don't pretend to complain that she Imprinted with you. You and I both know it just made the sex more pleasurable for you.'

'Well, I can tell you that it was damned inconvenient that you sent the gallant Erik to find his little girlfriend so soon. Couldn't you have given me a few more minutes to finish up?'

'I can give you all the time you want. Actually, I can leave right now and you can go find your little teenage lap dog and *finish up*.'

276

Loren sat up. Leaning forward he grabbed Neferet's wrist. 'Come on, baby. You know I don't *really* want her. Don't be angry with me, love.'

Neferet easily pulled away from him, but the gesture was more teasing than mad. 'I'm not angry. I'm pleased. Your Imprint breaking the bond with the human boy has left Zoey even more alone. And it's not like your Imprint with the chit is permanent. It'll dissolve when she Changes, or dies,' she finished with a mean little laugh. 'But would you rather it didn't dissolve? Perhaps you've decided you prefer youth and naïveté to me?'

'Never, love! I'll never want anyone like I want you,' Loren said. 'Let me show you, baby. Let me show you.' He moved quickly to the end of the bed and took her into his arms. I watched his hands roam down her body, a lot like he'd touched me not long before.

I pressed my hand against my mouth so I wouldn't sob out loud.

Neferet turned in Loren's arms and arched her back against him as his hands continued to moved all over her body. She was facing the doorway. Her eyes were closed and her lips were parted. She moaned in pleasure and her eyes opened slowly, almost sleepily. And then Neferet was looking directly at me.

I whirled around, ran down the stairs, and burst out of the building. I wanted to keep running away. Anywhere that was far, far away, but my body betrayed me. I was only able to stagger a couple steps from the door. I did manage to get to the shadows behind one of the well-trimmed holly hedges before I bent at the waist and puked my guts up.

When I stopped gagging and dry heaving I started walking. My mind wasn't working right. I was disoriented with terrible, whirling thoughts. I was feeling more than thinking, and all I could feel was pain.

The pain told me Erik had been right, except he'd underestimated Loren. He'd thought Loren was just using me for sex. The truth was that Loren hadn't even wanted me. He'd only used me because the woman he did want had put him up to it. I wasn't even a sex object to him. I was an inconvenience. He'd only touched me and told me all those things . . . all those beautiful things because he'd been playing a part given to him by Neferet. To him I meant less than nothing.

Stifling a sob, I reached up, yanked the diamond posts from my earlobes, and with a cry hurled them away from me.

'Damn, Zoey. If you were tired of those diamonds, you could have said something. I have some drop pearls that would go great with that dorky snowman necklace Erik gave you for your birthday, and I would have traded them for the rocks.'

I turned around slowly, like my body might shatter if I moved too fast. Aphrodite was just coming out of the sidewalk that led to the dining hall. She was carrying a weird fruit in one hand and a bottle of Corona in the other.

'What? I like mangos,' she said. 'The dorm never has them, but the vamps' kitchen fruit fridge always does. Like they'll miss a mango here and there?' When I didn't say anything, she continued, 'Okay, okay, I know beer's common and kinda

278

tacky, but I like it, too. Hey, do me a favor and don't ever tell my mom. She'd totally freak.' Then I saw her eyes widen as she got a good look at me. 'Holy shit, Zoey! You look awful. What's wrong with you?'

'Nothing. Leave me alone,' I said, barely recognizing my own voice.

'Okay, whatever. Go on about your business and I'll mind mine,' she said, and then almost bolted away from me.

I was alone. Just like Neferet had said, they were all leaving me. And I deserved it. I'd caused Heath terrible pain. I'd hurt Erik. I'd given away my virginity for lies. How had Loren put it? I'd sacrificed true love and a popped cherry to the god of deception and hormones. No wonder he was Poet Laureate. He definitely had a way with words.

And suddenly I had to run. I didn't know where I was going. I only knew that I had to move and move fast or my mind was going to explode. I didn't stop until I couldn't breathe anymore, and then I leaned against the bark of an old oak and gasped.

'Zoey? Is that you?'

I looked up, blinking through the fog of my misery to see Darius, the young, hot, warrior mountain. He was actually standing on top of the wide wall that surrounded our school, and he was studying me curiously.

'Is all well with you?' he asked in the weird, kinda archaic way the warriors all seemed to talk.

'Yes,' I managed between breaths. 'I just wanted to take a walk.'

'You were not walking,' he said logically.

'It's just a figure of speech.' I met his eyes and decided I was sick and tired of lying. 'I felt like my head was going to explode, so I ran as hard and as long as I could. This is where I ended up.'

Darius nodded slowly. 'It is a place of power. I am not surprised you were drawn here.'

'Here?' I blinked and looked around. And then – ohmygod – realized exactly where I was. 'This is the east wall near the trapdoor.'

'Yes, Priestess, it is. Even the barbaric humans sensed its power enough so that they left Professor Nolan's body here.' He motioned over his shoulder just outside the wall to the place Aphrodite and I had found Professor Nolan. It was also where I'd found Nala (or rather, where she'd found me), where I'd cast my first circle, had my first glimpse of what would turn out to be the undead dead kids, and where I'd called on the elements and Nyx to break through the memory block Neferet had placed on my mind.

It really was a place of power. I couldn't believe I hadn't realized it before now. Of course I'd been awfully busy with Heath and Erik and especially Loren. *Neferet had been right*, I thought with disgust. *I was ridiculously easy to lead astray*.

'Darius, do you think you could leave me alone here for a while? I'd – I'd like to pray, and I'm hoping Nyx will give me an answer if I listen hard enough.'

'And that would be easier to do were you alone,' he said.

I nodded, not sure if I could continue to make my voice mind.

'I will allow you privacy, Priestess. But do not stray far from here. Remember that Neferet has bespelled the perimeter, so if you use the trapdoor and cross the line of her spell, in moments you would be surrounded by Sons of Erebus.' His smile was grim, but kind. 'And that would not help you concentrate on your prayers, my lady.'

'I'll remember.' I tried not to flinch when he called me Priestess and my lady. No dang way I deserved either title.

With one fluid, unhurried movement, he vaulted from the top of the twenty-foot wall, landing neatly on his feet. Then he saluted me with his fist over his heart, bowed slightly, and disappeared soundlessly into the night.

It was then that my legs decided they wouldn't support me anymore. I sat heavily in the grass at the base of the familiar old oak, pulled my knees up to my chest, wrapped my arms around them, and began to cry, silently and steadily.

I was unbelievably sorry. How could I have been so stupid? How could I have fallen for Loren's lies? I really had believed him. And now I'd not only given the jerk my virginity, but I'd Imprinted with him, which made me a double idiot.

I wanted my grandma. With a little choking sob, I reached into the pocket of my dress for my cell phone. I was going to tell Grandma everything. It'd be awful and embarrassing, but I knew she wouldn't leave me or judge me. Grandma wouldn't stop loving me.

But my dang cell phone wasn't there. Then I remembered

it had fallen out of my pocket when I'd gotten naked with Loren. I must have forgotten to pick it up. Didn't that just figure? I closed my eyes and let my head fall back against the rough bark of the tree.

'Mee-uf-ow!'

Nala's warm wet nose poked against my cheek. Without opening my eyes I spread my arms so that she could hop up into my lap. She put her little front paws on my shoulder and pressed her face into the crook of my neck, purring furiously, as if the sound could force me to feel better.

'Oh, Nala, I've messed up so bad.' I held my cat and let the sobs shake my shoulders.

CHAPTER TWENTY-FIVE

WHEN I HEARD THE SOUND OF FOOTSTEPS APPROACHING I figured it must be Darius coming back to check on me. I tried to get myself under control, wiping my face with my sleeve and attempting to stop crying.

'Well, crap, Aphrodite, you were right. She does look majorly like shit,' Shaunee said.

I looked up to see the Twins descending on me with Aphrodite and Damien close behind them.

'Z, you have snot on your face,' Erin said to me, then she shook her head and told Shaunee, 'Sadly, I, too, must say Aphrodite was right.'

'Told you so,' Aphrodite said smugly.

'I do not think it's particularly appropriate to give accolades to Aphrodite for her being right that something is seriously wrong with Zoey.'

'Damien, I really wish,' Erin began.

'You'd stop with the damn Sylvan Learning Center vocab bullshit,' Shaunee finished for her.

'Would you two cease and desist, and perhaps get a dictionary?' Damien said primly.

I know it's weird, but their bickering sounded wonderful.

'You guys make a pathetic rescue squad,' Aphrodite said. 'Here.' She handed me a ball of (hopefully) clean Kleenex. 'I'm more nurturing than the three of you, and that's a damn shame.'

Damien huffed and moved the Twins out of the way so he could crouch beside me. I blew my nose and wiped my face before I looked at him.

'Something bad's happened, hasn't it?' he said.

I nodded.

'Well, shit. Is someone else dead?' Erin said.

'No.' My voice broke and I cleared my throat to try again. This time I sounded stuffy, but more like myself. 'No, no one's dead. It's nothing like that.'

'Go ahead and tell us,' Damien said, patting my shoulder lightly.

'Yeah, you know there's not much we can't handle together,' Shaunee said.

'Ditto, Twin,' Erin said.

'I may puke at the nerd herdishness of this,' Aphrodite said.

'Shut up!' the Twins said.

I looked at each of my friends. As much as I didn't want to, I had to tell them about Loren. I also had to tell them about Stevie Rae. And I had to do it before what Neferet said came true – before my lies and my secrets pissed them off so much that I lost them.

'It's messed up and complicated, and not very pretty,' I said.

'Oh, you mean like Aphrodite,' Erin said.

'No problem. We're getting used to that,' Shaunee said.

'Die Dorkamese Twins,' Aphrodite said.

'If you three would shut up, Zoey might be able to explain what's wrong,' Damien said with exaggerated patience.

'Sorry,' the Twins muttered.

Aphrodite just rolled her eyes.

I took a deep breath and opened my mouth to start the whole horrible story when Jack's perky voice interrupted me.

'Okay! I found him!'

Jack scampered up. His cute grin fading a little when he caught sight of me, proving that I really must look as bad as I felt. Then he hurried over to sit beside Damien, leaving Erik standing alone staring down at me.

'Go ahead, honey,' Damien said, patting my shoulder again. 'We're all here now. Tell us what's wrong.'

I couldn't speak. All I could do was stare at Erik. His face was a handsome, unreadable mask. Or at least it was unreadable until he started speaking, then his blank expression changed to disgust. His deep, expressive voice was a sneer.

'You want to tell them, *honey*, or should I?'

I wanted to say something. I wanted to yell at him to stop – to please forgive me – that he'd been right and I'd been so damn wrong that it was making me sick. But the only thing that came out of my mouth was a whispered no, so soft that I don't think Damien even heard me. Soon I realized it wouldn't have mattered if I'd shouted. Erik had come there to get back at me, and nothing was going to stop him.

'Fine. I'll tell them.' Erik looked at each of my friends. 'Our Z's been fucking Loren Blake.'

'What!' the Twins said together.

'Impossible,' Damien said.

'Nu-uh,' Jack sputtered.

Aphrodite didn't say anything.

'It's true. I saw them. Today. In the rec hall. You know, when all of you thought she was oh-so-upset because I'd Changed? Yeah, Zoey, I saw how *upset* you were. So upset you had to suck Blake's blood and ride him like a horse.'

'Loren Blake?' Shaunee said, sounding utterly stunned.

'Mr Luscious? The guy we've been talking about eating like he was a Dove chocolate bar all semester?' Mirroring her twin's tone, Erin gave me a shocked, horrified look. 'You must have thought we were completely pathetic.'

'Yeah, why didn't you say something?' Shaunee said.

''Cause if Zoey'd told you how *in love* they were, you might not have been cool with her using me and pretending like we were together so she could sneak around and be with Blake. And anyway, she probably liked laughing at you two,' Erik said cruelly.

'I wasn't using you.' I said to Erik, surprising myself with how strong my voice suddenly sounded. 'And I never laughed at you two, I promise,' I told the Twins.

'Yeah, and your word is something they can really trust,' Erik said. 'She's a lying slut. She used all of you just like she used me.'

'All right, time for you to shut up now,' Aphrodite said.

Erik laughed, 'Oh, that's perfect. One slut standing up for another.'

Aphrodite's eyes narrowed and she lifted her right hand. The branches of the oak closest to Erik's head swayed down toward him and I heard the warning sounding cracking of wood. 'You do not want to piss me off anymore,' she said. 'You claim to care so much for Zoey, but you've turned on her like a mangy-ass dog because she hurt your little ego. And I can verify for the masses that it is *little*. You did what you came here for, and now it's time for you to leave.'

Erik's brilliant blue eyes flicked back to me, and for a second I thought I saw the old Erik in them – the great guy who had been falling in love with me – but then the pain in his expression drowned out the last of his gentleness. 'Fine with me. I'm outta here,' he said before walking off.

I looked at Aphrodite. 'Thanks,' I said.

'No problem. I know what it's like to fuck up big time and have people hold it against you forever.'

'You've really been with Professor Blake?' Damien asked.
I nodded.

'Holy,' Shaunee said.

'Shit,' Erin said.

'He's really, really handsome,' Jack said.

I took another deep breath and blurted, 'Loren Blake is the biggest fucking asshole I've ever known.'

'Wow. You cussed,' Aphrodite said.

'So he was just using you for sex?' Damien said. He was back to patting my shoulder again.

'Not exactly.' I paused and wiped a hand across my face like I could make myself magically say the right thing. It was time to tell them about Stevie Rae. I wished I'd had a chance to practice what I was going to say. I glanced up to see Aphrodite watching me, and felt ridiculously glad she was there. At least she could back me up and maybe help Damien and the Twins understand.

Then a weird sound came from somewhere on the wall behind me. I wasn't sure I'd actually heard anything at all until Damien looked over my shoulder and said, 'What was that?'

'It's the trapdoor,' Aphrodite said. 'It's opening.'

A terrible premonition shivered down my spine. I was standing up, making Nala complain loudly and the Twins give me crinkled-forehead looks of confusion when Stevie Rae's voice came from the other side of the opening door.

'Zoey? It's me.'

I sprinted for the trapdoor, yelling, 'No, Stevie Rae! Stay on—'

And, frowning at me, Stevie Rae walked through the trap-door in the wall that surrounded the school. 'Zoey? I—' she started to say, then she noticed everyone who was standing behind me, and she froze.

On the ground beside me Nala yowled, and with a wickedly arched back she started to hurl herself at Stevie Rae, hissing and spitting like psycho cat. Thankfully, my fledgling reflexes allowed me to grab her before she got past me. 'Nala, no! It's just Stevie Rae,' I said, struggling with the freaked-out cat and trying not to get scratched or bit. Stevie Rae had lunged back and was crouching defensively in the shadow of the wall. All I could clearly see of her was the glowing red of her eyes.

'Stevie Rae?' Damien sounded strangled.

With a command to 'Be good, Nala!' I tossed my cat away so I could focus on my friends, but before I turned to face them I walked over to Stevie Rae. She didn't run away from me, but she definitely looked like she could bolt at any second. And she looked like crap, too. Her face was too thin and pale. She hadn't combed her curly blond hair and it looked matted and dull. Actually, the only thing shiny and healthy about her was her creepily glowing red eyes – and I already knew that wasn't a good sign.

'How are you?' I asked in a calm, quiet voice.

'Not good,' she said. Her eyes darted over my shoulder, and she cringed. 'It's hard to see them again, especially when I feel like I'm losing it.'

'You're not going to lose it,' I said firmly. 'Brace yourself. They don't know about you.'

'You didn't tell them?' Stevie Rae looked like I'd just slapped her.

'Long story,' I said quickly. 'Hey, why are you here?'

Her brow wrinkled. "Cause you texted me and told me to meet you here.'

I closed my eyes against a new wave of pain. Loren. He'd taken my phone. He'd text messaged Stevie Rae. Or more accurately, Neferet had probably done the actual texting. She hadn't known I'd be out here, but she had known – thanks to Loren – that I hadn't told my friends about Stevie Rae. She'd also known that Loren had no intention of making sure Erik didn't tell anyone about us. She knew he would freak and tell the world (or at least my friends) about Loren and me, and that secret would be out. Stevie Rae being discovered on campus would be yet another secret of mine discovered. I could almost hear my friends' thinking: *How can we ever trust Zoey again?* And feel them pulling farther and farther away from me.

Two points for Neferet. Zero points for Zoey.

I took Stevie Rae's unyielding hand, and even though I had to pull hard, I started walking with her back to where Damien, the Twins, Jack, and Aphrodite were standing – four of the five of them staring at Stevie Rae with their mouths open. Might as well get this over with before we were overrun with vamp warriors and the whole damn school found out everything and my life came crashing down around me.

'Stevie Rae isn't dead,' I told them.

'Yeah, I am,' Stevie Rae said.

I sighed. 'Stevie Rae. We are so not going to have this argument again. You're walking and talking. And you're solid flesh.' I held up our joined hands in demonstration. 'So you're not dead.'

Somewhere in the middle of my argument with Stevie Rae the sound of sobs registered. It was the Twins. They were still staring at Stevie Rae, but had clutched on to each other and were bawling like babies. I started to say something to them, but Damien interrupted me.

'How?' His face was stark white, completely drained of color. He took one hesitant step forward. 'How can this be?'

'I died,' Stevie Rae's voice was as pale and lifeless as Damien's face. 'Then I woke up like this, which, in case you can't already tell, isn't like I used to be.'

'You smell funny,' Jack said.

Stevie Rae turned her glowing eyes on him. 'And you smell like dinner.'

'Stop it!' I jerked on Stevie Rae's hand. 'They're your friends. You shouldn't be scaring them.'

She yanked her hand from my grip. 'That's what I've been trying to tell you all this time, Zoey. They're not my friends. You're not my friend. Not now. Not after what happened to me. I know you think you can fix this, but the only reason I came here tonight is to tell you that this has to end now. So, once and for all, either fix me, or leave me alone and let me finish becoming whatever bad thing it is I'm really supposed to be.'

'We don't have time for this. Neferet put a spell on the perimeter of the school to let her know when any human, vamp, or fledgling comes or goes from here. You crossed the perimeter, so any second the Sons of Erebus are going to show up. I think you should go. I'll come to you as soon as I can, and we can finish this then.'

'Hey, Zoey, I hate to contradict you, being as you're having a really shitty day, but I don't think the warriors are going to come because Neferet doesn't know Stevie Rae's here,' Aphrodite said.

'Huh?' I said.

'Aphrodite's right,' Damien said slowly, as if his brain was just then thawing out and starting to work again. 'Neferet bespelled the perimeter to tell her if it's breached by any human, fledgling, or vampyre. Stevie Rae isn't any of those things, so the spell wouldn't work on her.'

'Why is she here?' Stevie Rae said, glaring with hot red eyes at Aphrodite.

Aphrodite rolled her eyes, but I noticed she took several steps back so there was more space between Stevie Rae and her.

And then the Twins were suddenly standing in front of Stevie Rae. Shaunee and Erin were still crying, but quietly now, like they weren't even aware of it.

'You are alive,' Shaunee said.

'We missed you so much,' Erin said.

They threw their arms around Stevie Rae, who stood completely unmoving, like a statue of herself. Sometime in the middle of the hug Damien joined them. Stevie Rae didn't loosen up. She didn't put her arms around them. She closed her eyes and held perfectly still. I saw one blood-tinged tear spill from her eye and roll down her cheek.

CHAPTER TWENTY-SIX

'YOU HAVE TO LET ME GO, NOW.' STEVIE RAE'S VOICE WAS rough and strained and sounded totally unlike her. So it had the desired effect. Damien and the Twins instantly stopped hugging her.

'You do smell funny,' Shaunee said, trying to smile through her tears.

'Yeah, not to be mean or anything,' Erin said.

'But we don't care,' Damien added.

'Hey, nerd herd members who are still alive,' Aphrodite called from where she'd retreated to under the big oak tree. 'I suggest you step away from the undead dead kid. She bites.'

'You bite!' Shaunee snapped.

'Bitch!' Erin said.

'She's telling you the truth,' Stevie Rae said. Then she looked from Damien and the Twins to me. 'Explain it to them.'

'Stevie Rae has an issue with blood. She has to have it. Or she gets kinda cranky.'

Under the tree Aphrodite snorted.

'Tell them the truth,' Stevie Rae said.

I sighed in resignation and gave them the short version. 'She's just one of a bunch of fledglings who died and then came back like this. They're what killed those Union football players last month. And they almost killed Heath. Getting Heath away from them was how I found out about Stevie Rae. Only she *is* different than they are. She still has a hold on her humanity.'

'But it's slipping,' Aphrodite chimed in.

I frowned at her. 'Yeah, you could say that. So what we need to do is to heal Stevie Rae so she can be like she used to be.'

The Twins and Damien were quiet for what seemed like a long time. And then Damien said, 'You've known about this for a month and you haven't said anything to any of us?'

'You let us think that Stevie Rae was dead,' Shaunee said.

'You acted like you thought she was dead, too,' Erin said.

'Morons! She couldn't tell you. You have no idea what kind of forces are at work here,' Aphrodite said.

'You sound like a bad Sci-Fi Channel movie,' Shaunee said.

'Yeah, we're not buying, bitch,' Erin said.

'You've known about this for a month and you haven't said anything to any of us.' This time Damien didn't phrase it like a question.

'Aphrodite is right,' I said. 'I couldn't tell you about her. There were extenuating circumstances.' There still were. It was better for them not to know Neferet was behind the whole thing, even if it made them hate me.

'I don't care what Aphrodite said. We're your friends. Your best friends. You should have told us,' Damien said.

'Extenuating circumstances?' Erin said. 'Seems Aphrodite is suddenly a part of those circumstances.'

'Were there extenuating circumstances when you kept Loren a secret?' Shaunee said. Her voice was guarded. Her dark eyes narrowed at me warily.

I didn't know what to say. I could feel them slipping away from me, and the worst part of the whole thing was that I knew I deserved them to all turn their backs on me.

'How are we supposed to trust you if you keep things from us?' As usual, Damien summed up everyone's feelings in one simple sentence.

'I knew this was a bad idea,' Stevie Rae said. 'I'm outta here.'

'What? You got people to eat – places to terrorize?' Aphrodite said.

Stevie Rae spun around and snarled at her. 'Maybe I should start with you, hag.'

'Jeesh, relax. It was just a question.' Aphrodite tried to sound nonchalant, but I could see the fear in her eyes.

I grabbed Stevie Rae's hand again and held tight when she tried to pull away. Ignoring her, I looked from Damien to the Twins. 'Are you going to help me heal her or not?'

After only a little hesitation Damien said, 'I'll help you, but I don't trust you anymore.'

'Ditto,' said the Twins together.

My stomach had rolled back into a sick, tight little ball and I wanted to plop down right there in the grass and cry and beg them, *Don't stop being my friends – don't stop trusting me!* But I didn't. I couldn't. After all, they were right. Instead I nodded and said, 'Okay, let's cast a circle and get her healed.'

'We don't have any candles,' Damien said.

'I can run and get some,' Jack said. He didn't even look at me, but spoke directly to Damien.

'No. We don't have time for that,' I said. 'We don't need candles. We have the ability to manifest the elements. Candles are just ceremonial.' I paused and added, 'But I think you should probably go, Jack. I'm not sure what's all going to happen and I don't want to take a chance you might get hurt.'

'O-okay,' he stuttered. He put his hands in his pockets and walked slowly away.

'Looks like tonight we do away with ceremony,' Damien said, giving me a hard look.

'Yeah, tonight we do away with a lot of things.' Shaunee was watching me, but it felt like her eyes were those of a stranger. Erin nodded in silent but complete agreement with her.

I clamped my jaws shut to keep from screaming my pain and sorrow and fear. My friends were all I had. If I lost them, how would I survive? How would I stand against Neferet? How would I face Loren? How would I deal with the loss of Heath and Erik?

And then I remembered something I'd read in one of the old, musty books I'd been poring through when I was trying to find a magic bullet to help me heal Stevie Rae. A quote from one of the ancient vampyre Amazon High Priestesses had been written under her fierce, beautiful picture.

She'd said, *Being Chosen of our Goddess is as much pain as it is privilege.*

I was beginning to understand what that ancient priestess of Nyx had meant.

'Are we going to do this or not?' Aphrodite called from under the tree.

I pulled myself together. 'Yes, we are. North is that way.' I pointed to Aphrodite's tree. 'Take your places.' Still holding on to Stevie Rae's wrist, I walked to the center of the circle that was taking shape around me.

'If you don't let go of me, I can't go to the position of earth,' Stevie Rae said.

I stared into her red eyes, trying to see some trace of my best friend, but only another cold-eyed stranger looked out at me.

'You're not going to be earth. You're going to stay in the center with me,' I said.

'Then who's gonna complete the circle? Jack's gone, and anyway he's not exactly—' She broke off as her eyes went to the top position of the circle and she saw Aphrodite standing there. 'No!' Stevie Rae hissed. 'Not her!'

'Oh, stop it!' I shouted, causing the elements to stir the air around me in response to my anger and frustration. 'Aphrodite's standing in as earth. I'm sorry you don't like it. I'm sorry you don't like her. I'm sorry about a whole hell of a lot that I can't seem to do anything about. You're just going to have to deal with it, just like I'm dealing with it. Now stand here and be quiet and let's see if I can make this thing work.'

I knew everyone was staring at me. The Twins and Damien with the accusatory eyes of strangers, Stevie Rae with anger and what I knew was real hatred, whether it was just directed at Aphrodite, or at Aphrodite and me I wasn't sure. I took a quick glance at Aphrodite. She was standing in the northern position and watching Stevie Rae with wary eyes.

Great. Like this atmosphere was good for goddess worship?

I closed my eyes and took several deep, long breaths to center myself. *Nyx, I know I've messed up, but please be with me and my friends. Healing Stevie Rae is more important than the drama going on between us. Neferet wanted me separated from everyone so that I'd also separate myself from you. But I'm not going to stop depending on you . . . believing in you . . . ever.*

Then I opened my eyes and walked resolutely to Damien. He usually greeted me with a cute smile. Tonight he met my eyes steadily, but there was nothing sweet or friendly about him.

'As High Priestess in training for our Great Goddess Nyx, I use her power and authority to call to my circle the first element, wind!' I spoke with a strong, clear voice, raising my arms over my head when I said the element's name, and was unimaginably relieved when a powerful gust of air whirled around Damien and me, lifting our hair and making our clothes flap. I turned to my right and walked to Shaunee.

I didn't expect her to welcome me, and she didn't. She watched me silently with her dark, guarded eyes. I pushed back the despair her rejection made me feel and evoked fire.

'As High Priestess in training for our Great Goddess Nyx, I use her power and authority to call to my circle the second element, fire!'

I barely paused to feel the rush of heat that beat against my skin, but moved quickly to Erin, who was also silent and withdrawn.

'As High Priestess in training for our Great Goddess Nyx, I use her power and authority to call to my circle the third element, water!'

I turned my back on scents of the sea and walked over to Aphrodite. She met my gaze steadily and smiled grimly at me.

'It sucks to have your friends pissed at you, doesn't it?' She said it quietly, so that only I could hear her.

'Yeah,' I whispered back. 'And I'm sorry I had something to do with your friends getting pissed at you.'

'Nah,' she shook her head. 'It wasn't you. It was my stupid shitty choices. Just like it's your stupid shitty choices that got you into this mess.'

'Thanks for reminding me,' I said.

'I'm just here to help,' Aphrodite said. 'Better hurry this thing along. Scary Stevie Rae is losing it.'

I didn't have to look over my shoulder at Stevie Rae to know Aphrodite was right. I could feel Stevie Rae's restlessness increase. It was like she was a tightly wound rubber band that was getting ready to either break or zing out of control.

'As High Priestess in training for our Great Goddess Nyx, I use her power and authority to call to my circle the fourth element, earth!'

The clean, sweet scents of a spring meadow swirled around Aphrodite and me. I was still smiling when I turned to move back to the center of the circle and complete the casting by calling spirit when Stevie Rae broke.

'No!' The word was an almost unrecognizable snarl of rage and despair. 'She can't be earth! I'm earth! It's all that's left of me! I won't let her take it away!'

With blinding swiftness, Stevie Rae hurled herself on Aphrodite.

'No! Stevie Rae, stop it!' I cried, trying to pull Stevie Rae off her, but it was like trying to move a marble column. She was too strong. Aphrodite had been right. Stevie Rae wasn't human or fledgling or vampyre. She was something more – and that more meant more dangerous. She was holding Aphrodite in an ugly parody of an embrace. I saw the sharp glint of her fangs and then Aphrodite screamed as Stevie Rae buried her teeth into her neck.

'Help me get her off!' I yelled, looking desperately at Damien and the Twins as I kept trying to pull Stevie Rae from Aphrodite.

'I can't!' Damien cried. 'I can't move.'

'We can't either!' Shaunee said.

The three of them had been rooted into place by their elements. Damien was being pressed to the ground by a furious wind. Shaunee was surrounded by a cage of fire. Erin was suddenly encased in a pool of bottomless water.

'You have to finish the circle!' Damien yelled above the wind. 'Call all of the elements to help you. That's the only way you can save her.'

I ran to the center of the circle. Raising my arms over my head I completed the casting. 'As High Priestess in training for our Great Goddess Nyx, I use her power and authority to call to my circle the fifth and final element, spirit!'

Power surged through me. I gritted my teeth and tried to control the trembling within my body. Aphrodite's screams were getting weaker and weaker, but I couldn't think about that. I closed my eyes so that I could concentrate. Then I spoke the goddess-given words that drifted through my mind, like the sweet, sure answer to a child's prayer. My voice was magnified magically. I felt the words materialize, sparkling, in the air around me.

> *'Wind blow away that which is tainted*
> *Fire burn through the blackness of hatred*
> *Water wash clean evil intentions unsated*
> *Earth nourish her soul with darkness abated*
> *Spirit fill her so that from death she is emancipated!'*

Like I was throwing a ball, I hurled at Stevie Rae the sizzling elemental power that I felt between my hands. At that moment I felt a searingly familiar pain ripple from the base of my spine all the way around my waist. My scream echoed Stevie Rae's.

I opened my eyes to a bizarre sight. Aphrodite had fallen to the ground during Stevie Rae's attack. Stevie Rae's back was to me, so I could only see Aphrodite's face. At first I didn't understand what was happening. They were surrounded by a swirling, glowing ball of power made up of all five of the elements. The two girls kept fading in and out of focus as the power rolled and thickened around them. But I could see that Stevie Rae was no longer holding on to Aphrodite. Now it was Aphrodite who was clutching Stevie Rae and forcing her to keep drinking from the wound on her neck. Stevie Rae was still drinking her blood, but she was struggling to stop – trying to pull away.

I rushed forward to try to separate them again, but when I hit the bubble of power it was like walking into a glass door. I couldn't get through it, and I had no idea how to open it.

'Aphrodite! Let her go! She's trying to stop before she kills you!' I cried.

Aphrodite's eyes met mine. Her lips didn't move, but I heard her voice clearly inside my head. *No. This is how I make up for everything I caused. This time it's me who was Chosen. Remember, I made this sacrifice freely.*

Then Aphrodite's eyes rolled back in her head and her body went limp as the breath slipped from between her smiling

P. C. Cast and Kristin Cast

lips in a long sigh. With a terrible cry, Stevie Rae finally pulled away, collapsing on the ground beside Aphrodite's body. The bubble of power broke and then faded into nothingness. I knew the circle had been broken, too. I could feel the absence of the elements. I didn't know what to do. I didn't seem to be able to move.

Then Stevie Rae looked up at me. She was crying pink-tinged tears and her eyes were still a strange, reddish color. But her face was her own again. Even before she spoke I knew that whatever Neferet had broken in her when she'd caused her to become the walking, talking dead, had been healed.

'I killed her! I – I tried to stop! She wouldn't let me go, and I couldn't pull away! Oh, Zoey, I'm so sorry!' she sobbed.

I stumbled to her, Loren's words ringing in my head, *You should keep in mind that you're invoking powerful magic, and there's always a cost associated with that*. 'It wasn't your fault, Stevie Rae.' I told her. 'You didn't—'

'Her face!' Damien's voice came from just behind me. 'Look at her Mark.'

I blinked, not really understanding, and then I gasped. I'd been so busy looking into her eyes, so busy seeing the old Stevie Rae, that I hadn't noticed the obvious. The crescent moon that rested in the middle of her forehead had been filled in. A beautiful pattern of tattoos made of swirling flowers with long, graceful stems all twined together framed her eyes and stretched down her cheekbones.

But the tattoos weren't vampyre sapphire. They were the brilliant scarlet of new blood.

'What are y'all lookin' at?' Stevie Rae said.

'H-here,' Erin fumbled with her ever-present purse and pulled out a makeup mirror, handing it to Stevie Rae.

'Ohmygood*ness!*' Stevie Rae drawled. 'What does it mean?'

'It means you're healed. You've Changed. But what you've Changed into is a new kind of vampyre,' Aphrodite said, struggling to sit up.

CHAPTER TWENTY-SEVEN

'HOLY SHIT!' SHAUNEE SQUEAKED AND STUMBLED BACK, clutching onto Erin's arm to keep from falling over.

'You were dead!' Erin said.

'I don't think I was,' Aphrodite said, rubbing her forehead with one hand and gingerly touching the bite mark on her neck with the other. 'Ouch! Dammit, I hurt all over.'

'I'm really *really* sorry, Aphrodite,' Stevie Rae said. 'I mean, I don't like you, but I sure wouldn't bite you. Or at least not now I wouldn't.'

'Yeah, yeah, whatever,' Aphrodite said. 'Don't worry about it. It was all part of Nyx's plan, as painful and inconvenient as that might be.' She winced again at the pain in her neck. 'God, does anyone have a Band-Aid?'

'I have some tissue in here somewhere. Hang on and I'll see if I can find it,' Erin said, digging through her purse again.

'Try to find a clean one for her, Twin. Aphrodite has enough stress to deal with without a nasty infection.'

'Gee, that's so damn nice of you two,' Aphrodite said. She glanced up at the Twins with a half smile on her face, and I got my first good look at her.

My stomach dropped down somewhere around my ankles.

'It's gone!' I gasped.

'Oh shit! Zoey's right,' Damien said, staring at Aphrodite.

'What?' Aphrodite said. 'What's gone?'

'Ah-oh,' Shaunee said.

'Yep, it is gone,' Erin said as she handed Aphrodite some tissue.

'What in the hell are you guys babbling about now?' Aphrodite said.

'Here. Use this.' Stevie Rae passed the mirror to her. 'Look at your face.'

Aphrodite sighed, clearly irritated. 'Okay, I know I look like complete shit. Hello! Stevie Rae just bit me. Here's a news flash: Not even I can look perfect all the time, especially when—' As soon as she focused on the mirror and got a look at the reflection of her face, Aphrodite's words ended like someone had pushed her STOP TALKING button. With a trembling hand she reached up to touch the spot in the middle of her forehead where Nyx's Mark had been.

'It's gone.' Her voice was a hoarse whisper. 'How can it be gone?'

'I've never, ever heard of anything like this happening. Not in any book – not anywhere,' Damien said. 'Once you're Marked you can't just get un-Marked.'

'It's how Stevie Rae was healed.' Aphrodite sounded dazed, and she kept touching the empty spot in the middle of her forehead. 'Nyx took it from me and gave it to Stevie Rae.' A horrible shudder passed through Aphrodite's body. 'And now I'm nothing but a human again.' She scrambled to her feet, dropping the mirror. 'I have to leave. I don't belong here anymore.' She started backing woodenly toward the open trap-door, eyes wide and glassy.

'Wait, Aphrodite,' I said, starting after her. 'Maybe you're not human again. Maybe this is something weird that will go away in a day or two, and your Mark will come back.'

'No! My Mark is gone. I know it. Just – just leave me alone!' She ran through the door sobbing.

The instant Aphrodite passed through the perimeter of the school wall the air rippled and there was a distinctive cracking noise like something big had been dropped and broken.

Stevie Rae grabbed my arm. 'You stay here. I'll go after her.'

'But you—'

'No, I'm okay now.' Stevie Rae smiled her sweet, full-of-life smile at me. 'You fixed me, Z. Don't worry. I caused this to happen to Aphrodite. I'll find her and make sure she's okay. Then I'll get back to you.'

I heard noises in the distance, like something big was moving quickly our way.

'It's the warriors. They know the school's been breached.' Damien said.

'Go!' I told Stevie Rae. 'I'll call you.' Then I added. 'I *won't* text message you. Ever. So if you get a text message it will *not* be from me.'

'Okey-dokey-smokey, I'll remember,' Stevie Rae said and then grinned at the four of us. 'See ya'll soon!' She ducked through the door, closing it after her. I noticed that the perimeter warning didn't so much as ripple when she passed and wondered briefly what the hell that meant.

'So what are we doing out here?' Damien asked.

'We're here because Erik dumped Zoey,' Shaunee said.

'Yeah, she's upset,' Erin said.

'Don't tell them about Aphrodite or Stevie Rae,' I said.

My friends looked at me like I'd just said *maybe we shouldn't tell our parents about that little beer-drinking episode.*

'No shit?' Shaunee said sarcastically.

'We were just gonna spill our guts,' Erin said.

'Yeah, because we can't be trusted to keep secrets,' Damien said.

Well, crap. They were definitely still mad at me.

'So who do we say broke the barrier?' Damien asked. I noticed he didn't even look at me, but addressed the question only to the Twins.

'Aphrodite, who else?' Erin said.

Before I could protest, Shaunee added, 'Yeah, we won't say

anything about the disappearing act her Mark played. We'll just say she came out here with us and got annoyed at all of Zoey's blubbering.'

'And self-pity,' Erin added.

'And lies. So she took off. As per typical for Aphrodite,' Damien finished.

'She might get in trouble,' I said.

'Yeah, well, consequence is a bitch,' Shaunee said.

'A bitch who is clearly following some people pretty closely,' Erin said, giving me a sharp look.

Just then several warriors, led by Darius, burst into our clearing. With their weapons drawn they looked scary as hell and ready to kick some serious butt (potentially ours).

'Who broke the perimeter?' Darius practically barked the question.

'Aphrodite!' The four of us said together.

Darius made a quick gesture at two of the warriors. 'Find her,' he said. Then back to us, 'The High Priestess has called an assembly of the school. You are needed in the auditorium. I will escort you there.'

Meekly, we followed Darius. I tried to catch Damien's eye, but he wouldn't look at me. Neither would the Twins. It was like I was walking with strangers. Worse, actually. Strangers might at least smile and say hi. There was definitely no smiling or hi-ing going on with my friends.

We'd only gone just a couple of steps when the first of the pains hit me. It was like someone was driving an invisible knife into my stomach. I was sure I was going to be sick, and I doubled over, groaning.

'Zoey? What's wrong?' Damien said.

'I don't know. I—' I stopped being able to speak, and at the same time everything around me got ultrafocused. The pain in my stomach seemed to mushroom, and I knew the warriors were surrounding me, even as I reached out and grabbed hold of Damien's hand. Even though I knew he was still pissed, he hung on tight to me, and I could hear him telling me that everything was going to be okay.

Pain speared from my stomach to my heart. Was I dying? I wasn't coughing up blood. Could I be having a heart attack? It was like I had been thrust into someone else's nightmare where I was being tortured by invisible knives and unseen hands.

The searing pain that suddenly spiked through my neck was too much, and everything started to go black around the edges of my vision. I knew I was falling, but the pain was unbearable. There was nothing I could do . . . I was dying . . .

Strong hands caught and lifted me, and I was vaguely aware that Darius was carrying me.

Then there was a terrible wrenching inside me. I screamed over and over again. It felt like my heart was being ripped from my living body. Just when I knew I couldn't stand any more, it stopped. As abruptly as the pain had started, it went away, leaving me panting and sweating, but perfectly fine.

'Wait. Stop. I'm okay,' I said.

'My lady, you have been in terrible pain and you must be taken to the infirmary,' Darius said.

'Okay. No.' I was glad to hear my voice was completely back to normal. I thumped on Darius's overmuscled shoulder. 'Put me down. I mean it. I'm fine.'

Reluctantly, Darius stopped and put me gently on my feet. I felt like a science experiment as the Twins, Damien, and the other warriors all gawked at me.

'I am fine,' I said sternly. 'I don't know what happened, but it's over now. Really.'

'You should go to the infirmary. After the High Priestess is finished with her speech she will be there to check you out,' Darius said.

'No. Absolutely not,' I said. 'She's busy. She doesn't need to worry about a weird cramp or whatever that made my . . . uh . . . stomach hurt.'

Darius didn't look convinced.

I lifted my chin and swallowed every last bit of my pride. 'I have gas. A lot of it. Ask my friends.'

Darius turned to the Twins and Damien.

'Yep, she's one gassy girl,' Shaunee said.

'Miss Smelly, that's what we call her,' Erin said.

'She really is extraordinarily flatulent,' Damien added.

Okay, I realized that the troops hadn't rallied around me because all was forgiven and we were best buds again. They had simply grabbed an excellent opportunity to embarrass me.

God, I had a terrible headache.

'Gas, my lady?' Darius said, his lips twitching.

I shrugged and had no trouble at all blushing. 'Gas,'

I confirmed. 'Can we just go to the auditorium? I'm feeling much better.'

'As you wish, my lady.' Darius saluted me.

We all changed direction and started to the auditorium again.

'What was that all about?' Damien whispered, coming up beside me.

'I have no clue,' I whispered back.

'No clue,' Shaunee said quietly.

'Or you know but won't tell us,' Erin murmured.

I couldn't say anything. I just shook my head sadly. I'd caused this. Yeah, I'd had good reasons, at least for some of it. But the truth was that I'd been lying to my friends for way too long.

Like Shaunee had said, consequence was a bitch, and like Erin had observed, she was definitely following me around. No one spoke to me the rest of the way to the auditorium. As we walked through the front door, Jack joined us. He wouldn't even look at me. We all sat together, but no one talked to me. No one at all. The Twins chattered with each other as usual, clearly scoping the room for T. J. and Cole, who actually saw them first and rushed over to sit beside them. The flirting that ensued was almost gross enough to make me swear off dating forever. As if I had a choice.

I had been lagging behind everyone, so I was sitting in the last seat in the rear row. Damien was in front of me with the rest of the gang. I could hear him whispering to Jack and catching him up on what had happened with Aphrodite and Stevie Rae. Neither of them said anything to me, or even turned around to look at me.

Everyone was getting really restless, and it seemed like we'd been waiting forever. I wondered what the hell Neferet was up to. I mean, she'd called this big meeting. Practically the whole darn school was there even though I felt incredibly, miserably alone. I looked around to see if Erik was glaring at me from somewhere in the room, but I didn't see him anywhere. I did see poor little Ian Bowser, who was sitting in the front row, red-eyed and looking like he'd just lost his best friend. I definitely knew how he felt.

Finally there was a murmur in the crowd and Neferet entered the auditorium. She was followed by several of the senior professors, including Dragon Lankford and Lenobia; ringed by Sons of Erebus she made her way regally to the stage. Everyone got all silent and attentive.

She didn't waste time, but got right to the point. 'We have long lived in peace with humans, though they have insulted and ostracized us for decades. They envy our talent and our beauty – our wealth and our power. And their envy has been steadily growing into hatred. Now that hatred has shifted to violence perpetrated against us by people who call themselves *religious* and *righteous*.' Her laughter was cold and beautiful. 'What an abomination.'

I had to admit that she was incredibly good. She had the crowd mesmerized. Had she not been a High Priestess she could have definitely been one of the lead actresses of the age.

'It is true that there are many more humans than vampyres,

and because of our smaller numbers they underestimate us. But I promise you this: If they murder just one more of our sisters or brothers, I will declare a state of war against them.' She had to wait until the warriors' cheers quieted before she could continue, but she didn't seem to mind. 'It will not be an outright war, but it will be deadly and—'

The doors to the auditorium were flung open as Darius and two other warriors rushed into the room, interrupting Neferet. With the rest of us, she silently watched the grim-faced vampyre men approach her. I thought Darius looked weird. Not pale, but plastic. Like his face had turned into a living mask.

Neferet stepped away from the microphone and leaned down so that he could whisper to her the news. When he was finished she stood up very straight, almost as if she was holding herself so rigid because she was in terrible pain. Then she swayed and clutched her throat with one hand. Dragon stepped up beside her to steady her, but the priestess shook off his help. Slowly she returned to the microphone and in a voice like death she said, 'The body of Loren Blake, our beloved Vampyre Poet Laureate, has just been found nailed to our front gate.'

I could feel Damien and the Twins staring at me. I pressed my hand against my mouth to stifle my sob of horror, just like I had done when I saw Loren and Neferet together.

'That was what happened to you,' Damien whispered, his face gone almost gray it was so pale. 'You'd Imprinted with him, hadn't you?'

I could only nod. All of my attention was focused on Neferet, who had continued speaking. 'Loren was disemboweled and then decapitated. As with Professor Nolan, they nailed a foul scripture to his body. This one was from their book of Ezekiel. It said, *Take away all the detestable things thereof and all the abominations thereof from thence. REPENT.*' She paused and bowed her head, looking like she was praying as she collected herself. Then she straightened, lifting her face, and her anger was so bright and glorious that it made even my heartbeat quicken.

'As I was saying when this tragic news reached us, it will not be an outright war, but it will be deadly and we will be victorious. Perhaps it is time that vampyres take their proper place in this world, and that proper place is not being subjugated by humans!'

I knew I was going to be sick, so I ran from the auditorium, glad that my seat was at the end of the back row. I knew my friends wouldn't follow me. They would still be inside, cheering with everyone else. And I would be outside, having my guts turned inside out because I knew at a soul-deep level that war with humans was wrong. This was not Nyx's will.

I gasped, drawing deep breaths and trying to stop shaking. Okay, I might know war was not our Goddess's will, but what was I going to do about it? I was just a kid – and my recent actions proved I wasn't a very smart kid. Nyx was probably mad at me, too. She should be.

And then I remembered the familiar pain that had seared

around my waist. I glanced around, making sure I was alone, then I lifted the hem of my dress so that I could see my skin. They were there! My beautiful filigreed Mark had appeared around my waist. I closed my eyes. *Oh thank you, Nyx! Thank you for not leaving me!*

I leaned against the wall of the auditorium and cried. I cried for Aphrodite and Heath, Erik and Stevie Rae. I cried for Loren. Mostly I cried for Loren. His death had shaken me. My mind knew that he hadn't loved me. That he'd used me because Neferet had wanted him to get to me, but that didn't seem to matter to my soul. I'd felt the loss of him like he'd been ripped from my heart. I knew there was something wrong about his death, and the wrongness was more than his being murdered by religious freaks. And those freaks could be related to me. My stepfather could have caused Loren's death.

His death . . . Loren's death . . .

It hit me again. I don't know how long I leaned against the wall of the auditorium and cried and shook. I just knew that I was mourning the death of the girl I used to be as much as Loren.

'It's your fault.'

Neferet's voice sliced through me. I looked up, wiping my face with my sleeve, to see her standing there, red-eyed but tearless.

She made me sick.

'They'll all think you're not crying because you're brave and strong,' I said. 'But I know you're not crying because you don't have a heart. You're not capable of caring enough to cry.'

'You're wrong. I loved him, and he adored me in return. But you already know that, don't you? You watched us like the little sneak you are,' she said. Neferet glanced quickly over her shoulder at the doors and raised her index finger up, as if saying she needed a minute. I could see the warrior who had been about to come out to her stop and turn his back against the doors; obviously his job was to keep anyone from interrupting us. Then Neferet turned back to me. 'Loren's dead because of you. He could feel how upset you were, and when the perimeter was breached he assumed it was you running away from the little scene I orchestrated between you and *poor, shocked Erik.*' She said it with a sarcastic sneer. 'Loren went out to find you. And because he was looking for you, Loren was killed.'

I shook my head, letting my anger and disgust drown out my pain and fear. 'You caused all of this. You know it. I know it. And, more importantly, Nyx knows it.'

Neferet laughed. 'You've used the Goddess's name before to threaten me, yet here I am, a powerful High Priestess, and here you are, a silly, stupid fledgling who has been abandoned by her friends.'

I swallowed hard. She was right. She was all that, and I was nothing. I'd made stupid choices, and because of that I'd broken the trust of my friends. And she was still, well, in charge. I knew in my heart Neferet was hiding evil and hatred, but even I couldn't look at her and see it. She was bright and beautiful and powerful. She looked like the perfect picture of a High Priestess and someone Chosen by a goddess. How did I think I could ever stand up to her?

Then I felt the nudging of the wind, the heat of a summer's day, the sweet coolness of the seashore, the wild vastness of the earth, and the strength of my spirit. The new evidence of Nyx's favor tingled around my waist as the Goddess's words whispered from my memory: *Remember, darkness does not always equate to evil, just as light does not always bring good.*

I straightened my spine. Focusing on the five elements, I raised my hands, palms out, and without touching Neferet, I shoved. The High Priestess was thrown backward, stumbled, lost her footing, and fell smack on her butt. As several warriors burst out of the auditorium to help her to her feet, I bent, pretending like I was making sure she was okay, and whispered, 'You might want to reconsider pissing me off, old woman.'

'This isn't over between us,' she hissed.

'For once I totally agree with you,' I said.

Then I backed away from her and let the warriors and the rest of the fledglings and vamps who were swarming out of the auditorium mill around her. I could hear her reassuring them that she'd just broken a heel and tripped – that everything was okay – and then the crowd blanketed the sight and sound.

I didn't wait for the Twins and Damien to come out and ignore me. I turned my back on all of them and headed toward my dorm. I was brought up short when Erik stepped out of the shadows at the edge of the auditorium. His eyes were wide with shock, and he looked shaken and pale. Clearly, he had witnessed the entire scene between Neferet and me. I lifted my chin and met his familiar blue eyes.

'Yeah, there's more going on here than you assumed,' I said.

He shook his head, but more like in surprise than in disbelief. 'Neferet . . . she's – she's . . .' He stuttered, glancing over my shoulder at the mob that still surrounded the High Priestess.

'She's an evil bitch? Are those the words you're searching for? Yeah, she is.' It felt good to say it. It felt especially good to say it to Erik. I wanted to explain more to him, but his next words stopped me.

'This doesn't change what you did.'

I suddenly felt nothing but very, very tired. 'I know that, Erik.' Without another word I walked away from him.

Predawn was lighting the sky, giving the darkness the pastel tint of misty morning. I breathed deeply, taking in the coolness of the new day. The confrontations with Neferet and Erik had left me weirdly peaceful and my thoughts easily organized themselves into two neat little columns.

On the positive side: One, my best friend was no longer an undead dead blood-crazed monster. Of course, I wasn't really sure what she was, or, for that matter, where she was. Two, I no longer had three boyfriends to juggle. Three, I wasn't Imprinted with anyone, which was also a good thing. Four, Aphrodite wasn't dead. Five, I'd told my friends a whole bunch of stuff I'd wanted to tell them for a long time. Six, I wasn't a virgin anymore.

On the negative side: One, I wasn't a virgin anymore. Two, I no longer had a boyfriend. Not one. Three, I may have somehow caused the Vampyre Poet Laureate's death, and if I hadn't caused it someone in my family might have. Four, Aphrodite was a human, and clearly totally freaking out. Five, Most of my friends were pissed at me and didn't trust me. Six, I wasn't done lying to them because I still couldn't let them know the truth about Neferet. Seven, I was smack in the middle of a war between vampyres (which I was not one of yet) and humans (which I was no longer one of). And, for the grand prize winner: Eight, The most powerful vamp High Priestess of our time was my sworn enemy.

'Mee-uf-ow!' Nala's grumpy voice gave me enough warning to open my arms just before she launched herself at me.

I cuddled her. 'Some day you're gonna jump too soon and fall right on your butt.' I smiled, remembering. 'Kinda like Neferet fell right on her butt.'

Nala turned her purr button on and rubbed her face against my cheek.

'Well, Nala, seems I'm in the middle of some deep poo. The negatives in my life totally outweigh the positives, and you know what's weird? I'm starting to actually get used to it.' Nala kept up her purr machine, and I kissed her on the little white splotch over her nose. 'Hard stuff is coming, but I honestly believe Nyx has Chosen me, which means she'll be with me.' Nala made a huffy-old-lady cat noise, and I hastily

321

corrected myself. 'I mean *us*. Nyx will be with us.' I shifted Nala in my arms so I could open the door to the dorm. 'Of course, Nyx choosing me kinda makes me question her decision-making skills,' I mumbled, only half kidding.

Believe in yourself, Daughter, and get ready for what is to come.

I yelped as the Goddess's voice floated through my mind. Great. *Get ready for what is to come* did not sound good. I looked at Nala and sighed.

'Remember when we thought me having a sucky birthday was our biggest problem?'

Nala sneezed directly in my face, making me laugh while I said 'eew' and hurried into my room, going for the box of Kleenex I kept on my bedside table.

As usual, Nala summed up my life perfectly: kinda funny, kinda gross, and more than kinda messy.

About the Authors

P. C. Cast is an award-winning fantasy and paranormal romance author, who is heavily influenced by her long-standing love of mythology. She was a teacher for many years but now concentrates on writing and public speaking full time. Her daughter, **Kristin Cast**, attends college in Oklahoma and has won awards for her poetry and journalism as well as co-writing the *Sunday Times* and *New York Times* bestselling House of Night series.

For more information on the series visit www.pccast.net and www.houseofnightseries.co.uk

The story continues in

Untamed

Book Four of the
HOUSE OF NIGHT

P. C. Cast and Kristin Cast

Turn the page for an exciting preview ...

CHAPTER ONE

THE *CAW! CAW! CAWING!* OF ONE STUPID CROW KEPT ME UP all night. (Well, more accurately, all day – 'cause, you know, I'm a vampyre fledgling and we have that whole issue of day and night being turned around.) Anyway, I got zero sleep last night/day. But my crappy nonsleep is currently the easiest thing to deal with since life *really* sucks when your friends are pissed at you. I should know. I'm Zoey Redbird, currently the undisputed Queen of Making My Friends Pissed Land.

Persephone, the big sorrel mare who I could consider mine for as long as I lived at the House of Night, craned her head around and nuzzled my cheek. I kissed her soft muzzle and went back to brushing her sleek neck. Grooming Persephone always helped me think and made me feel better. And I definitely needed help with both of those things.

'Okay, so, I've managed to avoid the Big Confrontation for two days, but that can't continue,' I told the mare. 'Yes, I know they're in the cafeteria right now, eating dinner while they hang out together being all buddy-buddy and totally leaving me out.'

Persephone snorted and went back to munching hay.

'Yeah, I think they're being jerks, too. Sure, I did lie to them, but it was mostly by omission. And, yeah, I kept some stuff from them. Mostly for their own good.' I sighed. Well, the stuff about Stevie Rae being undead was for their own good. The stuff about me having a thing with Loren Blake – Vampyre Poet Laureate and professor at the House of Night – well, that was more for my own good. 'But still.' Persephone flicked an ear back to listen to me. 'They're being really judgmental.'

Persephone snorted again. I sighed again. Crap. I couldn't avoid them any longer.

After giving the sweet mare one last pat, I walked slowly out of her stall to the tack room and put up the array of currycombs and mane/tail brushes I'd been using on her for the past hour. I breathed deeply of the leather and horse smell, letting the soothing mixture ease my nerves. Catching my reflection in the smooth glass window of the tack room, I automatically ran my fingers through my dark hair, trying to make it look not so bedheady. I'd been Marked as a fledgling vampyre and moved to the House of Night just over two months ago, but already my hair was noticeably thicker and longer. And supergood hair was only one of the many changes taking place with me. Some of them were invisible – like the fact that I had an affinity for all five of the elements. Some of them were very much visible – like the unique tattoos that framed my face in intricate, exotic swirls and then, unlike any other fledgling or adult vampyre, the sapphire design spread down my neck and shoulders, along my spine, and most recently, had moved around my waist, a little fact no one but my cat, Nala, our goddess Nyx, and I knew.

Like who could I show?

'Well, yesterday you had not one, but three boyfriends,' I told the me with the dark eyes and cynical half smile that was reflected in the glass. 'But you fixed that, didn't you? Today not only do you have zero boyfriends, but no one will ever trust you again for at least, I dunno, a gazillion years or so.' Well, except Aphrodite, who totally freaked and took off two days ago because she might have suddenly been turned back into a human, and Stevie Rae, who was chasing said freaked re-humaned Aphrodite because she might have caused the fledgling-to-human issue when I cast a circle and turned her from creepy undead dead kid to odd-red-tattooed-vampyre-but-herself-again kid. 'Either way,' I told myself aloud, 'you have managed to mess up just about everyone who has touched your life. Well done, you!'

My lip had actually started to quiver and I felt the sting of tears in my eyes. No. Bawling my eyes red wouldn't do any good. I mean, seriously, if it did, then my friends and I would have kissed (well, not literally) and made up days ago. I was just going to have to face them and start trying to make things right.

The late December night was cool and a little misty. The gaslights lining the sidewalk that stretched from the stable and field-house area of the school to the main building flickered with little haloes of yellow light, looking beautiful and old-worldly. Actually, the whole campus of the House of Night was gorgeous, and always made me think of something that belonged in an Arthurian legend more than in the twenty-first century. *I love it here*, I reminded myself. *It's home. It's where I belong. I'll make it right with my friends, and everything will be okay then.*

I was chewing my lip and worrying about just exactly how I was going to make it right with my friends when my mental stressing was interrupted by a weird flapping noise that filled the air around me. Something about the sound sent a chill down my spine. I looked up. There was nothing above me but darkness and sky and the winter-bare limbs of the huge oaks that lined the sidewalk. I shivered, having a walking-over-my-grave moment as the night went from soft and misty to dark and malevolent.

Hang on – dark and malevolent? Well, that's just silly! What I had heard was probably nothing more sinister than the wind rustling through the trees. Jeesh, I was losing it.

Shaking my head at myself, I kept walking but had taken only a couple of steps when it happened again. The weird flapping above me actually caused the air, which seemed ten degrees colder, to flutter wildly against my skin. I automatically flailed a hand up, imagining bats and spiders and all sorts of creepy things.

My fingers passed through nothingness, but it was frigid nothingness, and an icy pain sliced through my hand. Completely freaked out, I yelped and hugged my hand to my chest. For a moment I didn't know what to do, and my body was numb with fear. The flapping was getting louder and the cold more intense when I finally managed to move. Ducking my head, I did the only thing I could think to do. I ran for the nearest door to the school.

After slipping inside, I slammed the thick wooden door behind me and, panting for breath, turned to peer through the little arched window in the center of it. The night shifted and swam before my eyes, like black paint poured down a dark page. Still, the terrible feeling of icy fear lingered within me. What was going on? Almost without realizing what I was doing, I whispered, 'Fire, come to me. I need your warmth.'

Instantly the element responded, filling the air around me with the soothing heat of a hearth fire. Still staring out the little window, I pressed my palms against the rough wood of the door. 'Out there,' I murmured. 'Send your heat out there, too.' With a whoosh of warmth, the element moved from me, through the door, and poured into the night. There was a hissing sound, like steam rising from dry ice. The mist roiled, thick and soupy, giving me a sense of dizzy vertigo that made me a little nauseated, and the strange darkness began to evaporate. Then the heat completely beat away the chill, and as suddenly as it had begun, the night was once again quiet and familiar.

What had just happened?

My stinging hand drew my attention from the window. I looked down. Across the back of my hand there were red welts, as though something with claws, or talons, had scraped across my flesh. I rubbed at the angry-looking marks, which stung like a curling-iron burn.

Then the feeling hit me strong, hard, overwhelming – and I knew with my Goddess-given sixth sense that I shouldn't be here by myself. The coldness that had tainted the night – the ghostly something that had chased me inside and welted my hand – filled me with a terrible foreboding and for the first time in a long time, I was truly and utterly afraid. Not for my friends. Not for my grandma or my human ex-boyfriend, or even for my estranged mom. I was afraid for myself. I didn't just *want* the company of my friends; I needed them.

Still rubbing my hand, I made my legs move and knew beyond any doubt that I would rather face the hurt and disappointment of my friends than whatever dark thing might be waiting for me in the concealing night.

I hovered for a second just outside the open doors to the busy 'dining hall' (a.k.a. school cafeteria), watching the other kids talk easily and happily together, and I was almost overwhelmed with the sudden wish that I could be just another fledging – that I didn't have any extraordinary abilities or the responsibilities that went along with those abilities. For a second I wanted to be normal so bad that it was hard for me to breathe.

Then I felt the soft brush of wind against my skin that seemed warmed by the heat of an invisible flame. I caught a whiff of the ocean, even though there is definitely no ocean near Tulsa, Oklahoma. I heard birdsong and smelled new-cut grass. And my spirit quivered with silent joy within me as it acknowledged my powerful Goddess-given gifts of an affinity for each of the five elements: air, fire, water, earth, and spirit.

I wasn't normal. I wasn't like anyone else, fledgling or vampyre, and it was wrong of me to wish otherwise. And part of my not-normal-ness was telling me that I had to go in there and try to make peace with my friends. I straightened my spine and looked around the room with eyes that were clear of self-pity, and easily found my special group sitting at our booth.

I drew a deep breath and then made my way quickly across the cafeteria, giving a little nod or small smile to the kids who said hi to me. I noticed that everyone seemed to be reacting to me with their usual mix of respect and awe, which meant that my friends hadn't been talking crap about me to the masses. It also meant that Neferet hadn't launched an all-out, open attack against me. Yet.

I grabbed a quick salad and a brown pop. Then, holding

on to my tray with such abnormal tightness that it was turning my fingers white, I marched straight to our booth and took my usual seat beside Damien.

When I sat down, no one looked at me, but their easy chatter instantly died, which is something I totally hate. I mean, what's more awful than walking up to a group of your supposed-to-be friends and having them all shut up so that you knew for sure they were all talking about you? Ugh.

'Hi,' I said instead of running away or bursting into tears like I wanted to.

No one said anything.

'So, what's up?' I directed the question at Damien, knowing that my gay friend was naturally the weakest link in the don't-talk-to-Zoey chain.

Sadly, it was the Twins who answered me and not gay, and therefore more sensitive and polite, Damien.

'Not shit, right, Twin?' said Shaunee.

'That's right, Twin, not shit. 'Cause we can't be trusted to know shit,' Erin said. 'Twin, did you know we're totally untrustworthy?'

'Not until recently I didn't, Twin. You?' Shaunee said.

'Didn't know till recently either,' Erin finished.

Okay, the Twins aren't really twins. Shaunee Cole is a caramel-colored Jamaican-American who grew up on the East Coast. Erin Bates is a gorgeous blonde who was born in Tulsa. The two met after being Marked and moving to the House of Night on the same day. They clicked instantly – it's like genetics and geography never existed. They literally finish each other's sentences. And at that moment they were glaring at me with twin looks of angry suspicion.

God, they made me tired.

They also made me mad. Yes, I'd kept secrets from them. Yes, I'd lied to them. But I'd had to. Well, mostly I'd had to. And their twin holier-than-thou crap was getting on my last nerve.

'Thank you for that lovely commentary. And now I'll try asking someone who doesn't have to answer in a stereo version of hateful *Gossip Girl* Blair.' I turned my attention away from them and looked directly at Damien, even though I could hear the Twins sucking air and getting ready to say something I was hoping they would one day regret. 'So, I guess what I really wanted to ask when I said 'what's up' is if you've noticed any scary, ghost-like, flappy weirdness outside lately. Have you?'

Damien's a tall, really cute guy with excellent bone structure whose brown eyes were usually warm and expressive but were, at this moment, wary and more than a little cold. 'A flappy ghost thing?' he said. 'Sorry, I have no clue what you're talking about.'

My heart squeezed at the stranger-like tone of his voice, but I told myself that at least he'd answered my question. 'On the way here from the stables, something kinda attacked me. I couldn't really see anything, but it was cold and it put a big welt on my hand.' I lifted my hand to show him – and there was no welt there anymore.

Great.

Shaunee and Erin snorted together. Damien just looked really, really sad. I was opening my mouth to explain that there had been a welt there just a few minutes ago, when Jack rushed up.

'Oh, hi! I'm so sorry I'm late but when I put on my shirt I found a ginormic stain right on the front of it. Can you believe that?' Jack said as he hurried up with his tray of food and sat at his place beside Damien.

'A stain? It's not on that lovely blue long-sleeved Armani I got you for Christmas, is it?' Damien said, scooting over to make room for his boyfriend.

'Ohmigod, no! I'd never spill anything on that one. I just love it and—' His words came to a staggering halt when his eyes flitted from Damien to me. He gulped. 'Oh, uh. Hi, Zoey.'

'Hi, Jack,' I said, smiling at him. Jack and Damien are together. Hello. They're gay. My friends and I, along with anyone who's not narrow-minded and utterly judgmental, are cool with that.

'I didn't expect to see you,' Jack babbled. 'I thought you were still . . . uh . . . well . . .' He trailed off, looking uncomfortable and blushing a pretty pink.

'You thought I was still hiding in my room?' I supplied for him.

He nodded.

'No.' I said firmly, 'I'm done doing that.'

'Well, la-te-da,' Erin began, but before Shaunee could do her usual chime-in act, a blatantly sexy laugh coming from the door behind us made everyone turn and gawk.

Aphrodite twitched into the room, laughing while she batted her eyes at Darius, one of the youngest and hottest of the Sons of Erebus Warriors who protected the House of Night, and did an excellent hair flip. The girl always had been good at multitasking, but I was totally shocked at how nonchalant and utterly cool and collected she looked. Only two days ago she'd been almost dead and then utterly freaked because the sapphire-colored outline of a crescent moon – which appeared on all fledglings' foreheads, Marking them as having begun the Change that would either end in becoming a vampyre or in becoming dead – had disappeared from her face.

Which meant she had somehow turned back into a human.

CHAPTER TWO

OKAY, I'D THOUGHT SHE'D TURNED BACK INTO A HUMAN, but even from where I was sitting I could see that Aphrodite's Mark had returned. Her cold blue eyes swept the cafeteria as she gave the watching kids a stuck-up sneer before turning her attention back to Darius and letting her hand linger on the big warrior's chest.

'It was ever so sweet of you to walk me to the dining hall. You're right. It shouldn't have taken two days to cut my vacation short. With all the craziness going on around here, it's best to stay on campus where we can be protected. And since you say you'll be stationed at the door of our dorm, that is definitely the most safe *and* attractive place to be.' She practically purred at him. Jeesh, she was stank. Had I not been so surprised to see her, I would have made appropriate gagging noises. Loud, obvious ones.

'And I must return to my posting there. Good night, my lady,' Darius said. He gave her a very sharp bow, which made him look like one of those romantic, handsome knights, minus the horse and the shining armor, from back in the day. 'It is a pleasure to serve you.' He smiled at Aphrodite one more time before turning neatly on his heel and leaving the cafeteria.

'And I'll just bet it would be a pleasure to service *you*,' Aphrodite said in her nastiest voice as soon as he was out of earshot. Then she turned around to face the gawking, silent room. She lifted one perfectly waxed brow and gave everyone her patented Aphrodite sneer. 'What? You look like you've never seen gorgeous before. Hell, I was only gone a couple of days. Your short-term memory should be better than that. Remember me? I'm the gorgeous bitch you all love to hate.' When no one said anything, she rolled her eyes. 'Oh, whatever.' She twitched to the salad bar and began to fill her plate as the noise dam finally broke and all the kids made rude sounds and turned back to their food dismissively.

To the uninformed, I'm sure Aphrodite looked like her usual haughty self. But I could see how nervous and tense she actually was. Hell, I understood exactly how she felt – I'd just walked through the gauntlet myself. Actually, I was currently stuck in the middle of it along with her.

'I thought she'd become human again,' Damien said under his breath to all of us. 'But her Mark's back.'

'Nyx's ways are mysterious,' I said, trying to sound wise and High Priestess in Training-ish.

'I'm thinking Nyx's ways are another M-word, Twin,' Erin said. 'Can you guess it?'

'Majorly messed up?' Shaunee said.

'Exactly,' Erin said.

'That's three words,' Damien said.

'Oh, don't be such a schoolteacher,' Shaunee told him. 'Plus, the point is Aphrodite is a hag, and we were kinda hoping Nyx dumped her when that Mark of hers disappeared.'

'More than kinda hoping, Twin,' Erin said.

Everyone stared at Aphrodite. I tried to force salad down my throat. See, here's the deal: Aphrodite used to be the most popular, powerful, bitchy fledgling at the House of Night. Since she'd crossed the High Priestess, Neferet, and been totally ostracized, she had been reduced to simply the most bitchy fledgling at the House of Night.

Of course, weirdly (and typically enough for me), she and I had kinda, sorta, accidentally become friends – or at the very least, allies. Not that we wanted the masses to know that. Nevertheless, I'd been worried about her when she disappeared, even though Stevie Rae had chased after her. I mean, I hadn't heard from either of them in two days.

Naturally, my other friends – namely Damien, Jack, and the Twins – hated her guts. So to say that they were shocked and not very pleased when Aphrodite walked directly to our booth and sat down beside me was an understatement almost as big as that knight in the *Indiana Jones* movie saying 'He chose poorly' when the bad guy picked the wrong goblet to drink out of and his body disintegrated.

'Staring isn't polite, even when it's at someone as stunningly beautiful as *moi*,' Aphrodite said before taking a bite of her salad.

'What in the hell are you doing, Aphrodite?' Erin asked.

Aphrodite swallowed and then blinked with fake innocence at Erin. 'Eating, moron,' she said sweetly.

'This is a no-ho zone,' Shaunee said, finally recovering her ability to speak.

'Yeah, it's posted back here,' Erin said, pointing at a pretend sign on the back of their bench.

'I hate to repeat a sentiment I've said before, but in this case I'll make an exception. So I again say: Die Dorkamese Twins.'

'That's it,' Erin said, barely able to keep her voice down. 'Twin and I are gonna smack that damn Mark right off your face.'

'Yeah, maybe it'll stay off this time,' Shaunee said.

'Stop it,' I said. When the Twins turned slant-eyed looks of pissed-off-ness on me, I felt my stomach clench. Did they really hate me as much as they looked like they did? It made my heart hurt to think about it, but I lifted my chin and stared right back at them. If I completed the Change to vampyre, I would someday be their High Priestess, and that meant they had damn well better listen to me. 'We've already been through this. Aphrodite is part of the Dark Daughters now. She's also part of our circle, being as she has an affinity for the element earth.' I hesitated, wondering if she still had that affinity, or had she lost it when she'd gone from fledgling to human and then, apparently, back to fledgling again, but that was just too confusing, so I hurried on. 'You guys know you agreed to accept her in each position, *without* name-calling and hateful remarks.'

The Twins didn't say anything, but Damien's voice, sounding uncharacteristically flat and emotionless, came from the other side of me. 'We agreed to that, but we didn't agree to be friends with her.'

'I didn't say I wanted to be your friend,' Aphrodite said.

'Ditto, bitch!' the Twins said together.

'Whatever,' Aphrodite said, moving like she was going to pick up her tray and leave.

I'd opened my mouth to tell Aphrodite to sit down and the Twins to shut up when a bizarre noise echoed down the hall and through the open doors to the cafeteria.

'What the—?' I began, but didn't get the whole question out before at least a dozen cats streaked into the cafeteria, hissing and spitting like crazy.

Okay, at the House of Night, cats are everywhere. Literally. They follow us around, sleep with, and in my cat Nala's case, often complain at, the fledgling of their choice. In Vamp Soc class, one of the first cool things we learned was that cats had long been familiars of vampyres. This meant that we were all majorly used to having cats everywhere. But I had never seen them act so absolutely insane.

The Twin's huge gray tomcat, Beelzebub, jumped right up between them. He was puffed up to twice his already ginormously large size, and he stared back through the open door to the dining hall with amber eyes slit in anger.

'Beelzebub, baby, what's wrong?' Erin tried to soothe him.

Nala leaped up on my lap. She put her little white-tipped paws on my shoulder and gave a scary, psycho-cat growl as she, too, stared at the door and the chaotic noise still coming from the hall.

'Hey,' Jack said. 'I know what that sound is.'

And it hit me at the same time. 'It's a dog barking,' I said.

Then something that resembled a large yellow bear more closely than a dog burst into the cafeteria. The bear-dog was followed by a kid who was being followed by several uncharacteristically frazzled-looking professors, including our fencing master, Dragon Lankford, our equestrian instructor, Lenobia, as well as several of the Sons of Erebus Warriors.

'Got ya!' the kid yelled once he caught up with the dog and came to a skidding halt not far from us while he swooped down, snagged the barking beast's collar (which I noted was pink leather with silver metallic spikes all around it), and neatly clipped a leash to it. The instant his leash was reattached, the bear stopped barking, plopped its round butt down on the floor, and stared, panting, up at the kid. 'Yeah, great. *Now* you want to act right,' I heard him mutter to the obviously grinning canine.

Even though the barking had stopped, the cats in the cafeteria had definitely not stopped freaking. There was so much hissing around us, it sounded like air escaping from a punctured inner tube.

'You see, James, this was what I was trying to explain to you earlier,' Dragon Lankford said as he stared, frowning, down at the dog. 'The animal just won't work at this House of Night.'

'It's Stark, not James,' the kid said. 'And like *I* was trying to explain to *you* earlier – the dog has to stay with me. It's just the way it is. If you want me – you get her, too.'

I decided that the new dog kid had an unusual way about him. It wasn't like he was being openly rude or disrespectful to Dragon, but he also wasn't speaking to him with the respect, and sometimes outright fear, with which the vast majority of newly Marked fledglings spoke to vampyres. I checked out the front of his vintage Pink Floyd T-shirt. No class insignia there, so I didn't have a clue what year he was and how long he'd been Marked.

'Stark,' Lenobia was saying, obviously trying to reason with the kid, 'it's just not possible to integrate a dog into this campus. You can see how much he's upsetting the cats.'

'They'll get used to him. They did at the Chicago House of Night. She's usually pretty good about not chasing them around, but that gray cat really did ask for it with that whole hissing and scratching thing.'

'Uh-oh,' Damien whispered.